Praise
The Corruptible

"Mark Mynheir is one of my new favorite authors. As a homicide detective, he knows his stuff and his characters reflect it. I'll be one of the first in line for his next book!"
—TERRI BLACKSTOCK, author of *Vicious Cycle* and *Predator*

"Because of the Night Watchman series, Mynheir has joined my short list of detective novelists I anxiously await new releases from, along with Connelly, Riordan, and Landsdale. If you demand both great plots and great characters from your thrillers, you need to spend some time with Ray Quinn and The Night Watchman Detective Agency."
—BRAD WHITTINGTON, award-winning author of *Welcome to Fred, Living with Fred,* and *Escape from Fred*

"In *The Corruptible* we find Mynheir at his best, providing a true insider view on the gritty world of the private investigator. Mynheir's world first whispers, then scratches its way to life with great characters. He mixes delicious evil and the slap of addiction with an even rarer ingredient in the world of crime fiction: the hope of redemption. I want more."
—HARRY KRAUS, MD, best-selling author of *The Six-Liter Club*

"Mark Mynheir knows how to deliver crime fiction with a punch—a terrific setup, strong characters, sparkling wit, crisp dialogue, and viable suspects that keep you guessing right up to the arrest. Put this one at the top of your 'must read' list."
—WANDA DYSON, best-selling author of *Judgment Day* and *Shepherd's Fall*

"With *The Corruptible*, Mark Mynheir scores a home run. This book is the perfect package of a broken hero to root for, a murder that spirals into so much more, and a tangled web of suspects and motives that literally kept me guessing to the bitter end. I loved it!"
—CARA PUTMAN, author of *Stars in the Night*

"Rich with realism and wit, Ray Quinn grips the crime scene and doesn't let you go until the murder is solved. Hold onto your seat!"
—DiANN MILLS, author of *Pursuit of Justice*

"With *The Corruptible*, Mark Mynheir has written another winning Ray Quinn Mystery. I love Mynheir's authentic police-crime details and complex, compelling characters. The plot never makes a false step or lags behind."
—LYN COTE, author of *Her Abundant Joy*

"With the return of beloved character Ray Quinn, *The Corruptible* is a prime example of a book that grabs you from the beginning and won't let you go. Don't miss this fantastic read!"
—ROBIN CAROLL, author of *Deliver Us from Evil* and *Fear No Evil*

"A first rate detective novel from a real detective. Mynheir tells a fast-paced, gritty tale of murder and money in Orlando, Florida. His characters are flawed, funny, and deeply human. *The Corruptible* is a winner!"
—RICK ACKER, author of *When the Devil Whistles* and *Dead Man's Rule*

"*The Corruptible* raises the stakes, intensity, and storytelling of crime fiction to a whole new level of amazing! The insider details immerse you in a dangerous world of high-adrenaline suspense and raise soul-stirring questions you'll wrestle with right alongside Ray Quinn."
—AMY WALLACE, author of *Enduring Justice*

THE
CORRUPTIBLE

OTHER BOOKS BY MARK MYNHEIR

Ray Quinn Mystery Series
The Night Watchman

Truth Chasers Series
Rolling Thunder
From the Belly of the Dragon
The Void

MARK MYNHEIR

THE CORRUPTIBLE

A RAY QUINN MYSTERY

MULTNOMAH
BOOKS

THE CORRUPTIBLE
PUBLISHED BY MULTNOMAH BOOKS
12265 Oracle Boulevard, Suite 200
Colorado Springs, Colorado 80921

The scripture quotation on page vii is taken from the Holy Bible, New International Version®.
NIV®. Copyright © 1973, 1978, 1984 by Biblica Inc.™ Used by permission of Zondervan. All
rights reserved worldwide. www.zondervan.com

ISBN 978-1-60142-074-9
ISBN 978-1-60142-286-6 (electronic)

Copyright © 2011 by Mark Mynheir

Cover design by Mark Ford

Published in the United States by WaterBrook Multnomah, an imprint of the Crown Publishing
Group, a division of Random House Inc., New York.

MULTNOMAH and its mountain colophon are registered trademarks of Random House Inc.

Library of Congress Cataloging-in-Publication Data
Mynheir, Mark.
   The corruptible : a Ray Quinn mystery / Mark Mynheir.—1st ed.
      p. cm.
   ISBN 978-1-60142-074-9 (alk. paper)—ISBN 978-1-60142-286-6 (electronic) 1. Private
investigators—Florida—Fiction. 2. Ex-police officers—Fiction. 3. Orlando (Fla.)—Fiction. I.
Title.
   PS3613.Y58C67 2011
   813'.6—dc22
                                  2010043880

Printed in the United States of America
2011

10 9 8 7 6 5 4 3 2

But God demonstrates his own love
for us in this: While we were still
sinners, Christ died for us.

—Romans 5:8

1

DYING ON THE TOILET was not how I envisioned leaving this world.

"Ray Quinn, you're a dead man!" The behemoth's rumblings reverberated off the bathroom walls like a fully throttled Harley-Davidson.

I locked the stall door and shuffled back against the wall, my good leg using the toilet to keep me upright. My balance was still suspect after the shooting that destroyed my hip and pelvis eighteen months before. I pulled out my phone and typed a hurried text message to my partner, Crevis.

Trapped in bathroom w/maniac. Get here now!

"Where are you, you gumshoe rat?" The goon kicked in the stall door three down from me. Keith Wagner, my large and socially challenged pursuer, didn't possess much of a sense of humor. His wife suspected he was being unfaithful and hired me to follow him. It wasn't a difficult job, as he possessed a predilection for young ladies and excessive amounts of booze. Easy money, I thought. Now it seemed Keith was going to extract from my body every dollar his wife paid me.

The lovely and gracious Mrs. Wagner hadn't thought it important to inform me that she confronted Keith and blamed everything on me until after she went to the gym and met some friends for a brunch date.

I got her flippant warning call as Keith followed me into the restaurant where I was meeting Crevis for lunch, so he was now on a quest to separate my head from the rest of my body. I ducked into the bathroom to avoid him. Not the smartest move I'd made in a while, because now I was cornered. And in my hobbled condition, I couldn't outrun anyone anywhere. I hoped Crevis got my message, or he would be looking for another employer soon.

"So you wanna ruin other people's marriages, do ya?" Another stall door fell victim to Keith's raging foot.

Pointing out that it was his serial adultery and boorish behavior that led to his personal problems probably wouldn't help the situation, so I remained quiet.

"You wanna stick your face into other people's business?" The walls rocked again as the stall next to mine endured his assault. I aimed the weighty brass handle of my cane toward the door. Whatever he wanted to do to me would come at great cost.

The door handle jiggled. "Thought you could hide, did you—Ray Quinn, private eye?"

The door exploded open, and I was face to face with Keith, who stood a solid six foot three with a thick lumberjack build that made me wonder if this whole private-investigator gig was worth it. He worked his hands in and out like he was warming up his forearms to throttle me. He smirked, and I hammered the handle of my cane into his bearded face.

A meaty thump filled the air as one of Keith's teeth smacked the mirror behind him and swirled around in the sink. Keith staggered back, blood pouring down his chin. He snarled—minus a front tooth—and charged back into the stall and snatched me by the neck, smacking the back of my head against the wall. He growled as his beefy hands wrapped around my throat; his crazed eyes widened as he squeezed down hard.

While trying to break his stranglehold, I reached back to my waistband holster for my Glock 9mm. Magilla Gorilla thumped my head against the wall twice more, trapping my pistol between my back and the wall. An uppercut to his man-spot elicited only a groan from him. A follow-up shot caused him to release his grip and stumble backward, hunched over and clutching his groin.

I stabbed the brass tip of my cane down on his foot with both hands, coaxing another yelp from him. He hopped backward on one leg, then fired a cranium-rattling punch into my cheek, knocking me down onto the toilet. He grabbed me by the shirt and jerked me out of the stall, launching me through the air and dropping me on the sink counter. My cane slid across the floor toward the bathroom door. One of the faucets snapped as we wrestled on the sink top, spraying water like a fountain.

As Keith raised his fist to pound me, the bathroom door smacked against the wall, and Crevis Creighton stepped in.

Crevis, in his gray suit and fedora, streaked toward us and nailed

Keith with his shoulder, driving him into the wall and off me. He locked Keith in a bear hug, pressing him against the wall. Keith pushed Crevis's face back and took a wild swing. Crevis broke away and bobbed under the punch, his much-loved fedora falling to the floor. He fired two deep uppercuts to Keith's floating ribs, just like I had coached him. Keith gasped and looped another much slower, feeble swing at Crevis, who stepped back out of range as the punch sailed past. Crevis snapped a round kick to Keith's jaw, knocking him back against the wall. He slid down to the damp floor, unconscious.

The water from the broken faucet drenched us as I lay on the counter like a slab of so much pounded beef, my hip throbbing in pain.

"You all right, Ray?" Crevis said as he snatched his hat from the floor and affixed it back onto his head. Oblivious to the torrents of water jetting around us, he was quick to my side, as usual. The kid was consistent if nothing else. The look of concern on his face was genuine, but he'd seen me battered and beaten before. I'd get up.

I always did—one of my many faults.

"I'll make it." I started to scoot myself off of the counter and swing my legs to the floor. A searing bolt of pain rocketed down my spine and hip. "Maybe I'll wait here for a minute."

The romantic notion of being a private investigator—righting wrongs, searching for justice, and all the other drivel that zipped through my brain on occasion—seemed a bit foolish as I rested on a bathroom counter, nearly drowning in cold sink water.

Crevis's gray suit was now a sooty black as the sink continued to spit water at us. Drops poured off the lip of his fedora like a rain gutter in a hurricane. My already broken body cried out again, even more than usual. I hoped Keith hadn't destroyed any of the doctor's work on my damaged hip and pelvis. When I caught my breath, I'd try to stand and test it out. But for a moment, I was quite comfortable lying there, taking an unplanned shower.

"You might want to call OPD before this goon wakes up," I said. "I don't think he'll be happy."

Sliding his arm underneath mine, Crevis tipped me up into a sitting position. He eased me off the counter, then stepped over Keith, who was still taking a tile nap, to retrieve my cane for me.

Crevis had packed on about twenty pounds since we'd started working together. The kid had been in the gym every day, lifting weights and doing heavy bag workouts. I'd been coaching him on his boxing and kick-boxing skills, which I recognized now as an investment in my own health. A 9mm bullet to my side had ensured I would never hit the ring again.

"Whose idea was this PI thing again?" I asked.

"Yours," he said.

"Remind me to never listen to myself again."

2

"DOES THIS HURT?" the paramedic said as he dabbed my cheek with a medical swab.

"Only when you do that." I pushed his hand back, antiseptic stinging in the wound. "I'll clean myself up."

The young, heavyset African American stood up and scribbled notes on his clipboard. "It's your choice, but I really think you should go to the ER and get checked out. Your hip could be fractured."

"I'm good." I held up my hand. "I just need a breather."

I'd don a tutu and enroll in ballet classes before I'd give Keith Wagner the satisfaction of knowing he'd put me in the hospital. I'd walked myself into this situation, and I was certainly going to walk myself out of it.

The paramedic had perched me on the stoop of the ambulance so I could keep the leg stretched out and drip dry in the afternoon sun. I worked the joint back and forth a few times, and even though it hurt—it always hurt—there was no need to get it checked out.

The road was blocked with two ambulances and a couple of Orlando PD squad cars. Curious spectators lined the sidewalks. The lunch crowd was thick, as both the federal and state courthouses were just a few streets over, and Church Street offered a diverse assortment of restaurants. Lots of suits and dresses hurried back and forth, gazing at the spectacle, like lawyers on parade.

Two more paramedics wheeled Keith Wagner out of the restaurant on a gurney, an Orlando PD uniform trailing him. His head jiggled as they rolled over the lip of the doorway and headed for the second ambulance. After he was cleared from the hospital, he'd be on his merry way to the 33rd Street Jail. At least his case was closed, and I could be done with him and his neurotic wife.

Crevis reenacted a blow-by-blow account to another officer on the sidewalk to my left, shadowboxing his way through the story in dramatic detail. I'd already given my statement and was ready to leave.

"Raymond Quinn," a female voice called from the side of the ambulance. "You're the only guy I know who can get into a fight at lunch. What did he do, cut you off in line for the salad bar?"

Pam Winters' voice was a welcome addition to the cacophony of emergency vehicles and passersby. She wore a blue skirt and a white blouse, and her sandy blond hair was pulled back. She'd apparently just left her teaching job at a local private school when I called her.

Pam's deep blue eyes narrowed at me, then eased up. "Are you okay?" she asked.

"I'll survive." I shrugged and pointed to Keith with my chin as he was being loaded into the ambulance. "I think I broke his fist with my face, though. That'll teach him."

"You're a mess, Ray." She rested her hand on my shoulder. "Can I do anything?"

"I'm gonna be out the rest of the day, so I figured you and Crevis could work together. And I have some phone records I need input on cases, if you're up for that. The disk is on my desk."

"I could use some more time to work on his grammar and reading." She straightened my collar and brushed some debris from my shirt. "His test is only a few weeks from now, and we have a long way to go. At this point, he's not ready. I can take care of the phone records too. I didn't have anything else planned today."

"It'd help me out a lot," I said.

I'd known Pam since I investigated her brother's murder six months ago. We started out on rocky footing, but she'd more than proved her mettle. Her brother had been a pastor at a ministry downtown and ended up shot to death in his condo alongside a prostitute—a salacious story the press had exploited. My old unit ruled the case a murder-suicide, but Pam knew her brother could never have done something as patently evil as that.

She convinced me to take the case. Although I gave her a ton of grief at first, she ended up being right. Her brother was a true victim and by all accounts the real deal as a pastor, a man every bit as committed to his faith as his sister and not the monster the papers made him out to be. While I didn't believe what Pam and her brother believed, they were both as sincere as they came.

Along with helping Crevis prepare for his written test for the police academy, which he'd failed twice already, she did some part-time work for me as well. I could always find something to keep her in the office a couple of hours a week, and she seemed amenable to the setup.

Maybe she hung around to pay me back for her brother's case, or maybe she was just a friend trying to help out our business. Either way, whenever I called, she showed up. That was big in my book. She was the only person other than Crevis who had a key to our office. She'd earned it.

Crevis joined us and pumped a couple of jabs in the air. "Not bad, huh, boss? I took that guy out with three strikes."

"Don't get cocky, Fist-of-Fury. You did all right, but if you were really on the ball, you could have dropped him in two." I stabbed my cane into the pavement and gripped the handle with both hands. Leaning forward, I eased off the bumper—planting both feet on terra firma. Crevis slipped his hand underneath my elbow and lifted. I shook him off and stood on my own power. I was unstable but vertical. My day was improving.

"There's just a little too much testosterone in this conversation for me," Pam said. "When you're ready to go, let me know. Do you want me to drive you back to your place? Crevis can bring me back here to get my car."

"I'll drive myself," I said. "If I let myself get stuck in the car with you, I'm afraid you'll spend the whole time praying for my heathen soul."

She smirked. "Maybe not the whole time. We could sing some hymns too."

"Funny," I said. "But I think I'm going to have to pass on the ride. I'm fine now, anyway. You and Crevis do what you have to do, and I'll get some rest at home. I feel better already."

Pam raised an eyebrow and seemed instinctively to know that I had just lied to her through my loose teeth. "I *will* pray for you anyway, Ray."

"I'd be surprised if you didn't," I said. "See you tomorrow."

She and Crevis headed down Church Street as I carefully wobbled my way in the other direction. I was glad someone was praying for me, because I wasn't inclined to do it for myself. Prayer, to me, was like surrender. And I'd rather be knocked out cold any day than quit.

3

"DETECTIVE QUINN," the man said as he burst into my office. "We need your assistance."

When I started the Night Watchman Detective Agency, I imagined a scenario like this, but it had played out a bit differently in my head: a leggy blonde wearing a sleek black dress sashaying through the door, easing a cigarette to her mouth in a sultry, alluring manner that hypnotized me—like something out of a Bogart film. She would entice me into a case that challenged me on every level.

A portly, balding guy in his late forties carrying a briefcase and wearing a crumpled suit didn't quite satisfy that expectation.

My chunky visitor sucked in a deep lung wheeze, as if the one flight of stairs to my office had winded him. He wiped his shiny forehead with a handkerchief.

"How can I help you?" I set down the book I was reading, *The Handbook for Private Detectives,* and swiveled my chair side to side. I'd spent most of the day skimming the book, recovering from my little donnybrook the day before with Keith Wagner, who went to jail for attacking me. My ribs were bruised, my cheek swollen, and my hip in no mood to be hopping up and down.

"We are in need of your services." He waddled to the edge of my desk and handed me a business card: Richard Wykoff, Esq., Mayer Holdings Inc. "My employer wishes to meet with you. It's very important."

"I'll set up an appointment." I tapped the top of my computer monitor with the tip of my cane. "I have some openings."

"I don't think you understand, Detective Quinn. Armon Mayer wants to meet with you *now.*"

He said the name like it should mean something to me. It didn't. I checked my watch and feigned an irked scowl, like I had more important things to do. "What does your boss need my services for?"

"He'll explain it when we arrive." He turned his bulbous body to face the entrance he had just walked through, as if I should jump up and sprint to the door.

I wasn't sprinting anywhere, but the urgency in his voice made a welcome addition to my office and hinted at a decent paycheck. Although I generally like to know what I'm walking into, I didn't have a lot of options, given my lack of disposable income. And besides, my interest was piqued.

With all the good press from solving Pam's brother's murder, I had assumed cases would pour in. Some had, like that of the perpetually dysfunctional Wagners, but they were small cases—cheating spouses and one corporate employee misconduct case. They were mere trickles when I desperately needed a cash flood to keep the business open. I hated worrying about those things. I just wanted to catch bad guys and do my job, but I couldn't neglect the business end—a consideration I hadn't fully evaluated before I opened the doors.

My office provided just enough space to accomplish the job without luxury and fluff. Crevis's desk stood next to mine, a computer on top of it. Several metal file cabinets lined the wall behind us. My front door had a glass window with a cool painting of a man with a cane and the words "Night Watchman Detective Agency" above it. The door faced Colonial Drive and the Amway Arena, the home of the Orlando Magic NBA team. Game nights could be loud and hectic outside—not necessarily a bad ambiance for the office.

A flat-screen television hung on one wall, and a large whiteboard covered the other, both for case presentations. My desk held two flat-screen monitors—one for my regular computer work and the other for any surveillance cameras I had out. Wireless remotes connected our entire system. I could place cameras at different locations and control them and watch everything going on from my desk. The newer technology made surveillance a whole lot easier. Our system had all the necessary—but pricey—accoutrements. Much better than sitting in a cramped car all night or hiding in a clump of bushes in the rain.

"Give me a second, so I can let my partner know I'm leaving," I said. I drew my phone from its pouch. *Find out what u can on Armon Mayer. We have a case,* I texted to Crevis.

I acquiesced to my fleshy visitor and locked the office. The afternoon sun energized me and eased the soreness from my beating. I paused on the walkway and let the warmth penetrate to my bones, like a lizard sunning itself on a branch. My office building was in a two-story complex just across Colonial Drive from Lake Dot, which was more of a pond. A computer repair shop, a telemarketing firm, and a CPA's office occupied the second floor with my office. The walkway and stairs were outside, which was pleasant when the weather was good and miserable when it was not so good.

I hobbled down the steps to my truck. Since my shooting, I didn't move with any kind of speed or efficiency. My right leg was a shriveled remnant of its former glory, the nerves and bone wrecked. The doctors had done all they could by inserting a plastic joint and enough metal to set off a security alarm at the airport. The leg did little more than fill my jeans and keep me from throwing one of my shoes away. Many years before, I used to kick-box and had a deadly right leg, rendering several opponents unconscious with well-timed, powerful kicks. Now the only thing I'd ever be able to kick would be the bucket when that time came.

Esquire Wykoff hurried over to his black Lincoln Town Car and opened the back door.

"How 'bout I drive myself?" I pointed to my blue pickup. I'd known this guy all of five minutes, so I wasn't about to get in the back of his mob-style car and ride anywhere with him. That was how people ended up in the trunk instead of the backseat. I'd made enough enemies in my nearly twenty years of law enforcement to be cautious. Although he didn't look like the Mafia thug type, I would just as soon give myself a ride to his place.

"I understand." He closed the door and circled around to the driver's side. "Follow me, please."

I loaded myself into my pickup, the only vehicle I could find after I was shot that I didn't have to bend down to get in. It was more for convenience than for looks.

Wykoff drove east on Colonial Drive underneath I-4 to Orange Avenue, then south for less than ten minutes into the heart of downtown. We zigzagged through stop-and-go traffic to the corner of Orange Avenue and Washington Street.

He pulled into the parking garage of a red-faced glass-and-steel monolith that was the pinnacle of the Orlando skyline. In all my years on the force, I'd never been inside this building. Wykoff stopped at the gate and spoke with the security guard. The guard glanced back at me and raised the bar. We both drove in.

The darkness of the garage swallowed me as if I'd driven into the mouth of a waiting giant. I flipped on my headlights and continued to follow Wykoff. He pulled into a spot with his name on a placard next to an elevator. A black Lamborghini was parked next to it—Armon Mayer's name marked that spot. You don't see a lot of Lamborghinis in Orlando. Minivans loaded to the hilt with screaming kids en route to Mickey Land, yes. Cars worth three hundred thousand dollars, no.

I found the visitors' spot and took my time adjusting myself. My phone vibrated with a text from Crevis.

A very rich dude.

OK, I messaged back to him, as if I couldn't tell that now.

Wykoff held the elevator door for me. As I entered, he punched a security code into the keypad and pushed the penthouse button. I committed the code to memory. The elevator rose smoothly and effortlessly. Wykoff didn't speak but did smile on occasion.

The door opened to a view of a wall emblazoned with the Mayer Holdings Inc seal—two hands holding the world. Nice.

A secretary's desk faced us as we exited the elevator, an enormous set of oak double doors looming behind it.

"Richard," the brunette said in a professional tone. A gentle smile leaked out before she regained her stoic expression. In her early thirties, she had soft green eyes, and her hair was tied back off her shoulders. She wore a yellow dress and a wireless headset. She rose from her chair as we approached, and her smooth tan skin and lithe figure kept my attention.

"Megan, can you let Mr. Mayer know we're here?" Wykoff said.

She held her earpiece. "Mr. Mayer, Richard and the private investigator are here."

"Ray Quinn," I said. "My name is Ray Quinn."

"Excuse me." She grinned. "Private Investigator Ray Quinn is here to see you."

I winked at her. A coy smirk crossed her face as she opened the set of double doors that were easily twelve feet tall.

Wykoff and I entered a boardroom two stories high with rectangular windows on either side that stretched from floor to ceiling like enormous fingers holding the penthouse aloft. An oblong walnut table large enough to double as an indoor track dominated the middle of the room. More than two dozen plush black chairs surrounded it.

A set of smaller doors stood at the opposite end, probably Armon Mayer's office. Photos of Armon with famous folks dotted the room—several actors and sports figures, and many others I didn't recognize but probably should have. All the photos appeared to have been taken in this room.

Two men peered out one of the heavily tinted windows, surveying the Orlando skyline below. Another younger man sat at the end of the table with a laptop computer open before him.

Armon Mayer stood farthest from me. Although not a large man—several inches shorter than me, with a modest build—his bearing and poise were those of someone in charge. Armon wore an olive green coat with an unusual weave—hemp, I suspected—and a black pullover shirt, and his hair was dark, though thinning along his forehead. A tightly woven ponytail hung just past his shoulders, and he had a close-cropped, salt-and-pepper beard. An impressive array of shimmering gold rings with thick stones adorned his manicured fingers, and a single diamond stud pierced his right ear. He turned toward me and then focused again out the window to the world beneath him.

The man next to him, a little taller than my six feet, approached us.

"Jack Gordon." He extended a hand. "Chief of Security for Mayer Holdings Inc."

Like I couldn't tell. A pistol bulged underneath his navy blue suit coat on his right-hand side, and unless he had elephantiasis of the left ankle, he stashed his backup there. A folding knife was clipped to the inside of his belt next to his cell phone. He was in his late thirties and sported the kind of build that could only be honed by an hour or two in the weight room every day. He had a brown

flattop haircut as tight as a boot brush and a chin cleft deep enough
to hide a TV remote. A Marine Corps pin kept his tie from flopping
around.

He squeezed my hand harder than necessary and locked me into
a stare. "Thanks for coming. Please have a seat."

Wykoff pulled out a chair for me. I regarded it but caned down
two seats closer to Armon and took my own chair, the Wagner beating still fresh on my bones. Armon made no effort to extend a greeting and shuffled even farther away from me.

"I am looking for someone." Armon twisted one of the rocks
around his pinky. "I've been told you can help me find him."

"You can find just about anyone on the Internet," I said. "There's
a number of sites that will help you do that. I solve cases."

Armon side-eyed first me and then Jack Gordon.

"Do you know an ex-cop named Logan Ramsey?" Jack picked
up a file from the table. "He used to work for the Orlando Police
Department."

"I do," I said. "We ran in some of the same circles. I had just
started in OPD's narcotics unit when he was leaving, maybe a dozen
years ago. He did the undercover operation that brought down the
Rebel Soldiers motorcycle gang. It was a great case."

"Yes, he was a hero for his undercover work and was fired soon
after for leaking information to a drug dealer about ongoing police
operations." Armon sauntered to a small shelf in the corner of the
room, pulled an antibacterial wipe from a dispenser, and rubbed it
across both hands. I spotted at least two more such stations around
the room. He tossed the used towelette into a wastebasket.

"I think we're talking about the same guy." I rested my cane against the smooth table. Logan had ridden the publicity of that case for a couple of years. He'd been featured on all the top cop shows and documentaries as one of the few police officers to ever successfully infiltrate a criminal biker gang undercover.

I knew Logan better than I let on. We worked a couple of cases together when I first started in the unit. He could walk into any bar and in an hour have everyone there buying him drinks and selling him a kilo of cocaine.

"Why are you looking for Logan?" I asked.

"Even though Logan showed an extreme lack of ethics and sound judgment during his time as a police officer, *someone* in my employment still thought it would be a good idea to hire him as a security officer here at Mayer Holdings." Armon shifted his body toward Jack Gordon. "Logan's ways have not changed. He has stolen some assets that must be returned."

"What kind of assets?" I asked.

"The valuable kind." Armon looked at Jack, who handed me the file. "He's commandeered a large number of clients' personal and investment information. We don't know if he's going to sell the information or try to exploit it in some other way for his own gain. Find Logan, and you will find what he stole."

I opened the file. A picture of Logan lay on top of the stack of papers.

"This is Derek Strickland from our IT department." Jack pointed to the anemic-looking young man with the laptop. He had light brown hair and skin the color of skim milk. He had yet to look up from the screen since I entered the room. "He can fill you in on the sequence of events."

"Two days ago, Monday, Logan downloaded some very sensitive material from his computer to a portable storage device," Derek said, still not engaging me with eye contact. "It's a 300-gig hard drive that can store up to—"

"No need for the computer mumbo-jumbo," Jack said. "Just stick to the facts."

"Okay. He penetrated a firewall-protected area of our network and downloaded all the client files at 9:47 a.m. According to our surveillance cameras, he left the building at 10:02 a.m. and has not been seen since. He was carrying this satchel when he left, and we believe he had the external hard drive in the satchel."

I examined the security photo—Logan Ramsey walking with a brown satchel in his hands. His once sharp and hard facial features appeared softened by time and the weathering effects of his hedonistic approach to life, but he was still built like a Viking, imposing and dominant in any room he entered. His blond hair was short now, and he wore blue jeans and a brown leather coat. He was walking through the downstairs lobby.

Armon dipped his head to Wykoff, who pulled a check from his top pocket and laid it on the table before me. As I picked it up and assessed the number, my stomach fluttered. The ability to finally swim out of the ocean of debt lay before me.

For a few embarrassing seconds I brushed aside my many questions and the cop alarm sounding off in my psyche. I paused with the tantalizing piece of paper in my hand, tickling my expectations.

I swallowed hard and placed it back on the table, facedown, and slid it toward Wykoff.

"The amount does not suit you?" Armon said.

"It's not the amount." I drew my cane toward me and rested both hands on it. "I don't take cases where I'm not being told everything up front. Client information can't be worth what you're looking to pay me for this job, especially when you can shoot off one call to OPD and have Logan picked up for grand theft. You have all the evidence you need. They'll put a warrant out for him, and he'll be arrested. Problem solved."

"Do you know what Mayer Holdings Inc. does, Detective Quinn?" Armon steepled his gaudy hands but still remained at a distance.

"I can't say that I do."

"I will give you a brief overview. We invest, support, and manage assets from all around the world. Many prominent people in the public spotlight are our clientele. Do you know why we are able to do this?"

"Enlighten me." I shrugged, already tiring of his babble.

"Reputation. Mayer Holdings has a stellar reputation for the safety and security of the assets we manage, and I will not allow our standing in this industry to be destroyed by a rogue, morally challenged ex-cop. I don't want law enforcement involved, or any publicity. I want Logan found and my assets returned—discreetly. And I do not care how you do it. My security is not suited for situations like this."

He stopped his soliloquy and glanced toward Jack with a not-so-veiled look of disgust. "You have contacts with the police department

and are familiar with Logan. I am prepared to compensate you gen-
erously and cover your expenses because I want results, and I want
them now. I know my business, Detective Quinn. You're the right
person for this case."

The bloated check lay before me, but Armon's homily had not
alleviated all of my concerns. On the other hand, I really did need
the business. If I opened that door, I would discover what they
weren't telling me soon enough.

I grabbed the check, folded it, and slipped it in my pocket. "I'll
call some sources and start tracking him today. I'm gonna need his
employee file, any notes or personal information on him. I'll fax you
a contract. I can take this case."

"Very good," Armon said. "Jack will help you with what you
need."

He eyed the door, which told me our meeting was over, and I
had a new client. Armon made no attempt to cover the forty feet to
shake my hand and see me out. I gathered my carcass and headed for
the exit.

Jack outpaced me and held open the door for me, pseudosmile
in place. He followed me out into the lobby.

"Call me first if you stumble onto anything." He handed me his
business card, which listed his cell and office numbers.

"If I stumble onto anything, you'll be the first one to know."

Too bad for Jack that I never "stumbled" onto anything.

4

THE NEXT MORNING we got an early start, and Crevis and I arrived at Logan's house on the west side of Orlando. Not a real stretch in investigative techniques, but it was always a good idea to start where the person lived and work your way out from there.

Logan's house was a small, unassuming two-bedroom chalet with a carport instead of a garage. The lawn was more than ready to be mowed, and a Harley-Davidson skeleton with the gas tank ripped off balanced on cinder blocks in the carport. An assortment of parts lay strewn about, and two full trash cans stood against the wall—beer cans, whiskey bottles, and fast-food wrappers overflowing onto the ground. Logan's Jeep Cherokee wasn't there, but we still needed to check the house.

"Watch your step." Crevis stepped over an oil stain on the ground. "There's junk everywhere."

"Yeah, Logan's not strong on yard maintenance." I nudged a KFC bucket to the side, and a bevy of cockroaches scattered in all directions. The information in Logan's employee file was thin: only his home address, a criminal history report, a credit check, and the

address of his daughter, Cassandra Ramsey, in Clermont. I planned
to visit her later. For now, we needed to see if Logan had found his
way home.

We followed the walkway to the front door. I had already called
Logan's cell and house numbers. He didn't pick up either, so I left
messages for him. If he was on the run, he still might talk to me.
He'd need an old friend right now, and that was the line I played. I
told him I had some PI work for him, if he was interested. I just
wanted him to get in touch with me. Once I got him on the phone,
I was sure I could convince him to meet with me and put this case
to rest.

I knocked once and waited. The front door was closed, but the
frame was split from the doorknob to the floor. I pushed the door,
and it swung open with ease.

Crevis went to step inside, but I grabbed his arm.

"Logan," I called. "It's Ray Quinn. You home?"

I wasn't about to burst through the door of an ex-cop's house.
Odds were good he was packing and might be skittish, especially
since the door looked like someone had already put their boot to it.
We would move smart, not fast.

Using the tip of my cane, I pushed the door open farther. The
living room was in shambles—papers strewn on the floor, the cabinet doors of the entertainment center open, and cushions from the
couch removed and tossed on the floor. CDs and the DVD player
had been shoved from their original positions on the shelf.

I drew my pistol and regarded Crevis, who followed my lead.

"Logan?" I entered the house with my cane in one hand, pistol in the other.

"This guy is really a slob." Crevis followed me, his pistol wandering wherever he looked. The barrel of his .40 caliber passed across my body several times.

"I don't think this is how it normally looks. Someone did this on purpose." I reached out and put my hand on his wrist, pushing his gun down. "And please keep that thing down at your side. I'm in front of you, remember?"

"Sorry." He shrugged and lowered his gun.

We checked the small kitchen. More beer cans populated the counter and table. Someone had rummaged through the drawers and cabinets as well. Nearly every cabinet door hung open.

We moved down the hallway to the back bedroom. I stayed clear of the doorway and used my cane to nudge it open. The king-size bed was unmade and a large lump filled the middle. Crevis and I crept in.

"Logan, it's Ray Quinn." I probed the lump with the cane. No movement. "Everything okay?" I pulled the bedspread off, revealing a pile of dirty clothes. All the drawers had been removed from the dresser and emptied on the floor and bed.

Pictures of Logan covered one wall: some with him in uniform, one with him holding an armload of pot plants from a big bust, and another with him in full biker-gang attire as a Rebel Soldier. He really looked the part, wearing the traditional jacket with the symbol for the Rebel Soldiers. I removed the photo from the wall. Logan wore a helmet with horns protruding from the sides and had his arms around a horde of Rebels. If I didn't know who he was, it would have been tough to spot the cop. I laid the photo on the dresser.

A computer station was set up in the corner of the room. The archaic monitor sat on the desk, but the CPU was missing. No disk or thumb drives were around either. I'd bet anything that whoever shook Logan's house down had taken the CPU as well.

Crevis stepped over another load of clothes on the floor. "Who did this?"

"I don't know. But we're not the only ones looking for Logan."

5

"RAY! GREAT TO SEE YOU." Sergeant Oscar Yancey twisted around in his chair and faced me as I stood in the doorway of his office. "How are things?"

"I'm doing okay."

In his early fifties, the African American sergeant had been in charge of Homicide for nearly a dozen years. The Orlando Police Department's Homicide Unit, tucked away on the second floor of police headquarters on Hughey Street, had remained virtually unchanged from the days when I stomped around case after case—a bullpen of cubicles for the detectives, with a conference desk set in the middle to hash out any current cases.

Oscar's office sat off from the bullpen with a window to keep watch on the host of feral detectives that made up the homicide unit. The logout board was still mounted on the wall. Each detective had to sign out whenever they left and state where they were going, or they'd face the wrath of Oscar.

At the conclusion of Pam's case, in which I solved three murders—one being that of my former partner, Trisha Willis—the city officials, in their infinite wisdom, chose to give me back my access key to the department. Since they were feeling magnanimous about everything, I pushed for consultant status. Now I could assist on cold cases as well as current ones and had free rein at the PD. I figured it would come in handy sometime. I just didn't think "sometime" would come so quickly.

"How's your partner...Cravis?" Oscar said.

"It's Crevis, like a crack. He's hanging in there. Saved my crippled butt again the other day."

"I heard. You're not paying him enough, especially if he has to keep you outta trouble. You better watch yourself, Ray. Chasing cheating husbands can be dangerous."

"So's chasing ex-cops." I rested my hands on the handle of my cane.

He pushed his glasses up on his nose and got out of his chair. In one step from his desk, his lean six-three frame met me at the door, and his hand engulfed mine. He poked his head into the hallway, checked up and down, and then pulled me into his office and shut the door behind us. "I don't like the sound of that. What are you working on?"

I took a seat in front of his desk, which was organized and clean. An in-box and a computer occupied the only space on an otherwise pristine desk top. Pictures of Oscar and his family hung on the wall behind him—his wife, Mimi, and their two daughters. Alyssa, his older, had just gotten married about two months before. A picture of her and Oscar dancing together at the reception held a prominent place next to the family photo. His younger daughter, Amy, was still in college—the University of Florida, I thought.

Oscar updated me on their lives whenever I saw him. Not that I asked. It was just important to him. They were his life; police work was his job. He was one of the few cops I knew who was still married to his first wife. I often wondered how he managed that, not only as a cop, but a homicide sergeant.

"When was the last time you saw Logan Ramsey?" I said.

Oscar removed his glasses and pinched the bridge of his nose. "I haven't seen him in a long time. Not since he left here. Man, that must have been over ten years ago. What did he do this time? Somethin' stupid, I imagine."

"I'm looking for him." I laid my cane across my lap. "My client's got a beef with him."

"What kind of beef?" Oscar said.

"It would be highly improper of me to tell you the reason my client has hired me," I said. "Especially if Logan had stolen some valuable information from my client, who wants it back. Bad."

"I see." Oscar stretched back in his chair. "Some folks just don't change. He's always been a dirty dog."

My *Handbook for Private Detectives* specifically warned against revealing a client's interest in a case. But the handbook didn't reveal how to get cops to work with you, something I did know. I was fixing to hit Oscar up for some favors, and he wasn't obliged to share anything with me. I needed to toss a juicy morsel his way.

Besides, I trusted Oscar more than anyone else on the planet, except maybe Crevis. The difference between Oscar and Crevis, though, was that Oscar had the good sense to know what could be spread around and what had to remain confidential. We were still working on that with Crevis.

"Do you know anyone close to him?" I said. "Anyone who stayed in contact with him after he left?"

"I can check around. I don't know anybody who would even talk to him. Not after what he pulled. I can tolerate a lot of things but not a dirty cop. Who knows how many people he could have gotten killed. I've got no use for that man."

"I still need to find him," I said. "I'm gonna see if I can get a copy of his personnel file and the Internal Affairs case."

"The personnel file should be easy. I'll take care of that. Good luck getting any info out of I.A. They hold on to that stuff like it's their own."

"Sergeant Phillips still run I.A.?"

"Unfortunately."

"Swell. I'm sure he'll be happy to see me again. If you get any leads on Logan, let me know."

"No problem. Just promise me you'll quit brawling in bathrooms."

"I'll see what I can do."

6

THE WELL-TROD ROUTE from Homicide to Internal Affairs was as familiar to me as my own way home. To say I'd been to Internal Affairs a few times would be a gross understatement and do extreme violence to the truth. I used to have my own chair there, as well as seven or eight department policies named after me. Not everyone could say that.

"Sergeant Phillips, catch any cops taking a discount on their meals lately?"

"What's that supposed to mean, Quinn?" he said as I caned my way into his office. "And what are you doing here? Didn't we fire you or something?"

"Medically retired, actually. Glad you're keeping up." I eased into the chair in front of his desk—the Chair of Forgetfulness, as it was called. A cop in trouble would show up in Phillips's office, plop down in that chair, and systematically forget everything the allegation was about.

Not me. I'd tell him everything I'd ever done in great, dramatic detail. While I could be a bit off-color at times and maybe a little short with people once in a while, I never did anything I was ashamed of. A couple dozen memories came flooding back as I sat in front of Phillips. I once got a day off without pay for swearing at a murderer as I tossed him in a cell. He'd shot his girlfriend and left her to die on the side of the road like an animal. I gave Sergeant Phillips a detailed statement of the incident, maybe even embellishing it a bit. The day off was worth it, and I'd do it again.

The gelatinous mass of cop regarded me as he crossed his arms and bared his predatory teeth, which gave him great pleasure when he sank them into wayward cops. His supersized suit was wrinkled, and a shaggy, unkempt throw rug covered his head. The office reeked of a noxious mix of old leather and pork rinds. Case files overflowed on top of each other, and papers, driver's license photos, and computer printouts blanketed his desk.

"Heard anything from Logan Ramsey lately?" I asked.

A *tss* sound seemed to be all he could manage as he swatted his paw in the air. "He's been gone awhile. We worked up a good case on him. Wasn't hard. He was as dirty as they come. Why do you want to know?"

"I'm looking for him, that's all. Just thought you might have heard something. Maybe I could take a peek at his I.A. file and see if something there can point me to him?"

"Maybe you can hobble your butt right out of my office. The files are sealed, and you or anyone else don't get to 'look' at them."

"I'm a consultant with the department now." I waved my ID card, which I wore on a lanyard around my neck, and smiled large, aping my goofy photo. "It's all professional."

"Yeah, sell it to someone else, Quinn," he said. "I know you too well."

I wished Phillips were as dumb as he looked, but that wasn't the case. He'd been around a long time and was pretty sharp. I'd have to switch tactics. I drew my cell phone out and dialed Oscar.

"Hey, Oscar," I said. "I'm up here with Sergeant Phillips, and he won't turn over any of Logan's notes or files. Would you like to talk with him?"

I stood, handed the phone across the desk to Phillips, and grinned. "Sergeant Yancey from Homicide would like to talk with you."

He snatched the phone from me with fat fingers that resembled potato wedges. "What gives, Yancey? I know…I know. This ain't your area… You wouldn't dare… Fine! But I'm holding you responsible for him and anything he does." He hung up and pitched the phone back to me, then stood and stormed out of the office without saying anything.

After about ten minutes, Sergeant Phillips returned with a thick manila folder. He dropped it in my lap with considerable force as he breezed by me and plopped back into his chair.

"Not one piece of paper will be disturbed. Do you understand? I will receive it back in the exact condition I gave it to you." He pointed a meaty digit at me. "And tell Yancey he's a dirty dog for pulling that."

"I'll give him the message." I stood, switched the file to my right hand, and steadied myself. "I don't know about you, but I feel kind of nostalgic. You know, like the old days."

"Shut it and get out of my office." He pointed the way.

"Like I said." I aimed a finger at him with my thumb up like a pistol. "Just like the old days."

7

I HURRIED BACK to my office to pick up Crevis. I had as much information on Logan as I was going to get. Now I needed to contact his friends and associates to see what I could dig up. He hadn't just fallen off the face of the planet. Somebody knew where he went and what he was up to. It was just a matter of finding that someone and compelling them, by whatever means necessary, to tell me.

I wanted to write a court order to ping Logan's cell phone and get a good location for him, but I wasn't sure Oscar could sneak it through the state attorney's office for me. Logan was shrewd and would know not to use his phone if he wanted to disappear anyway, and it was enough that Oscar had run interference for me with Phillips. I was dying to know what he said to him.

My leg reminded me why I wasn't on the force anymore as I scaled the stairs to my office with great care, toting the files from the PD. I'd been on my feet all day, and my hip was in full mutiny, throbbing rhythmically with the beat of my heart and giving me that tender feeling it does when I'm exhausted, like it was ready to give out at any moment. I stopped at the top of the stairs to catch my breath and balance. I tended to forget—more out of want than necessity—that I was a scuttled ship. I'd medicate later, in the pool with my pal Jim.

As I entered the office, Pam sat next to Crevis's desk while he bent forward, scribbling along a line. She wore blue jeans and a black button-down shirt. She'd recently turned thirty, a solid ten years younger than me, though she didn't even look that.

"Hi, Ray." She pointed to a problem on the page for Crevis.

"Pam." I hobbled past them and stacked the files on my desk.

"What's this word?" Crevis said, pointing to the book. "I can't figure it out."

"Sound it out," she said.

"See Dick run—" I said.

"Raymond Quinn!" Pam aimed a focused finger and an ice-pick glare in my direction, threatening to wound me on the spot if I completed the sentence. "You'd better not even think it."

"All right, all right." I raised my hands. "I was just playing around. And it's Ray, never Raymond. You know that."

Her claws retracted as she turned back to Crevis. "Sound it out."

"You two need to finish up." I tapped my watch. "This is duty time, Cowboy, and I need you on the street. Just 'cause you're trying to be a cop doesn't mean you can fool around in here all day."

"All right. I could use a break anyway." Crevis rubbed his forehead. "What do you want me to do?"

"You need to get eyes on an address in Clermont." I handed

Crevis the printout with the address and map. "It's Logan's daughter, Cassandra Ramsey's house. If it looks like she's home, I'll meet you out there."

"I'm on it. See ya tomorrow, Pam."

"You're doing great, Crevis," she said. "I'm really proud of how hard you're working."

He grinned as he removed his coat from the back of his chair and slid it on. He tightened his tie and plopped the fedora on his head. He slid his paddle holster with his pistol underneath his belt and hurried out the door, a fully accessorized Crevis.

"Do you really think he'll pass it this time?" I took a seat at my desk and fired up the computer.

"He's getting there," Pam said. "His reading comprehension isn't terrible, considering his education level, or lack thereof. He reads slowly, but he remembers most of what he's read. It's his spelling and handwriting that's really holding him back, which is common for dyslexics. He's really very bright. But he could use encouragement, not teasing."

"He's a tough kid." I typed in my password, and my computer came to life. "He can take it. Besides, he's gonna experience a whole lot worse if he does pass that test and gets on the streets. It's a cruel world, especially a cop's world, and no one is going to cut him any slack."

"He admires you, Ray." She opened a black briefcase and slid the reading workbook inside it. "Every once in a while, it wouldn't kill you to tell him how proud you are of him. It'll go a long way. He's never had anyone support him before."

"I promised to teach him how to become a cop, not baby him."
I clicked into my e-mail. "He'll be fine."

"Think about it, Ray. That's all I ask."

"You coming back tomorrow?"

"Yes, unless you're kicking me out for good."

"I suppose I can release Crevis for a little while."

"See you tomorrow, Ray Quinn." She closed her briefcase, gathered her purse, and stowed the laptop in a black case. She waved at me as she left the office.

I had my doubts that Crevis would pass the test, but having Pam visit the office on a regular basis wasn't the worst thing I could think of. The schoolmarm had grown on me.

I checked my e-mail, and an address I wasn't familiar with popped up. I opened the message.

Dear Friend,

I write to seek your cooperation as my foreign partner and your assistance to enable us to own properties and invest in the stable economy of your country.

My names are Mr. Chaka Nomvete. We are making this venture proposal to you in strict confidence. As senior civil servant in the South Africa Government, the South African civil service laws (Code of Conduct Bureau) forbid us to own a foreign account. The money we have in our possession is an overdue payment bill totaling Twenty Six Million, Four Hundred and Twenty Six Thousand US Dollars (US$26,426,000.00) which we want to transfer abroad with the assistance and cooperation of a company/or an individual to receive the said funds, via a reliable Bank Account.

If you will like to assist us as a partner, then indicate your interest after which we shall both discuss on the modalities. All other information to facilitate the remittance of the funds will be revealed to you in due course. For your assistance, you shall receive 30% amounting to US$7,927,800.00 will be used to settle taxation and other miscellaneous expenses in the course of transferring the funds to your account.

A swift acknowledgment on the receipt of this mail will be appreciated.

Thank you and God bless you.

Best regards,

Mr. Chaka Nomvete

Most of my scam e-mails came from Nigeria, or so they said. This one piqued my interest. Mr. Nomvete was creative enough to come up with a new spin on an old trick, which angered me all the more. Since I felt a bit testy, I decided to create a separate e-mail account and respond.

Dear Mr. Nomvete,

Thank you so much for contacting me! I don't hear from people very often, so I was so excited to get your e-mail. I'm very sorry for the difficulties you're experiencing. I'd love to help you, but I don't know how to begin. You see, my son runs all of my finances now, and he's placed me in this retirement home with only my computer. You were very kind to offer the money, but I really don't need it. My son says we have access to upwards of 30 million dollars in our estate. I really can't believe it either, but my husband was very wealthy before his untimely death. I will see if my son will give me the account numbers, so I can help you. I hope this works out.

God bless,

Marion Simpkins

Scams like that tend to work because of the greed of the victims. No matter how crazy it sounds, the thought of receiving millions for doing absolutely nothing is too good to pass up. But that doesn't alleviate the responsibility these guys have for being scumbags and taking advantage of people.

I sent the e-mail. Nothing wrong with a little payback.

After messing with the South African, I started to review the Internal Affairs report on Logan's investigation and firing. Not a pretty read.

My cell phone vibrated. I checked the screen.

"Hey, Oscar," I said. "Long time, no hear."

"I have some interesting news."

"Great."

"I found Logan, and I'm with him right now."

"Keep him there. I'm on my way. Where are you?"

"The Sand Dollar Motel. He won't be going anywhere, even if he wanted to."

"Why's that?"

"Because he's been murdered."

8

CRIME SCENE TAPE encircled the Sand Dollar Motel like a ribbon on a present, but this was no birthday party. The motel was just a few miles east of my office, on Colonial, toward the University of Central Florida. Two white crime scene vans were parked in the lot along with several derelict vehicles. The two-story L-shaped motel was infamous in the area for catering to a less-than-desirable crowd and renting rooms by the hour.

As I passed the motel, searching for a place to park, Oscar was talking with a woman just outside the front office, which was positioned at the entrance of the parking lot. In her late fifties and wearing a pink flowery gown, she had brown hair streaked with gray. Her hands flailed about as she told her story to Oscar.

I found a spot in an adjacent lot, and Crevis, who I'd diverted from Cassandra Ramsey's house, met me there. I grabbed my case file, as thin as it was, and met Crevis on the sidewalk.

"Come on, Ray." Crevis locked the company van with the remote. "You gotta buy a better car. I gotta check my man card before I get into this thing. I can't be seen in this. It'll kill my rep."

"I hate to be the bringer of bad news, Stallion, but you don't have a rep to ruin. And it's a minivan, not a chick magnet," I said. "It's a great surveillance vehicle. We're not making so much money that we can afford a fleet, so unless you're willing to buy your own car and use it, I suggest you just get used to the soccer-mom mobile."

A Hispanic patrol officer held his hand up as we approached on the sidewalk. I pulled my badge and ID card from my wallet. As I showed them to him, Oscar called out, "Log them in and let them pass."

The officer jotted our names and the time on the crime scene log. Oscar handed the woman a business card and hurried toward us. His shirt-sleeves were unbuttoned at the wrist and rolled up to his elbow. His coat was off, and his gun and badge were clipped to his belt. An OPD badge tack pinned his tie to his shirt. The late afternoon sun glinted off his graying temples.

I shook hands with Oscar. "What happened?"

"Looks like some of Logan's bad habits caught up with him." Oscar posted his hands on his hips as he shifted toward the room roped off with crime scene tape. "He's in room 107. I'll let you take a look. Just don't start searching or do anything crazy that I have to explain later."

"No problem." I pulled out my phone and captured a quick video of the scene. Some habits were hard to break. I liked having something to look at when I wrote my reports. I'm a visual guy. "Do you mind if Crevis comes in? It would be good training."

"He can step in the door and get a look, but he can't go any farther than that, and definitely don't let him touch anything. Bowden's going to be lead on this. We're buried in other cases, so I'll be his backup and walk him through the investigation." He pointed to Detective Greg Bowden, who was taking a statement from a middle-aged black male in the doorway of a second-floor room.

Bowden was still pretty fresh in Homicide, but Oscar said good things about him. As large as a football lineman, he stood a solid six-one with thick, well-muscled arms that looked like they could pull off a car door. He wore a white long-sleeved shirt with a blue tie. His brown hair receded on his forehead like a tide that had gone out and never come back. Bowden acknowledged us and then continued talking to the witness.

"I'll stay out here, Ray." Crevis took two steps back and crossed his arms. "I can help guard the scene."

"You need to come." I dug the tip of the cane into the craggy pavement. "It's good training."

"Really, Ray. I can stay out here."

"Let me rephrase that—you're going in. If you're going to be a cop, you need to get used to dead people. It's kind of a prerequisite."

"Okay."

His head drooped, and he shuffled behind me and Oscar toward room 107, which was on the first floor and faced Colonial Drive. A petite female patrol officer with short black hair stood guard just outside the open door. No cars were parked in front of the room or close to it.

"What did the management have to say?" I asked Oscar.

"A woman checked into the room two days ago, late Tuesday night. She registered under the name Savannah Breeze. No ID, of course, and the manager doesn't remember much about her. House-keeping found him today."

"Savannah Breeze?" I stepped up onto the walkway. "Original, anyway. I get the feeling we're going to have a hard time finding any Savannah Breezes in the databases."

"You think?" Oscar said. "An alias if I ever heard one."

Crevis trailed us, remaining quiet.

Oscar reached in his pocket and pulled out a pair of rubber gloves. He worked them onto his large hands. I didn't have any with me and really didn't want to hobble back to the truck.

"Hey, Katie," Oscar yelled into the room. "Can you come out here for a second?"

Katie Pham appeared in the doorway, decked out in her white crime scene suit, complete with booties and rubber gloves. A camera dangled around her neck. "Ray! What are you doing here? I'd give you a hug, but I'm all geared up." She feigned an air hug toward me. Of Filipino descent, Katie had a sleek, fit frame that could make even the most prosaic crime scene apparel look like runway model clothing. Her chocolate brown hair was tied back, and her blue eyes beamed. She seemed legitimately happy to see us.

Our friendship had a volatile beginning, but she really pulled through on Pam's case. I was able to keep a couple things out of the final report that could have caused her grief at her job, mainly her connection to Club Venus. Everyone had a past, but that didn't mean it had to be exposed. Katie was a class act and had put herself on the line to catch a killer. I wasn't about to toss her overboard for that. I was glad she was working the scene.

"Crevis, it's great to see you too," she said. "What are you guys doing here?"

Crevis feigned a smile, but his head drooped again. He shifted his weight from one foot to the other.

"We've got a case with Logan," I said. "Looks like our case has just gotten a little complicated."

"I didn't know Logan before, but I'm sure he looked better than he does now." Katie snapped the lens cap on her camera. "It's a bit of a mess in there."

Crevis's face flushed, and he held his stomach. "I don't think I'm gonna make it."

"Do you have some gloves and booties we can use?" I held up my hands. "I need to come in."

"Sure, Ray." She eyed Oscar.

"It's okay. They're consulting on the case." He lifted one foot and slipped a paper boot over his shoe, then did the same with the other foot. "I still can't believe you talked the brass into approving you as a consultant. You solve one good case and suddenly you're an expert."

I shrugged. "They felt guilty about me being crippled, so I took advantage of it. I don't care what they call me, as long as I can get access."

"You're somethin' else, Ray," Oscar said.

Katie handed me the gloves, and I gave a set to Crevis and put on mine. Crevis did the same.

"I'm going to need some help, Crevis."

I leaned hard on my cane, and Crevis bent down and wrapped

a bootie over my left foot. I stepped into the room and lifted my right foot as much as I could. I teetered and used the wall to keep myself vertical. Once the bootie was on my right foot, I swung it into the room, my file folder still in tow.

Crevis slipped on his booties and stopped outside the door. I shuffled forward and waved at him to follow me. He sucked in a deep breath and stepped in.

The dank, cramped room reeked of mold and soiled laundry. The dark wood paneling along the walls gave the room a cave appeal. A 1970s television sat on a rickety stand, rabbit ears protruding. The multistained curtains were drawn, and the window air-conditioner did little to temper the heat.

Logan was on the bed, lying on his back with his arms at his sides.

I eased closer to the bed, making sure I wasn't trampling any evidence. Logan wore blue jeans and a white T-shirt. A red button-up shirt hung on the bedpost, and his brown leather jacket lay on the dresser. He didn't have any shoes on but was wearing socks. His brown work boots sat next to the bed. He'd probably just kicked off his boots and lay down to rest when he was attacked.

He'd have looked fairly peaceful if it weren't for the silver-handled knife with a skull at the end buried to the hilt in his chest. The skull had red luminescent eyes that peered at me.

Logan's waxy face showed the wear of a life lived too hard. His physique was still well muscled, but it too suffered the degenerative disintegration of ascending years and descending sobriety. The worn ink of a "Rebel Soldiers" tattoo graced his forearm, accompanied by some barbed wire around his right bicep. "L.O.V.E." was spelled out on the knuckles of his right hand, and "H.A.T.E." on his left, a combination that described Logan in a frighteningly appropriate way. Logan had played the role of outlaw biker back then. Maybe too well. Maybe he wasn't playing, only behaving, which could explain his troubles.

I'd seen hundreds of dead folks in my time, killed in every manner possible, but the other victims were just business for me, no different than an accountant reviewing a spreadsheet. It was just part of the job. But Logan and I knew each other. We'd spent time in each other's company, and now he lay before me, perforated with a creepy knife in a nasty hotel room. His glazed, vacant eyes were fixed toward the heavens. What had brought him to this? And what a lousy place to die.

Crevis groaned.

"Don't lose it." I leaned forward, examining the scene as best I could.

Crevis bolted from the room, hand over mouth. A guttural heave emanated from him as he launched his lunch into the parking lot with a splash.

I shrugged. "At least he didn't goo up the crime scene."

Oscar chuckled and elbowed me. "Rookies."

At least five more small tears were apparent in Logan's shirt, like the marks of a tiger's claw. Probably more stab wounds to the chest. Knife attacks were usually very personal: an up-close weapon. The multiple wounds indicated extreme passion. This was more than stolen assets or a robbery gone bad.

The white shirt was remarkably free of the crimson notice of most stab wounds, which were characterized by copious amounts of blood. I saw only small slits in the shirt with trace amounts of blood around them.

"Not much blood for a stabbing." I took more video with my phone and snapped a couple of stills as well.

Crevis hurled again, the noise barely rising above the rattling air conditioner.

"Yeah, but it looks like the knife is right in his heart." Oscar shuffled to my side. "That'd make him DRT, Dead Right There. He bled internally. I bet when the M.E. opens him up, his chest cavity will be full of blood. That's why we don't see much here."

"Looks like whoever did this nailed him where he's at. Nothing in the room is overturned or looks like a struggle took place." I stepped to the edge of the bed. "No apparent defensive wounds to his hands or forearms either. It just seems weird."

"His lividity is consistent with his body position," Oscar said, pointing to where blood pooled underneath the skin at the neck and arms, making his exposed skin look like a large pink bruise. In fact, his skin seemed excessively pink, although it could have been the lighting.

"Whoever did this either snuck into the room and caught him off guard or was with him the whole time," Oscar said. "He was a tough cop and would have fought back. I agree that it doesn't look right. Not sure why yet."

"Whoever did this must be someone he knew and was comfortable enough with to rest like that before he was attacked." I pointed out the wounds with the cane. "Maybe someone who goes by Savannah Breeze?"

"She'd be a good place to start." Oscar forced his hands into his pockets, a good habit for a cop in a scene, so you don't mess with things.

Katie snapped a photo. "Is Crevis going to be okay?"

"He's fine," I said. "He just can't seem to get used to dead things. We're working on that."

A bottle of Jack Daniel's lay on the floor at the foot of the bed. It had been opened, but only a couple of fingers were missing. Two glasses were on the floor next to it. Logan could put it away in his day. I much preferred Jim Beam myself, although if they were investigating my death, I'm sure the bottle would be empty.

Logan's suitcase was on the floor near the foot of the bed, a small bundle of shirts, jeans, and his shaving kit visible. The brown satchel from the surveillance photo from Mayer Holdings was nowhere in sight.

An open pizza box covered the surface of the nightstand next to the bed. Three pieces were missing.

"Katie, can I get a copy of all your photos and video for my case?" I said.

"Sure. I'll e-mail them to you when I get back."

"Also, if you find a brown leather satchel or any electronic storage devices—thumb drives, external hard drives, even iPods or phones—let me know." I pulled the surveillance photo from my file and showed them what I was looking for.

"No problem, Ray." She snapped two more pictures. "I'll keep an eye out for everything."

"Has anyone found his phone?" I asked.

"It's on the dresser, and the battery's dead," Oscar said. "We'll power it back up when we get it to the station. Then we can check his last calls."

"Oscar, I'll make a deal with you," I said.

"I don't like your deals, Ray." Oscar crossed his arms. "I always come out on the short end of them."

"Not on this one," I said. "I have an agreement with a private DNA lab in North Carolina. I can get my results back in days, not months like the state labs. If Katie can do extra DNA swabs for me, I'll send them off to my lab, and I'll share the results with you. My client is willing to pay whatever it takes to get his property back, so I'm willing to spend whatever it takes of his money to get it done."

"And what do you want in return?" Oscar raised an eyebrow.

Crevis launched into his third and what I hoped was his last round of chumming the parking lot.

"Just share anything you come up with," I said. "We'll work it together. You catch his killer, and I get my client's information back. It's win-win."

Oscar rubbed his chin and sighed. "If I do this, you can't tell everyone. It could taint the case for court. And you can't go all rogue Ray Quinn on me either, or we'll part ways. I've got a responsibility to do this right. The brass is going to be watching, since Logan used to be one of us."

"I'll be on my best behavior." I raised my right hand.

"I don't want your 'best' behavior," he said. "I want better behavior. Much better. No tasering witnesses, impromptu wiretaps, hacking computers, or transporting prisoners in your trunk. You need to do everything right."

I had forgotten about the prisoner in the trunk.

"My best behavior," I said, forming my right hand into the three-fingered Boy Scout pledge sign. "Scout's honor."

"Ray, we both know you were never, ever a Boy Scout."

9

CREVIS WAS HUNCHED OVER with his hands on his knees, his gloves and booties still on, much to the amusement of the female officer standing watch next to him.

"Are you about finished?" I said as I exited the room. "I figured we'd get some barbecued pulled pork and greasy cheese fries for dinner."

"Not funny, Ray," he managed. He spit twice, never looking up at me.

Since Crevis was temporarily out of commission and unable to lend a hand, I poked the tip of my cane into a paper bootie and pushed it off my foot. I did the same with the other, then used the cane to slide the booties out of the way. Katie or someone else in Crime Scene would pick them up later and dispose of them.

Oscar and I huddled in the parking lot. Greg Bowden finished up with the man on the second floor, walked down the stairs, and approached us.

"I just spoke with a guy named Pat Collins," Bowden said, reading off his legal pad. "He's been staying here for four days. This morning at about 2:20 a.m. he was just going to sleep when he heard what he thought was a scream. He looked out his window." Bowden pointed to the second-floor motel room, one down from being above Logan's room. "He saw a female running through the parking lot from the area of Logan's room. She was white and wearing dark clothing—probably jeans and a shirt, but he couldn't be sure. He saw her from behind as she ran, so he won't be able to do a lineup. That was all he could tell us."

"Did he see a car or anything?" I asked.

"Nope," Bowden said. "He figured it was a lovers' spat and went back to bed."

"How credible does he seem?" Oscar asked.

Bowden shrugged. "Seemed pretty credible."

Crevis staggered over and joined the huddle, wiping his mouth on his sleeve. He seemed to be attempting to work some color back into his face.

"Has anyone searched Logan's car?" I said.

"We've run the tags in the parking lot," Bowden said. "None of them came back to Logan. We still have a lot of work to do. I'm going to call in more detectives to help with everyone in the motel. Then we have to search the Dumpsters and stuff, plus what still has to be covered in the room. It's gonna be a long night."

"I guess we can assume his car is missing then," I said. "It wasn't at his house. We were there earlier."

"We'll input it into NCIC/FCIC, so if patrol runs the tag, they'll know to stop it," Oscar said. "Maybe whoever did this stole it as well."

"Or maybe Logan just parked it somewhere else, so whoever was looking for him wouldn't see it. Someone's tossed his house. Every room was turned upside down."

"If he wasn't there, how did you get in?" Bowden asked.

Oscar sighed and rubbed his chin. "I don't think I want to hear this."

I snapped to attention. "Upon arriving at his residence, from our position at the door, I could see that some dastardly person had kicked in the door. Fearing for the safety of Logan Ramsey, I and my trusty assistant, Crevis Creighton, entered the residence to ascertain if Mr. Ramsey was indeed unharmed. In the process of conducting that safety search, we observed that the house was in disarray—in other words, had been tossed."

"Wow. That's the biggest load of garbage I've heard in a long time," Bowden said.

"You're very astute. But that's how my report is going to read." I flashed him a full-toothed grin.

"I've called out the rest of the unit to get the neighborhood canvass done," Oscar said. "We'll wait until they arrive."

The nice part about being a consultant and a PI was that I could leave the scene anytime I wanted. Bowden had a good grasp of the case and had Oscar to help him through any tough spots. My client needed to know what was going on. Logan's death changed the dynamics of the case considerably.

Katie walked from the motel room and hurried over to us. "I thought you might find this interesting," she said. She held out a three-by-five-inch picture. "I found it in his coat pocket."

The photo showed Logan sitting in a recliner with a young girl, maybe nine or ten years old, sitting in his lap. Logan had a beer in one hand and his other arm around her. She was hugging him and pulling his face close to her, smiling the kind of smile that only a child's love could manage. Her features mirrored his except for her shiny black hair. Definitely his daughter.

"Has anyone made contact with the next of kin?" I said.

"Not yet," Oscar said.

"Do you want us to do it?" I held up the file. "I have the daughter's information. Crevis and I were going to talk with her anyway. I can get a statement from her and see if she knows anything. I know you're short-handed."

Bowden paused for a moment. "Yeah, Ray. That's no problem. I hate doing death notifications, so I won't wrestle you for it. And we've got a lot more to do here tonight. Just let me know what she says."

I wished he had wrestled me and won. I had no desire to tell Cassandra Ramsey her father had been murdered.

10

CREVIS AND I DROVE out to Cassandra Ramsey's neighborhood in Clermont, a sleepy hamlet west of Orlando.

Finding Logan and retrieving the stolen property at first seemed easy, quick, and lucrative—but had morphed into something wicked and hideous. Logan's house had been tossed, and he was taking an eternal dirt nap. My client did need to know the latest information on the case, but I wasn't inclined to trust the man completely. So when the time came, I'd figure out how much to tell him—and how much not to.

I pulled Cassandra's information from the file. Thirty-one years old. Never married. One car, a Honda Civic, and it appeared she lived alone. No criminal history. Graduated from the University of Miami with an engineering degree. Sounded like she was a pretty boring young lady.

A knot formed in my gut, knowing I had to tell her that her father was dead, murdered in a sleazy motel. One of the lousier jobs in police work. And I wasn't even a cop anymore. I should bill Armon extra for this.

I took out my phone and speed-dialed Wykoff. I didn't have a number for Armon.

"Detective Quinn," he said.

"I have some good news and some bad news."

"Good news first, please," he said.

"I've found Logan."

"Great work, Detective Quinn," he said. "Mr. Mayer will be so pleased. Have you recovered the items?"

"Well, that's where the bad news comes in." I held the phone between my shoulder and ear as I shuffled through the file. "Logan's been murdered. Someone plunged a knife into his chest at the Sand Dollar Motel. No sign of the satchel or any of the stolen property."

"So you haven't recovered the information?" he asked.

"No. I haven't recovered the information. Did I mention that Logan's dead?"

"Very tragic. What are you doing to recover the hard drive? Do you have any indication of what he might have done with it?"

"I have a couple of leads. I'm working on them now," I said. "You need to let Armon know this could get costly. I'm working alongside the homicide unit. They're gonna give me full access."

"That's why we chose you," Wykoff said. "For your contacts with the police department."

"I'm sending some DNA swabs from the scene to a private lab. It's a lot faster than waiting for the state lab to get to anything. If I pay their hurry-up price, it will only be a few days before I have results."

"Whatever you need to do, Detective Quinn," he said. "This matter must be resolved as quickly as possible."

"I don't want to hear any complaining later about the bill," I said. "I'm fair, but I'm thorough. The lab test could get expensive."

"Mr. Mayer made it perfectly clear. He wants his information back. Do whatever you need to make it happen."

"Good enough for me," I said. "I'll keep you posted."

I hung up.

"So what'd he say?" Crevis asked.

"He gave us carte blanche to solve this thing," I said.

"Cart what?"

"It means an open checkbook." Armon's money funding the investigation struck me as ironic on a number of levels. Not that I'm so altruistic I didn't think of the payout for me and Crevis, but doing investigations on the cheap just doesn't work. If you're too worried about expenses, you cut corners, and that's when things get missed. While Wykoff eased some of my concerns, he raised a few more. Something about him saying they "chose" me didn't settle well with me.

We arrived at Cassandra's house, a two-story home squeezed into a neighborhood with about three feet between each house. The lower half of the home was covered in brick while the top half was light blue wood siding. Two children on bicycles passed my truck before we got out. A family neighborhood.

"So she doesn't know he's dead?" Crevis said.

"Not yet," I said. "We're going to tell her."

"What are you gonna say?" he said.

"Just watch and be quiet. We can't make it any better for her, but we'll try not to make it worse. Just follow my lead."

Her blue Honda was parked in the driveway. I listened at the door for a moment, a cop habit that followed me into this job. No matter the reason I was there, I liked to know what I was walking into. It was 6:00 p.m.; I could hear a television. I expected her to be home from work, school, or whatever.

I knocked once and saw movement through the full-length window that ran alongside the door. A woman with pitch-black hair, wearing brown pants and a white blouse, walked to the door and peered out the side window.

"Who is it?" She squinted and moved her head around for a better look.

"Cassandra Ramsey," I said, "I'm Detective Ray Quinn. I need to speak with you about your father. It's very important."

She opened the door a crack but kept her body behind it. "What's happened? What's wrong?"

I held up my badge, and Crevis did the same. "We're private investigators. I have something very important to talk to you about."

She stepped back and opened the door fully. Crevis and I walked inside. In an office to our immediate right, a computer was on. Her diploma from the University of Miami hung on the wall, as did several awards from her company.

"Please come into the living room." She hurried ahead of us, down a narrow hallway that opened into a large living room on the left and a kitchen on the right. About five-eight or five-nine, Cassandra was tall for a woman and unfortunately built like her father, with large bones and broad shoulders. Her black hair was trimmed short, just above her ears.

"Something's happened to him, hasn't it?" she said.

"Why don't you have a seat, Cassandra?" I pointed to the couch.

"It's Cassy." She faced us. "I'll stand. What's going on?"

"I'm very sorry, Cassy." I placed both hands on my cane. "Your father is dead."

She swallowed hard. Her eyes moistened, but she seemed to be fighting the tears, not wanting them to roll in front of us. "I knew this day would come. The way he was and all. I knew someday someone would come to tell me this. What happened?"

"It appears that he's been murdered."

As much as I wanted to sugarcoat it for her and gloss over the fact that her father was the victim of a homicide, there was no good way to do it. I'd learned through the years to be as clear and plain as possible. Her father was dead, murdered. No amount of euphemism would dull that reality or blunt the oncoming agony.

"Who did it? Who murdered him? Why?"

"We don't know yet, but we're working with OPD to find out. I know this is a difficult time, but do you think you could answer some questions?"

She nodded, a disconnected stare glazing her eyes.

"Do you know anyone who would want to hurt your father?"

She released a nervous chuckle. "A better question is who *didn't* want to kill him. Did you know my father?"

"I worked in the narcotics unit with him at OPD just after he broke the Rebels case. I knew him a little."

"Then you know how many lives he destroyed." A multicolored cat whose breed I couldn't identify sauntered toward her. She picked it up and stroked it. She pointed to a picture of her with a woman I assumed to be her mother. "He broke my mom's heart. He cheated on her so many times and always promised not to do it again. She would take him back, and he would be right back at it. He was rarely sober, especially after that stupid biker case. He was bad before that, but all that time working undercover ruined him—and us. He was never the same after that. We all fell apart."

"I'm very sorry," I said. "When was the last time you heard from him?"

"He called me about three days ago," she said. "He was babbling about something he had to do. I asked if he was drunk. He said he'd been sober for a couple weeks." She shook her head. "I've heard that from him before, many times. He said he'd call me back the next day but never did."

"Did he say anything else?" I asked. "Did he seem concerned about anything?"

"Just that he had something he had to do," she said. "For him to mention it like that, it had to be pretty important. But when he didn't call me back, I just figured he was on a binge again. Nothing he does surprises me anymore."

"When was the last time you saw him?" I asked.

"He came by three weeks or a month ago." She eased the cat to the floor; the beast sprinted between Crevis's legs and disappeared into the kitchen. "He's been trying to call or come by more. He said he wanted to make up for not being there for me when I was young. We talked a little. He seemed sincere, but he was more salesman than cop. He could talk paint off a car, if you know what I mean."

She knew her dad well. Even though I worked in the narcotics unit with him, I was no Logan Ramsey. Homicide was my thing, but Logan could work undercover like no cop I'd ever seen before. I occasionally drove through some of the drug areas, bought dope off street dealers, and made busts that way. That was easy. The street dealers would sell anything to anyone who pulled up. That wasn't working undercover.

Logan went deep undercover, living a whole other life in an outlaw biker gang. He was able to put them at ease and thrive in that lifestyle without tipping them off that he was a cop. He talked the talk and walked the walk. He was a master actor, and because of that, he brought down some real thugs. The Rebel Soldiers were pushing large amounts of meth and guns through their club. Fourteen club members and their girlfriends were federally indicted on gun and drug charges, which added significantly to the number of people who wanted to skewer and fillet him.

"Why are private investigators involved in this?" She wiped some tears off her cheek and pushed her hair back.

"The Mayer people, your dad's employer, asked me to look into some issues with him," I said, being intentionally vague. "Then this happened."

"He was in trouble with them too? He said he liked that job. Made him feel like he was back in police work again. I knew he'd do something to ruin it."

"Does he have any property or personal items here?" I asked.

"No," she said. "He never left anything but a bad taste."

"I would like to get a sample of your DNA if I could," I said. "To compare against any evidence found. Would that be okay?"

She agreed.

I put on rubber gloves and removed two sterile swabs, like long Q-tips, from their packaging. Cassy opened her mouth. I ran the swab along the inside of her cheek and twisted it for about ten seconds to collect buccal mucus for the DNA test. I repeated the action with the second swab on the other cheek.

I would start a databank for this case with my lab and use it to compare any potential evidence collected. The DNA testing was so sensitive now that technicians could find DNA on items that were just touched or brushed against. The technology had come a long way in a very short amount of time, and I would use that to my advantage.

"Again, I'm very sorry for everything." I handed her a business card with my cell phone number on it. "I would like to talk with your mom, if that's okay. Maybe she could give me some insights on the case."

"That's not possible," Cassy said. "She died almost four years ago. Cancer. I always felt it was the stress of the divorce and the drama Dad put her through that wrecked her health. Now he's not even around for me to be angry with anymore."

I promised I would contact her if we found anything more. Crevis and I left Cassy to her cat and her grief.

11

WE ARRIVED AT the office at about 9:00 p.m. Some event was going on at the Amway Arena across the street, and a cascade of red brake lights backed up Colonial Drive, which made us ten minutes later to our office than we should have been—a factor I did not consider when I chose the location. After negotiating through the horrendous traffic, we finally turned into the office parking lot.

Swaying and teetering, I crept up the stairs, cane in one hand, railing in the other. The hum of the cars and occasional horn blast added to the chaos in my head. I'd pushed myself too hard again. I unlocked the office door and punched the security code into the alarm system's keypad.

The talk with Cassy disturbed me more than expected. I'd witnessed loved ones crumple on the floor or jump up and down, crying out in pain when I delivered the news of an untimely, felonious death. Cassy displayed little emotion to what should have been a catastrophic loss. Logan's waywardness and capricious affections had severed the natural bonds of a daughter to her father.

I didn't have children and, growing up in foster care, I'd never experienced the special union of parent and child, but I'd still expected something resembling extreme sorrow from her. Logan and Cassy's fractured relationship moved me into a melancholy mood as I settled into the office.

Crevis worked on his homework while I finished reading the Internal Affairs report on Logan's fall. Frustrating stuff, like something you'd read in a cheap, tawdry novel. If I wasn't careful, I'd drain the whole bottle of Jim Beam tucked away in my desk just to stomach the foul tale.

After the Rebel Soldiers case, Logan had an informant named Nicole "Nikki" Bray. Logan and Nikki's relationship drifted ever so carelessly from professional to personal. Nikki's boyfriend at the time was a slug named Jason Santos. OPD's narcotics unit worked a case against Santos. When the S.W.A.T. team hit his house to serve the narcotics search warrant, they found that a shotgun had been propped up, facing the front door, with a cord attached to the trigger—a death trap for the cops who entered the home. If S.W.A.T. hadn't entered through the rear door, there would have been a police funeral to attend.

Santos was arrested for the gun charge and said in his formal statement that Nikki told him the cops were coming for him. The case was tainted, though, by all the drama, and Santos cut a deal for five years in federal prison so the prosecutors didn't have to rehash all the dirty details of the case in court. According to Santos, Logan disclosed the case against him during some "pillow talk" with Nikki; she then tipped off Santos.

The internal investigation was long and painful. Sergeant Phillips was as rapturous as if he'd won a lifelong pass to an all-you-can-eat buffet. Logan copped to an "inappropriate relationship" with his informant but denied he intentionally revealed anything to her about ongoing investigations. It didn't matter. His career was over, and the shroud of suspicion that he was complicit in nearly getting some S.W.A.T. guys killed never lifted from him. Logan dropped off the face of the earth, until he dropped dead at the Sand Dollar Motel.

I considered toasting Logan but stopped short, conflicting thoughts sparring in my head. Part of Logan I despised in an intense way. He'd let himself get entangled in the filth of the world we were fighting against. His betrayal stung on a personal level. He was one of us, the police, the Good Guys, supposedly.

The other part of me was saddened by his wasted life, the family he'd destroyed, and the way he died—alone in a filthy motel room.

A scary realization I didn't want to acknowledge probed the perimeters of my mind: I understood Logan with frightening clarity.

Police work could eat away at you with the malignancy of an unrelenting cancer until it destroyed everything you once were. I knew what that felt like. Witnessing the constant pain and misery of others, fighting to save a world that didn't want to be saved, and crashing hard on some terrible event—for Logan, being fired in disgrace. For me, being shot twice and left for dead just feet away from the woman I loved.

Either way, the job changed us both forever and not for the better. It had buried Logan, and there were times when I felt like I wasn't far behind.

I focused my thoughts back on the case and spent the next thirty minutes printing off pictures and information from what I knew so far. Grabbing my stack of papers, I caned over to the whiteboard mounted on our wall. Some random scribbling still covered it from the Wagner case. I wiped it clean, then smacked Logan's picture in the center.

"Okay, Crevis." I picked up a marker. "Today's lesson is on victimology."

"Victim what?"

"Victimology. The detailed study of a person's life, habits, and hobbies that help identify who would want to dispatch said person to the netherworld. So, let's start by breaking Logan's life down a bit."

The marker squeaked along the board as I drew a line off to the side. "Logan put a good number of biker scum in federal prison." I jetted an arrow from Logan to the Rebel Soldiers. "He leaked information to a drug dealer about OPD's narcotics operations, which didn't endear his name to anyone in the police world and infuriated every cop in the area. He had numerous affairs and girlfriends in life, leaving a trail of broken, angry women behind him. He stole assets from his employer, for which I'm sure someone tossed his apartment. And finally, he was a chronic alcoholic." By the time I'd finished the last sweep of the high-pitched marker, Logan's picture and wrecked life had grown monstrous spider legs on the board.

"What does all that mean?" Crevis scratched his chin. "Who do you think killed him?"

"Well, judging from our hastily drawn chart, I'd say we have approximately five hundred thousand very solid suspects. Basically, anyone in the greater Orlando area who Logan pissed off or wronged in some way."

"What do we do now?"

I settled onto my desk top, easing some of the pressure off my hip, which burned from the pace of a chaotic day. I opened my bottom drawer, moved my *Handbook for Private Detectives,* and grabbed the fifth of Jim Beam and a glass. I poured myself a taste. Crevis eyed me.

"We're done for the day, and my hip is killing me," I said. "Do you have a problem with that?"

He sighed. "No problem. Unless you need me, I'm headin' home. Pam's going to meet me here early tomorrow."

"For your book learnin'." I raised the glass again.

Crevis snarled.

"Tomorrow we'll coordinate with Oscar and his crew." I topped off my drink. "I think we need to vet some suspects."

"Who?"

"I don't know yet." I held up the stack of reports I had on Logan. "I'll review these tonight and get a better idea."

"How ya getting home?" Crevis spun his keys on his finger. "I can come back later and pick you up. You shouldn't drive tonight."

"I'll be fine, Mother Hubbard," I said. "Get home and get some sleep. I don't want Pam giving me grief about you not getting to bed at a good hour on a school night."

"If you get a DUI, don't call me to bail you out. I'll leave you there for the night."

"Let me worry about that."

Crevis headed out the door and down to the van. His taillights melded with the scarlet stream on Colonial Drive.

I sucked down two gulps of Jim that made my eyes water. The throbbing pulse of my hip, though blunted, kept me focused. The pain pills numbed me and messed my head up so much I couldn't think. At least with Jim, I could function. I'd deal with the aftermath of a little too much of him in the morning. A few aspirins and a gallon or two of coffee, and I'd be on track. The pills never felt right. Jim was a much better traveling partner.

I checked my e-mail. Along with the normal junk, I had a reply from my new friend—Mr. Chaka Nomvete.

Dear Mrs. Simpkins,

Greetings and blessings from South Africa! I hope today finds you well. I knew when I sent my message to you that you would be the one who could help us out of our terrible mess. I understand the problems you seem to be having with your son. But are you not his mother? You could ask him for such a simple request to help us out, and in return we can compensate you and your son in an enormous manner. If you can get a bank account number to us, we can deposit the money immediately! I feel very blessed to have contact a woman such as yourself. Please contact me soon.

God bless you!

Chaka Nomvete

My good friend had been sufficiently drawn in. He didn't seem skittish at all about the true identity of Mrs. Simpkins. His e-mail brimmed with excitement and nudged me a little out of my glum mood. I hoped to whet his appetite for the vulnerable Mrs. Simpkins just a little more.

Dear Mr. Nomvete,

It's so good to hear from you. I did discuss the matter with my son today, and he just doesn't seem to understand the dire nature of your situation, even though I explained it to him again and again. He doesn't want to give me the account numbers because he thinks I will do something to spend our great wealth. I've assured him that you're a good man in need of our help. He wasn't convinced. He needs some sort of good faith effort on your part before he'll consider releasing the account numbers to me. I just don't understand him sometimes. But he does have the control of the entire estate. Please give me something that I can convince him with. I will continue to pray for you and this situation. I look forward to hearing from you.

Blessings,

Marion Simpkins

I wasn't sure what kind of "good faith" offering I was looking for, but it was fun to ask. Who knew what he would send. I had to keep Mrs. Simpkins believable and yet still draw him in. We'd see if it worked.

12

I ROLLED INTO Crevis's and my apartment complex, Hacienda Del Sol, at oh-dark-thirty. Our little slice of heaven sat just off of John Young Parkway. I'd arrived home intact, unarrested, and at least working my way toward sober.

The horseshoe-shaped, two-story complex was being renovated; most of the other apartments were empty. We were one of the few tenants, and if I had anything to do with it, we'd be gone as soon as possible. We were on the first floor facing the pool, so I didn't have to dislocate my hip hiking the stairs every time I went home. An iron gate enclosed the pool area and small courtyard. Our one-bedroom flat had a living room—where Crevis slept on the couch—a kitchen area, and a master bedroom the size of a closet.

Jim had numbed my leg enough to get me up and moving from the office without getting too plowed under to make it home, in spite of Crevis's dire warnings. He was crashed on the couch when I opened the door. We'd been roommates for about six months. He started living with me after someone attempted to blow me away in my own place when I was investigating Pam's case. Now I'd have to get a restraining order to get him out.

The lone object of any real value in the entire abode was my shrine to John Wayne—a painting of the Duke on his trusty mount and a collector's envy of DVDs on two shelves on either side of our television. I'd found every movie the Duke ever appeared in and placed them in chronological order.

Whatever else I was immersing Crevis into, at least I was getting this right. He was becoming quite the aficionado of fine Duke films, though he lacked a deeper understanding and appreciation for the earlier movies like *Stagecoach*. We were working on that.

I grappled through a few hours of fitful sleep—the case and my chronic insomnia chatting with each other until the early hours of the morning. During those hours of erratic slumber, the direction of the case became apparent. We would visit Mr. Jason Santos in the morning.

Crevis and I started moving about the same time that morning. Neither of us were too talkative, which was good. He'd have been homeless if he pestered me before my morning coffee.

I got up, took my jeans from the closet, and laid them on the floor. I used the handle of my cane to cinch them up to where I could grab the waistband and work them around my hips. I was getting better at it—one of the many adjustments in my life since my injury.

I caned out of my room and down the short hallway to the living room and kitchen area. A leather heavy bag hung from the ceiling. Crevis pounded out combinations and worked drills I'd prepared for him to sharpen his skills. When I was feeling particularly brave, I slipped on the bag gloves and went a round or two on the bag. If I didn't fall on my face like an idiot at least once during the workout, I didn't think it was worth it. The management hadn't said anything about the bag or the thunderous jolts when Crevis hit it, but we didn't have any neighbors yet to complain.

I passed Crevis on my way through the kitchen and gave him a nod. I went straight for the coffee and scooped enough Joe into the filter to bury a body. It was a necessity to get moving. Jim to get to sleep, and Joe to get moving. And Crevis as my bodyguard. Life could take weird, unexpected turns at times.

Crevis sported his gray suit with a thin black tie and the sharp-rimmed fedora as we rode to a neighborhood in West Orlando off Rio Grande. It didn't matter the temperature or the weather, he would "Bogey up," as he called it.

"As soon as the coffee kicks in, we're gonna visit a potential suspect."

"Who is this guy?" Crevis asked.

"Jason Santos." My plastic coffee mug was filled to the top, and I sipped it so it wouldn't spill. "I reviewed the I.A. file on Logan last night, and he was the drug dealer Logan gave information to through his informant Nikki Bray. Jason was a pretty bad dude and did time for weapons violations, drugs, and assault, so keep your eyes open."

Crevis checked his hat in the mirror and adjusted it around his crimson cranium. "Not to worry, boss. I got you covered. I'm a weapon of death and destruction."

"Great," I said. "I feel much better about this now."

13

SANTOS'S ADDRESS WAS in a decent middle-class area. The houses were close together, and sidewalks and streetlights lined the road. His single-story tan stucco residence blended in with every other cookie-cutter home on the street. A basketball goal was mounted above the garage door, a tricycle sat in the front yard, and several plastic toys littered the side of the driveway.

We parked on the street a house away so we could approach from a relative distance, paying attention to the target. Maybe it was the fact that I had been ambushed walking up to a suspect's house once before that gave me an abundance of caution on this day. My cane wobbled as we entered the archway to the front door. I made sure Crevis couldn't see it.

After a couple of knocks, a woman in her midthirties answered the door. She had a soft, round face and was a little taller than Pam, about five-five or so, and her straight brunette hair reached to the small of her back. She wore shorts and a white T-shirt with tiny finger smudges all over it and propped a kid on her hip.

The child, maybe two years old, suffered from an explosion of curly black hair and a wild-eyed gaze that fixed on Crevis, who waved at her and flashed an equally dopey expression back. I'd talk with him about that later. The chaotic chatter of several other children spilled out of the house.

"Can I help you?" she asked.

"I'm Detective Ray Quinn." I showed her my badge. "I would like to talk with Jason Santos, please."

She eased the child to the floor. "Go in the kitchen, honey. I'll be there in a second." The imp fled, bare feet slapping the tile. After stepping out on the porch, she slammed the door behind her, crossed her arms, and faced me. "What's this about?"

"It's about talking to Mr. Santos." I eased my wallet into my back pocket. "My business is with him."

"I'm Mrs. Santos, and I'm telling you to leave my property now." She squared her eyes on me and shifted into a fighter's stance. "I'm tired of all you cops from his past coming back here and harassing him. He's paid his debt and changed his life. Can't you get that through your thick skulls? He has a family and responsibilities and is a taxpaying citizen. His old life is long behind him; I've made sure of that. So take your friend and get off my porch before I call the chief of police and have you both fired."

"Call whoever you like." I discovered another nugget of joy in working for myself. No Internal Affairs, and no supervisor to scrutinize my every move or have me fired should I anger the wrong person. I breathed in a stimulating whiff of fresh, unrestrained air. "I came here to talk with Mr. Santos, and I'm not leaving until I do. I know he's home, so tell him to come out and talk with me for ten minutes, like a man, and I'll be out of his life."

"This harassment is going to stop. You'll be out of his life right now." She pointed toward the street, as if I didn't know where it was. "I'm going to call 911 and have you removed. Get off my property."

The front door opened and a man appeared. I almost didn't recognize him. Jason Santos stepped out onto the porch, an older child clinging to his leg. With the gentle skill of an experienced father, he pried her arms off and directed her back into the house before he shut the door behind him. Jason's facial features were the same, though softer. He wasn't nearly the hardened felon his pictures and history painted. A tan smock wrapped around his blue jeans and he wore a blue shirt with an American flag on it. His black hair was cut short, almost to his scalp, with the voided patterns of a receding hairline. Other than a couple of jailhouse tats on his forearms, he looked like a dad.

"I'm Jason Santos." He wiped his hands on the sides of his jeans. "What do you want?"

"You don't have to talk with them." His wife pushed against his chest, trying to turn him back inside. "They're just going to keep harassing you until you take a stand."

"Cindy, go inside." He took her hands in his and locked eyes with her. "I'll take care of this. It's going to be okay. Trust me."

"I do trust you. It's these guys I don't," she said. "They'll never stop."

"It'll be okay." He opened the door and pushed her gently on the shoulder. "Please. Let me handle this. I know what I'm doing. Just watch the kids until I'm finished."

The first child had returned to the doorway. Cindy scooped her up as she stormed back into the house, taking time to assault me with her glare.

Jason sighed. "I'm sorry. She's very protective of me, of all of us. A lot's been going on lately."

"Do you know why we're here?" It was a good question to start with, to set the tone of the interview.

"I imagine it's about Logan Ramsey," he said. "I read about it in the paper this morning."

"You're a good guesser." I scribbled down the date and time on a legal pad. "When was the last time you saw Logan?"

Jason paused and shifted his eyes from Crevis to me. "What agency do you work for?"

"We're private detectives," I said. "We're assisting in the investigation."

"You're not OPD?"

"Nope," I said, keeping mum that I used to be OPD and was still a consultant. "Does it matter?"

"Probably not." He leaned back against the doorframe. "Look, if you know anything about me at all, you know about my past. That's not who I am now. I did my time in prison and got my life right. You see I have a family and a life now. I own my own business, doing sculptures and jewelry repair and all sorts of things. I have a shop out back. Like I said, I'm not what I was. I'm very blessed in a lot of ways. I'm not involved in all the drama with Logan and that group. That's ancient history."

"Since we're on the subject, what were you?" I said.

"I was a drug dealer, meth head, and a lot of other things I don't care to go into." He crossed his arms. "Prison got my attention and straightened me out. I got clean, and I'm never going back to that life. And I'm certainly never, ever going back to prison."

He'd passed my first test and was being straight about his past. Not a bad start.

"So, back to the original question," I said. "When did you last see Logan?"

The front window curtain jostled. The gracious Mrs. Santos watched me with a stare that could have been chiseled out of Mount Rushmore.

"He came by here about a month ago." Santos's lungs deflated. "I hadn't seen him since I got arrested. When I was with Nikki, years ago. That's why Cindy's so freaked right now. He just showed up at our door, like you. And he waved a badge around too."

A souvenir from his cop days, I wagered. "What did he want?"

"He was really drunk. Said he was going to ruin me like I had ruined him. He'd hooked up with Nikki again, and if it was the last thing he did, he was going to see me back in prison forever."

"What did you do?"

"I tried to tell him how my life had changed and reason with him, but he was really pissed. I told him to leave, and he grabbed me and threw me around. He's a big dude."

"Did you call the police?"

"Yeah, right." He chuckled. "Me—the ex-con on lifetime probation—call the cops on an ex-cop. I think we know how that would have turned out."

"You're still on probation?"

"Yep. One wrong step, I go back to prison for a very long time. That's why I make every appointment with my probation officer, take a drug test twice a month, and am in the house after sundown. I'm not doing anything stupid to ruin what I got."

Another test passed. I already knew his probation status.

"I guess you had good reason to be angry with Logan, then?" I said. "He could have destroyed everything you have, taken it away in a heartbeat."

He raised his hands and stepped back. "I know what you're thinking, but I didn't have anything to do with his murder. And I don't like the way this conversation is going."

"Well, if you're not comfortable, we can call your probation officer and have him hold your hand while we talk." One of the stipulations of probation was that he had to cooperate with the police in any investigation. I could flip a switch with his probation officer, and he'd be locked up for as long as I liked.

"We don't have to do that." He lowered his hands and shoved them in his pockets. "I'm just telling you that I didn't have anything to do with Logan's murder. That's all I'm saying."

Now that we had the pecking order of the conversation established, I continued with my interrogation. "Where were you the night before last?"

"I was here watching the kids. Cindy goes to class on Mondays and Wednesdays for the nursing program at UCF, so I watch the kids until she gets home around ten o'clock. I did some work in my shop after that."

"Can we see your shop?" I asked.

"Sure," he said. "It's around back. I think Cindy would appreciate it if we walked around the house, not through it."

Jason led us around his garage to the side of the house and through a wooden privacy fence. He headed for a large aluminum shed at the rear of their backyard. We passed a swing set, and Crevis pushed one of the empty swings high in the air.

The door was unlocked, and he opened it wide for us. A metal statue of a woman, crouched down and holding a child, stood in the middle of the floor. The metal was smooth with a dark blue hue. I'm not much of an art guy, but the detail of the faces of both mother and child was incredible.

A workbench was off to the left, with a station of magnifying glasses and a vise for smaller items, probably where he worked on the jewelry. Stacks of metal and supplies lined the wall in front of us. A blowtorch and a propane tank were next to the statue. Several cabinets covered the other wall, and metal shavings gave the floor a grayish tint.

"It stinks in here." Crevis waved his hand in front of his face. The biting chemical smell made my eyes water too.

"Sorry. I usually have the ventilation on when I'm working." Jason beamed at his creation and brushed his hand along the woman's shoulders. "This is where my angst goes now, Detective. I discovered in prison that I work well with metal. I have a gift, one not to be wasted. It just kind of came to me. Now I sell my art and work on jewelry for local jewelers. I'm not getting rich, but I get to work from home and build my life—free. I'm not risking this for anyone, Detective Quinn, and I mean that."

I nodded. I didn't want to get too giggly over his statue, although it was clear Santos had talent. He was also still a felon with a good motive against Logan. I hoped what he was telling me was true.

"That's nice work." I needed to get him back on task. "Is there anyone who can verify your whereabouts Wednesday?"

"Just my kids." He toyed with the ties on his smock. "And Cindy after ten. I didn't plan on needing an alibi."

"When was the last time you talked with Nikki?"

He shrugged. "It's been years. I think we've both moved on."

"I'm gonna need to get some DNA to rule you out," I said.

He agreed, and I had Crevis take the sample quickly, anticipating another go-around with an angry middleweight named Cindy Santos, who I imagined would appear at the workshop at any moment. I got Jason's cell phone number and vital information.

"For what it's worth," Jason said, "I really do feel bad about what happened to Logan, and I hope you find who killed him. When he showed up here, he was just so angry and bitter. That's no way to go through life. It's been a dozen years, for goodness' sake, and I'm the one who went to prison."

"OPD's gonna want a formal statement from you," I said, not wanting to go into Logan's self-destruction. I handed him a business card; I'd scribbled Bowden's and my cell phone numbers on it. "You need to call this guy and set up the appointment yourself. That way they don't show up here and stress out your wife."

He held up the card. "I'll call him. I just dream of the day that all this is behind me."

14

I'D SENT CREVIS OUT to check all the Dumpsters in the area of the Sand Dollar Motel and down Colonial Drive as far as he could go. We needed to find our satchel and hard drive, and I didn't want to lose it if Logan's killer had tossed it in the trash after a hasty retreat. After I dropped him off, I hurried to OPD.

Oscar and three other Homicide detectives milled around the bullpen, their own version of a flow chart up on the whiteboard. Oscar parked on a desk as he chatted with Detective Steve Stockton, a longtime homicide guy from my day. A decent man who smiled more than a cop in Homicide should, Steve would never be accused of being an intellectual. He was a good worker bee, though—maybe a bumblebee, considering his waistline—and would do whatever was asked without too much complaining, which was a hard thing to find with cops. Since he kept Oscar happy, he was a mainstay in the unit. His drab, worn yellow jacket was a size too small for him, and his thick brown pelt was frizzed.

Detective Rita Jiminez stalked around the bullpen like a caged animal. She'd spent eight years in the Special Victims Unit, where she gained a reputation for emasculating male offenders at an astounding rate. Her no-nonsense reputation got her into Homicide—and was the very reason some wanted her out. Her brown hair didn't come close to her thick, broad shoulders, and she wore a brown jacket with brown pants and shoes that were a case study in frumpiness. She'd been partnered with Stockton since Pampas left the unit with a little nudge from me.

Okay, it was more of a full push off a cliff than a nudge, but he had it coming. One of the few good things that came out of Pam's case.

The buzz of the bullpen during a homicide case stirred my blood and made me feel like a cop again—until, quite stupidly, I glanced toward the picture and deflated like a punctured balloon.

A portrait of Detective Trisha Willis, a black ribbon around the frame, hung on the wall with a proclamation from the governor on one side and the state of Florida on the other, acknowledging her for heroism and service.

Just so many words on paper now. She was still gone and wasn't coming back. In the photo, she wore her dress uniform and smiled. That smile dominated my dreams. The ache in my heart at that moment hurt worse than my hip ever did.

Greg Bowden's loud voice drew me back from my memories. He sat at his desk, on the phone, rubbing the back of his neck. I winked to Trisha and got my head back in the game. She would have appreciated that.

"I talked with Jason Santos," I announced to the bullpen. "He said he was home at the time of the murder but didn't have much of an alibi. His wife got home about ten o'clock, and they stayed there the whole night. He's going to call Bowden and give a formal interview."

"What's your gut tell you?" Oscar asked.

"Hard to tell right now." I picked at the carpet with the cane. "He didn't look like he was in the drug world anymore, but Logan came by to see him about a month ago. He threatened Santos and tossed him around the yard in front of his wife. Could be good enough reason to bump him off. People have done more for less."

"We did a neighborhood canvass of the entire area around the motel." Oscar glanced toward the flow chart. "The only person who saw anything is Pat Collins, who heard the scream and saw a woman run from Logan's motel room."

Greg slammed the phone down and threw his hands in the air like he'd just scored a touchdown. "Nikki Bray's going to be here in ten minutes."

Bowden had been in Homicide about a year and was still green and untested. His desk was well ordered and sported a couple of pictures of him with his young blond wife and two towheaded children, both under ten. He stood, rubbed his hand across his sparse hair, and straightened his tie. "We downloaded the call log from Logan's cell phone, and Nikki was the last person he talked with, at 8:00 p.m. the night before. She's agreed to come in for an interview."

"Katie said she found some fingerprints on the whiskey bottle and glasses at the scene." Oscar checked his watch. "She thinks the prints are too small to be Logan's, so we might have a shot of them belonging to Nikki."

Nikki's ten-minute ETA turned into forty-five before she arrived in the lobby of the PD. Not a surprise. People in her world were rarely punctual. Taking advantage of the extra time, I skimmed her file. Knowledge is power, especially in an interview. The more information the detective had, the better. I used to find out as much as I could about someone before I spoke to them—who they associated with, where they lived, what schools they attended. Then, during the interview, I'd toss tidbits of their life back at them. The person often assumed I knew everything, bringing them closer to confessing. It was a great advantage.

Nikki's sorrowful life read like a tabloid newspaper—crime and drama from front to back. As a teen, she got locked up for shoplifting, then burglary and drug possession. She ran away from home. Got arrested for more crimes, ranging from assault to attempted murder on an old boyfriend. That report made for an interesting read. Then she hooked up with Jason Santos and ran drugs for him. In her earlier arrest photos, she was an attractive young girl, a face full of life and vigor. She did some prison time and some recreational drug use that would bankrupt a pharmacy. Her latest driver's license photo was a sad portrait of a life squandered.

I examined the photo of the knife lifted from Logan's chest: a dagger with a grinning skull fixed at the butt of the handle. The deep-set red eyes peered through me. It looked like the kind of knife someone would pick up at a flea market or specialty store.

"I want you to interview her," Oscar said to Bowden. "Ray can go in with you, but this is your case. Just get a good time line from her, her whereabouts that night. If you see an opening, go for the confession."

Oscar had made a good decision. A lot of supervisors would put a more experienced interviewer in with Nikki, but Oscar liked to train his people and let them get their own experience. I'd try to keep my mouth shut as long as I could. That wouldn't be easy.

Bowden agreed but didn't say much after that; he seemed to be processing everything. The pressure of being lead on a big case could build quickly.

"Anything to add, Ray?" Bowden asked.

"I just read the report where she was arrested for tying a former biker boyfriend to the bed and beating him with a baseball bat. She's volatile and loves bad men. Get her to talk about her relationship with Logan. Get her in the emotional area and bring her into depression. That's where you'll see the real Nikki."

"Thanks," he said, swallowing hard. His phone vibrated. He read the text. "Nikki's in the lobby. I'll go get her. Wish me luck."

"You make your own luck," I said.

15

"NIKKI BRAY." She extended a petite hand to me. Her blue jeans were ripped at the knees, and her black T-shirt was more like a napkin that refused to cover her navel, which was pierced with a green hoop of some sort. Her sun-soaked skin wrinkled at the cheeks, her face showing the wear of a wasted life. Her brown hair frizzed as if we'd just woken her. She eyed the cane, which was good. People tend to underestimate a cripple in every situation. Her clammy hand trembled as I shook it.

"Ray Quinn." I pointed to Bowden. "You know Detective Bowden."

We led her upstairs and made some small talk to get her used to us. We got situated in the small, drab interview room, its gray walls designed to depress the mood of the suspects. Nikki's chair was small and hard, like a grade-schooler's. The two front legs had been shortened, making the chair lean slightly forward so the person sitting in it could never really get comfortable. Bowden's chair and mine were cushioned and soft with armrests. Nothing wrong with a little psychological edge, especially since cops were always playing catch-up to the bad guy. Or girl.

"So why did you call me?" She brushed a lock of hair behind her ears. "I haven't seen Logan in weeks."

"We're talking with everyone who knew Logan or had contact with him," Bowden said. "You're next on the list."

Bowden read her the Miranda rights. She wasn't under arrest, but given that she was the last person we knew of to have contact with Logan, it was wise to have her rights read to her in case she spilled something incriminating. Bowden schmoozed her for a few minutes, then got around to the questions. Softballs at first, to make her comfortable and get her used to answering questions, even if the answers didn't matter yet. Once she was at ease, he'd turn up the stress.

"When was the last time you talked with Logan?" he asked.

"Um…maybe two or three weeks ago." She crossed her legs and her arms and tried to lean back in the chair, away from Bowden.

He slid a piece of paper toward her. "His phone records show you talked with him two nights ago, at about 8:00 p.m. You talked for almost eight minutes. That's a lot of talking."

"So what? We talked." She canted her body toward the door to the interview room, as if she'd sprint out at any second. "It's not against the law to talk to someone."

I let Bowden lead for a while, wanting to let him go as far as he could for experience. But after a while I couldn't help myself.

"You two are an item again, I take it." I scooted my chair a few inches closer to her.

"We've been seeing each other a little. He just couldn't stay away from me. He called me months ago, wanting to see me, so we went out every once in a while, got some drinks or something. Had some fun. That's not illegal either."

"Did you meet him Wednesday night?" I said. "Go out for drinks or anything?"

"No. No! I wasn't *anywhere* near him."

"What did you talk about, then?" I pressed. She was hiding something.

"He said he'd stopped drinking and didn't want to live like that anymore. He was sick of his life, sick of being angry and always thinking about the past and what happened. He wanted a fresh start, wanted to do something good again, like when he was a cop. He…" She stopped and pushed back in the chair, her eyes welling up.

"He…what?" I said.

"He didn't want to see me anymore." Her face contorted as she scowled at me. "He said I brought him down. He bounced back into my life, used me, and thought he would just leave again."

"And you weren't about to take that, were you?" I said. "I know why you did prison time. You tied your last boyfriend to a bed and beat him with a baseball bat because he was cheating on you. Good thing *he* didn't die."

"I didn't kill Logan, I swear."

"What's going to happen when we compare the DNA on the handle of that knife against yours? You and I both know what the results will be. You need to come up with a much better story than the one you're selling now, because you know we're going to put you at the scene. You were the last one he had phone contact with, and he used you and tossed you aside again. Kicked you to the curb like the rest of the trash in his life."

"He had no right!" she hissed as she rose in her seat like a provoked cobra. "No man is gonna treat me that way, no one."

"The DNA is gonna prove you killed him, isn't it? It's gonna put you right there with him, and you know it."

"He wasn't going to get away with that. He wasn't just going to do that to me again and walk away."

Nikki Bray sobbed and crumpled in her chair, her head nearly on her knees. I rolled my chair forward and rested a hand on her shoulder.

"Tell us what really happened, Nikki."

"I just didn't want him to leave me." She snorted and wiped her forearm across her nose. "I snuck into his room while he was asleep and killed him. He would never hurt me again."

"How many times did you stab him?" I asked.

"I don't know." She thrashed a fist in the air half a dozen times. "I just kept stabbing him. He didn't move. I knew he was dead."

I had her describe the knife she used. It fit ours perfectly, even the piercing red eyes on the skull. Those details had never been released to the press. We had the right person.

"Did you take anything from the room, anything from Logan's room? An iPod, computer stuff, a satchel?"

"No, I just did it and left." She crumpled in the chair. "I didn't take anything."

"What time did this happen?" I asked.

"About an hour after I called him," she said. "I was driving from Tampa."

"Did you check Logan into the hotel?"

"No," she said. "I found out he was there that night."

"Does the name Savannah Breeze mean anything to you?"

She shook her head.

I got up and caned out of the room. I'd let Bowden finish with her, getting the details of the crime. I met Oscar in the adjacent room, watching the interview on a monitor.

"Nice work," he said. "You still got it."

"Yeah, but I still don't have my client's property," I said. "That strikes me as kind of odd. And if what she says is true, she killed Logan around 9:00 or 9:30 p.m. The witness heard the screaming at 2:20 a.m."

"Look at her." Oscar tapped the screen focused on Nikki. "She's high. Was probably high when she did it. She couldn't tell you what time it is right now, much less what time it was on Wednesday. We'll arrest her and book her. Bowden can write a search warrant for her house, and we'll see what we come up with. If we find your client's stuff in the process, so be it."

"That works for me," I said. "But it still seems odd. The time line doesn't seem to work, and—"

Katie Pham hurried down the hall toward us, carrying several fingerprint cards. "Hey, Ray." She held out the cards. "I was able to lift some prints off the bottle and the glasses at the scene."

"Let me guess; they match Nikki Bray," Oscar said.

Katie arched her eyebrows. "Well, not exactly."

"Not exactly." Oscar placed his hands on his hips.

"Actually, not at all." Katie handed me the print cards and her comparison workup. "I have good, identifiable prints, but they definitely aren't Nikki's. I still think they belong to a female because they're so small. Unless we have a wee-little-man killer out there."

"Everyone's a comedian," Oscar said. "Even if they're not her fingerprints, we still have Nikki's detailed confession. We prove it's her knife and her DNA on it, then we try to find out who else was in Logan's room."

Greg Bowden finished with Nikki and got a DNA reference swab from her. He came out to powwow with us.

"Seems pretty open and shut." He rubbed both hands across his face and sighed. "I'm gonna arrest her now and finish up what we have here."

"Clean this thing up and get a good night's sleep," I said. "We've got the autopsy tomorrow."

16

CREVIS WAITED ON the corner of Colonial Drive and Summerlin Avenue. His camo pants and dark blue T-shirt bore the stains of a fine day of Dumpster diving. His red hair twisted in the breeze like orange peels dancing on his head. I pulled up alongside him.

"Still liking this PI job?" I asked.

He paused before answering. "I crawled in every Dumpster from here to the motel. I checked every trash can and wooded lot, every gutter and back alley. Nothing. I wasted my whole day playing in other people's garbage."

"It's not a wasted day." Stretching across the seat, I pushed the passenger door open. "We now know a hundred places the satchel and hard drive are not. Get in."

He plopped down and stared straight ahead. "Let's go home. I need a shower."

"We need to make a stop first."

I filled him in on the chat with Nikki and her murder confession, and in fifteen minutes we were cruising the underground garage at Mayer Holdings, looking for a parking spot. His Majesty would want to know the latest developments. I could have called and given the details on the phone, but I was tired of going through Wykoff. I wanted a little more face time with Armon to get a feel for him. Besides, it was good training for Crevis. He needed to learn how to read and deal with people.

"Since she confessed, doesn't that mean our case is over?" Crevis picked a piece of lettuce off his shirt, opened the window, and tossed it out. "Logan's dead, and his killer is arrested. Who cares where the stolen junk went?"

"We care." I pulled into a spot near the elevator. "More importantly, our client cares. Until the hard drive and items are accounted for, the potential for his clients' banking information to be leaked is huge. They should have been in his house or in the motel room, but they weren't in either place. Bowden's writing a search warrant for Nikki's apartment, so when we're done with Armon, we'll meet him there."

We rode the elevator to the penthouse, Crevis's body odor nearly chasing me out. The doors opened to the attractive yet confused face of Armon's secretary, Megan.

"Private Detective Ray Quinn." She stood and clasped her hands in front of her. She wore a yellow skirt with a white long-sleeved shirt that seemed tailor-made for her. I wasn't all that into clothes and fashion, but her lithe figure and alluring smile made it tough not to notice.

"Secretary Megan." I spun my cane once before returning it to the floor. "It's good to see you again. Can I speak with Armon for a moment?"

"He doesn't like seeing anyone without an appointment." She rolled her eyes and smirked.

Along with being easy on the eyes, she had a bit of attitude. I liked her more and more each moment.

"Let him know I'm here and that it's important," I said.

"With pleasure." She raised her hand to her headset. "Mr. Mayer, Detective Quinn is here with an urgent request to see you." She smirked at me. "Yes sir… I'll let him know." She lowered her hand. "He'll be with you in a few moments," she said to us. "Can I get you anything while you wait?"

"I'll take a soda," Crevis said.

I jabbed his foot with the tip of my cane.

"Ouch." He shuffled back a step. "What? I'm thirsty."

"He's fine," I said. "We'll just wait for Armon."

"Do you have any more news about Logan?" Her countenance shifted and a pall shrouded her face like a veil.

"A little," I said. "I have to fill Armon in on some things."

"He was so nice." She sat down and rested her elbows on her desk. "I can't believe anyone would want to kill him."

I shrugged, unwilling to defend Logan's niceness. It probably had something to do with the fact that she was an attractive young woman. If she were sixty-five and obese, with only a few teeth and bad feet, I was sure Logan wouldn't have given her the time of day. No need to damage her memories, though.

The elevator door chimed, and Jack Gordon galloped out like a horse out of the gate at the first shot. "I told you before to go through me on any new developments," he said to me. "I don't like to be blindsided."

I tapped my chin a couple of times and let my eyes drift skyward. "Oh yeah, I think I remember something about that."

"I don't like your attitude, Quinn," he said.

"I don't really care, *Gordon*." I posted both hands on my cane. "My business is with Armon. If I want your opinion about something, I'll ask. So far, I haven't asked."

"That's one of the things I can't stand about police officers. You lack any kind of discipline. I had my reservations about hiring Logan in the first place, and I should have listened to my gut. Cops are just too unreliable and undisciplined."

Jack stood nose to nose with me, his garlic lunch breath assaulting my sense of smell. Crevis stepped forward, growling. I rested my cane handle on his chest to back him down, lest there be bloodshed in the penthouse.

"You better protect your guy." Gordon straightened his tie and eased back. "You're both out of your league right now."

"I wasn't protecting *him*," I said. "Now get out of my face before I take my cane and—"

Armon's office door opened, and Wykoff exited. "Mr. Mayer will see you now."

Jack pushed past us into the boardroom, Crevis and I close behind. Armon hovered at the end, like a knight of the oblong table. I made it a point to hobble straight up to him.

"You have good news for me, I assume, Detective Quinn?"

Armon said as he shuffled to the other side of the table, keeping it between us. He wore a black long-sleeved shirt, dark dress slacks, and a tattered pair of Converse high tops. He possessed all the fashion sense of a bag lady.

"OPD made an arrest on a suspect for Logan's murder," I said. "I've sent off some DNA samples to the lab for comparison. We'll see what comes up."

"Have you recovered my information?" Armon said.

"Not yet," I said. "The detectives are preparing a search warrant for the suspect's, Nikki Bray's, house, and I'll go with them to see if anything's there. She confessed to murdering him but denied taking anything from him. I'm inclined to believe she didn't take the hard drive. She'd have no use for it. It doesn't fit, anyway. It was a crime of passion, and she appears to know nothing about or have any contact with your group that I can tell."

Armon rested his hands on the back of one of the chairs and engaged me with his eyes for the first time. "What else do you have to tell me? I sense there is something you are holding back."

He was at least perceptive.

"There are some questions about Logan's last hours," I said. "We should have come across something more concrete by now. It's strange that Nikki confessed to killing Logan but the satchel is gone. There's a disconnect between the two. I have to flesh out Nikki's contacts. Some other oddities have surfaced as well."

"Like what?" Jack asked.

"Like odd things within the case," I said, not bothering to look his way.

"I'm growing impatient with the pace of this investigation." Armon pulled a wipe from a dispenser and worked it across his hands and between his fingers before discarding it in a wastebasket. "My information should be back in my possession by now. The longer their information is out there, the greater the risk for my clients. I can't have that."

"Well, Logan's murder has thrown a monkey wrench in the situation," I said. "Since he can't tell me where he hid the hard drive, it's gonna take a lot more digging."

"The quicker you find my items, the more inclined I'll be to give you a bonus."

"A bonus doesn't help me solve the case." I rested my entire body weight on the cane. "I need time and patience to work through every lead and vet every suspect. The amount of commas in a check doesn't change that."

"Money changes lots of things, Detective." Armon steepled his spiffy clean hands. "It can help change the outcome of your investigation too. You need to work smarter and use that to your advantage."

"I understand." I sniffled, then feigned a sneeze.

Armon stepped back even farther, and an odd grimace crossed his face. "Unless you have something else to share, you may leave."

"I'll be in touch."

I waved with the hand I used to cover my fake sneeze, then touched the top of every chair I passed on my way out. Armon pulled two more wipes out of the dispenser as I left the room. If my assessment of him was correct, he'd have the entire place disinfected in an hour.

I was getting a better feel for Armon. He didn't mince words, but I was still missing something with him. And I didn't like Jack Gordon—mainly because I just didn't like the guy. Hanging out with him was about as fun as sprinkling salt in my eyes.

Megan caught my attention as we passed her desk. She offered to shake my hand again, and as I accepted, she slipped me a piece of paper and held my hand longer than necessary, her emerald eyes calling to mine. I discreetly slipped the note into my pocket and caned toward the elevator.

Jack held the elevator door. "Going down, Quinn?"

"Not yet." I smiled, mumbling unmentionables under my breath. We'd take the next one. Jack smiled as the door closed, and I pressed the down button again. Less than thirty seconds later, the elevator returned.

"What's that dude's problem?" Crevis held the door for me. "He's supposed to be on our side."

"His first problem is he's a jerk." I stepped into the elevator and pushed the button for the garage level. "But the second and most important reason is that he messed up by hiring Logan in the first place and allowing all this to happen on his watch. At some point he's gonna pay for that. I doubt Armon will keep him as head of security when the dust settles on this case, so he's trying to salvage what he can of his career. If he can glean any info from us and bring it to his boss like it's his own, it'll look like he's making amends for his screw-up."

"Yeah, but he still doesn't have to be an idiot."

"Well, that's not likely to change." I tapped Crevis's leg to get him to focus. "Just watch yourself around him. I don't trust the guy. There's meanness behind his eyes."

"I'd take him out in a flash." Crevis smacked his fist into his hands. His hubris worried me at times. When I was a rookie and training every day, young and strong, I didn't think anything would ever bring me down. Now I've got a plastic hip, constant pain, and a hundred other reminders of my mortality. Before he donned a police uniform, I hoped Crevis got to that place of understanding so he didn't end up like me...or worse.

I eased the note Megan had given me out of my pocket, holding it so Crevis couldn't see it. *Call me,* it said, and her cell number was scribbled on the back. I wasn't sure whether it meant *call me, I have information for you,* or *call me and we'll have a couple of drinks.*

Having never been much of a chick magnet, the fact that an attractive woman a good ten years my junior would hit on the crippled guy raised many tantalizing questions in my mind—questions I couldn't wait to try to answer. I'd call her later, away from Crevis.

"We've got Logan's autopsy tomorrow," I said.

"Great." Crevis sighed and hunched forward. "Do I have to—"

"It starts at 9:00 a.m. We'll both be there."

Since I'd never attended an autopsy of someone I knew, it had an eerie factor for me too, but I wasn't about to let Crevis know that. He wasn't wiggling out of this. He could stand in the corner and hurl in the sink if he needed to, but he had to build his tolerance to the dead.

17

CREVIS AND I WOUND through the evening traffic to Nikki's apartment, which was off Sand Lake Road near Orange Blossom Trail. The late evening traffic was sparse, as it was well past rush hour.

Oscar had Steve Stockton write the search warrant for her place while Bowden booked her. It took more than one detective to work any kind of crime. A team approach worked best with the major crimes—depending, of course, on who was on your team. Back in the day, I preferred to work with Trisha and Oscar. The three of us could get anything accomplished. In comparison, I was working uphill now, it seemed.

Nikki's abode was in a dumpy set of apartments that had no problem a good arsonist or air strike couldn't cure. This blighted complex had constant foot traffic, mostly drug fiends looking to get high. Her single-story wood-faced building housed four apartments clustered together. Hers was number 102, but the original metal numbers on the door had been ripped off, leaving only peeled-paint traces. Crime scene tape draped across her door like an award from a Most Likely to Be Condemned contest, and an OPD uniform stood watch on the sidewalk so no one disturbed the scene.

Oscar arrived about the same time we did and found a spot in the lot among the burgeoning myriad of police and resident vehicles. He removed his jacket and tossed it without care into the backseat of his dark blue Suburban. As he approached, he unbuttoned his sleeves and rolled them halfway up his forearms.

"Stockton should have the warrant signed soon," Oscar said. "Then we'll get a look around. We'll collect whatever clothes we think she was wearing that night, shoes and stuff."

"Can you collect hard drives and computers too?" I adjusted the file folder in my hand. "Logan's computer is missing from his house, so any electronic storage devices are in play."

"Pretend for a second, Ray, that we've done this before. It's all part of the warrant." Oscar checked his watch and scanned the entrance. "We got it covered. And you owe Bowden and me big for this. Lunch. At a nice place. Not the cheese-ball dives you used to take me to."

"I'll take care of you both. I can write it off my taxes now."

"Always got an angle, don't you?"

"I've got to consider these things." I glanced toward Crevis. "I'm not on the government dole anymore. Every penny matters. Not exactly what I expected."

"Being your own boss isn't all it's cut out to be."

Rita Jiminez and Steve Stockton rolled into the lot in their unmarked vehicles. Rita had an older black Crown Vic, and Steve drove a silver Buick Century. Katie Pham backed the white crime scene van into a spot. Life returned to Crevis's face at the sight of Katie, and he puffed out his chest and meandered toward her. The two talked out of my earshot.

"I'm seeing more of you now than when you worked for us, Ray-Ray." Steve slipped on his form-fitting jacket. He approached us with a copy of the warrant in hand.

Rita grimaced, alternating her glare between Crevis and me. She sighed and shook her head. She didn't work in the unit when I was there, so we only knew each other in passing. Maybe she didn't respect PIs. Cops are weird that way. Or maybe she was just that way all the time. Hard to tell.

Katie entered the apartment first, videotaping her way through each room, documenting everything before we got started. A standard procedure to show how it looked before and after the search, to prove that the police didn't come in and trash the house or steal anything. I had Crevis stay outside because the warrant stated that only Orlando PD personnel could enter and search. As a consultant, I could help, but I didn't want to push the legality by including him.

When Katie finished, we filed into Nikki's one-bedroom apartment. The kitchen was just off the front door to the right. Dishes and pans were stacked up on the counter, and various forms and colors of growth covered the remaining food. The kitchen area faced a half-sized living room with a tilting plaid couch and a TV/DVD unit on a dilapidated entertainment shelf. An ashtray sat on the coffee table. A mound of cigarette butts rose from it as large as an African anthill. Her apartment bore all the markings of a drug addict's burrow, used only to lay her head for a time before the next high. I was glad Katie had videoed the entry. No one would believe this disaster wasn't done on purpose.

"Of course Bowden's gotta miss this part of the case." Rita picked up a pair of jeans from the floor with a gloved hand. "Leaves all this nastiness for us to go through. He should be here."

Oscar gathered everyone into the living room and doled out assignments: Steve got the kitchen, Oscar took the living room, and Rita won the top prize of the day—the master bedroom. Katie set up a laptop with a small printer on the kitchen table, a stack of paper and plastic evidence bags on the floor next to her. Any blood or DNA evidence would go in the paper bags, so as not to degrade the DNA; other evidence could go in the plastic. She would catalog any evidence seized and print out a receipt to be left at the scene, although I didn't think Nikki would be returning any time soon to review it.

"Great," Rita said, shaking her head as she trudged back into Nikki's lair. I slipped on a pair of rubber gloves and followed her.

Nikki's bedroom was to our left. It shared all the ambience, décor, and aroma of the rest of the apartment. The color of the carpet couldn't be determined because there wasn't a spot on the floor that wasn't covered by dirty clothes. The bed was a rumpled, twisted mess with sets of dresser drawers flanking it on either side. A bathroom lay off the bedroom to the left. Cosmetics and tissues littered the counter, and the sink had brown water stains. I didn't dare raise the toilet seat, in utter fear of what I might discover.

Rita opened the top drawer of the dresser on the other side of the bed from me.

Reaching down, I eased open one of the drawers on my side, revealing Nikki's underwear and lingerie. I could have gone my whole life without seeing that.

"You aren't supposed to be touching anything," Rita said, not even looking my way. "It could ruin the case."

"I'm not touching anything." I closed the drawer without going through it. "Just looking."

"Don't 'look' at anything either." She patted down a pair of jeans and pulled the front pockets inside out. "Go in Oscar's room and do that stuff. He's your buddy and will let you get away with whatever. Not gonna happen in this room. I'm responsible for what happens in here."

"Lighten up, Rita. It's been a long day already. I was working Homicide when you were still in the academy. I know what I'm doing."

"Even though Ramsey was a dirtbag, we still gotta make sure we do this right. Having you in here is a bad idea. A good defense attorney will have a field day with this. And I don't like you in here while I'm trying to do my job."

"I'm here, like it or not. The chief was kind enough to make me a consultant for the department and give me access to major case investigations, so if you have any issues, take it up with him."

"Whatever. Just don't put your fingers on anything I have to answer for."

"Fine." I paused long enough to let the terse comments run their course. "I guess there was no love lost between you and Logan."

"He was a scumbag with a badge, a player. As far as I'm concerned, stabbing was too kind a fate for him. I had a lot of friends on S.W.A.T. back then and could have lost one of them because he sold us out. We got into it a few times when I was on patrol too. He was a criminal with a badge. Made us all look bad."

I decided to keep my mouth shut.

"Looky here." Rita lifted a knife sheath off the nightstand. Its length and markings were consistent with the murder weapon. Katie photographed it and logged it into evidence.

For three solid hours, we searched every article of clothing, every pocket, and every cupboard, stirring the pungent funk of the apartment. A host of DNA swabs were collected, as were numerous shirts and pairs of jeans and a couple of pairs of tennis shoes with interesting stains on them that could have been spilled food or spilled blood. The lab would figure it out.

There was no satchel and not even a hint of computers or storage devices. Nothing at all related to Mayer Holdings.

18

CREVIS AND I KEPT time with the late-night traffic. I was pooped, and Crevis didn't seem very chatty, which meant he was probably spent as well. I had forgotten how exhausting a homicide case could be.

I used the time to get my mind right and sift through the case. Why was Nikki such a good fit for the homicide but had no apparent connection to or knew nothing about the theft? And who had plundered Logan's house before we got there, and what had happened to his computer? I didn't believe that was Nikki's doing. Why would Logan steal client information from Armon and then be murdered by a crazed biker chick? Was she a patsy in all this? Did she have more to tell us? I had a headache and was in desperate need of relaxation.

Crevis and I arrived back at the office at nearly 10:00 p.m. Pam's blue Toyota was parked in our lot, and the office light was on. Crevis bounded up the stairs with an ease that made me envious.

I waited until he was in the door before I dialed Megan's number.

"Hello," she said.

"Megan?" I switched the phone to my left hand. "This is Private Investigator Ray Quinn. I got your note."

"I'm glad you called, PI Ray Quinn," she said in a tone significantly different, and more inviting, than when she answered. "I was wondering if we could meet sometime. Maybe go out for some drinks or something. Talk a little."

"I'm a pretty busy guy, but I think I could fit in a night out between my triathlon training and rigorous meeting schedule."

She laughed. "You crack me up, Ray. How's tonight sound? I was just getting ready to head out. It's early enough to get a head start on the partying."

"Sounds like fun. I'll need some time to get ready."

We agreed to meet in an hour and a half at Jay Jay's on East Kaley Street, which was about halfway for both of us. Her *call me* note was more pleasure than business, which I had to admit was intriguing.

I felt wide awake and refreshed now. Since my shooting, I'd practically been a hermit. There were very good reasons for that, but it was getting old. Trisha had been gone for over a year and a half. I couldn't stay like this forever. I didn't do crowds well at all—the thought of them forced my heart rate up—but at some point, I had to try again. The doctor had told me as much. Maybe tonight was that time.

I hobbled and wobbled up the steps, taking my time, my mind only half on the case. Pam and Crevis worked at his desk. Pam's blond hair bounced around her shoulders, and she wore blue sweatpants and a gray workout shirt. She must have been running before

or something. Few women I'd ever known would show up somewhere wearing what they felt comfortable in. Pam would, though.
She was comfortable with herself and never seemed to be trying to
impress anyone. That impressed me.

"Ray," Pam said, looking over Crevis's shoulder. She'd just had
him open his workbook to a page for diagramming sentences, very
short ones it seemed, identifying the subjects and the verbs. He'd
probably enjoy Logan's autopsy more than that. From what I could
discern, he was about fifty-fifty on understanding it, which didn't
instill me with confidence about his test. I wondered if all his efforts
were going to be for naught.

While sitting at my desk, I opened my bottom drawer, where I
kept my dart gun. It fired spongy darts with rubber suction cups on
the end. The range wasn't bad, and I could nail Crevis coming
through the door on a good day.

I loaded a dart without Crevis or Pam hearing the spring. I took
aim and locked in on my target, the back of Crevis's head, and let the
dart fly. With the precision of a cruise missile, it whacked Crevis just
behind the ear.

"Stop it, Ray." He swatted his hand back without looking. "I'm
trying to finish this."

Pam picked up a stapler and pointed it in my direction. She
made no verbal threat, but I understood with great clarity that I was
not to fire another round or staples would cover my body from head
to toe. I relented and replaced the pistol in the drawer.

Since both of them were too busy to chat, I logged in and
checked my e-mail. My South African friends hadn't seen fit to

respond to me yet. I wouldn't push it, though. It would require time and an extreme amount of patience to get them to bite. Maybe they would, maybe they wouldn't. Either way, the thrill of the hunt provided me with a bit of joy.

After knocking down a couple of Sudoku games on the computer, I dropped a few loud, laborious sighs until Crevis finished his lesson.

He finally got the hint and closed his book. He said he had some business to take care of but didn't elaborate before leaving the office. I guessed it had something to do with his parents but couldn't be sure. I left him alone with that stuff.

Pam stacked her books in her book bag and brushed a lock of hair from her face.

"He's doing much better," she said. "He's progressed about three grade levels in the past two-and-a-half months."

"So he's at about a third-grade level now?"

"It's not funny. He's working hard, really hard. I think he's going to make it."

I located my bottle of Jim in my top drawer. A man must always be prepared. Since I was technically off-duty and my leg just flat-out hurt, I filled my glass with about three fingers and washed the day down.

Pam stared at the glass. She'd seen me drink before, a lot, and I was comfortable enough with her not to put on airs anymore, even though she was a teetotaler.

She cast the book bag over her shoulder. "How about I give you a ride home? It's getting late and—"

"I'll be fine," I said. "I'm just priming the pump. I'm going out for a little while. I need to blow off some steam."

"Crevis says you've been priming the pump a lot lately. Are you sure you should be doing that right now? Especially if you're going to be driving?"

"Have you and Crevis been plotting against me?" I pointed at her with my glass.

"We've talked about it. He cares about you. We both do. We just want to make sure you're all right, that this isn't getting out of control."

"Is this an intervention?" I said, smirking. "You know, where you ask me to pour out my demon rum?"

"No. Not yet anyway." She took a couple of steps closer to my desk. "And don't try to throw me off track with your psychological tricks and smart-aleck remarks. I'm worried about you, Ray. You're drinking more and more lately."

"Look, Pam, you have no idea what it's like dealing with this every day. My hip and leg send shots of throbbing pain up and down my leg all day. The nerve damage is extensive, and there's nothing the doctors can do. Nothing. I've tried the pain meds, but they're narcotics and make me loopy. When I'm on them, I can't concentrate or focus at all. I hate the feeling. I'm used to the Jim. I know exactly how much I need to numb the pain and still keep moving. I can't do that with the pills. Besides, it helps me relax after days like this. I know what I'm doing. I've got it under control."

"I just don't want to see you in trouble or wrapped around a tree or something," she said. "God's got a larger plan for you than this, and we have recovery ministries at our church. I want to help you, Ray. Like you helped me—"

"I've got it under control," I said, interrupting her umpteenth "thank you" for catching her brother's killer and restoring his ministry. We didn't need to travel that road again. Especially since I'd never told her that the case helped me more than it ever did her. I kept that part to myself.

"Okay." She stepped back. "Just promise me that if something happens and you need a ride or help, you'll call me. Please. That's all I ask. I'll come get you no matter the time. I'll make sure you get home safe. And I won't give you a hard time, or preach to you, give you scriptures, or anything. I promise."

"Really? You expect me to believe you won't beat me down with the God stuff?" I laughed out loud. "I know you too well, Miss Pamela Winters."

"Maybe I'll give you a little grief. But only a little. Think about it." Her smile warmed me because I knew that even as stubborn and hyper-religious as she was, she meant every word.

"I will."

"Have you had a chance to look at your file yet?"

"Which file?" I shuffled some of the loose papers on my desk. "We have a couple open cases."

"Don't play your answer-a-question-with-a-question games with me, Ray," she said. "You know perfectly well which file I'm talking about."

She didn't let me get away with much, but it was fun trying. She pestered me now and then about the file she gave me from my time in foster care, which remained unopened in my file cabinet.

"I've been busy with cases that actually pay. I don't have time to dig through ancient history."

"It's your history. I had to call in some favors to even get my hands on that information. It could help you find out who your parents are and why you went to foster care in the first place."

"I'll get to it when I get to it." I checked my watch. "Speaking of getting, I have to get ready. I'm meeting someone in a little while."

Pam adjusted the bag's strap on her shoulder and then pulled her cell phone from its holster on her belt and dangled it in my face. "Remember what I said. If you need help, call me." She smiled and headed out the door.

I waited until I was sure she was down the steps, and then I opened the bottom drawer of the file cabinet and pulled out the file in question, from the Florida Department of Children and Families. It was only half an inch thick, so there couldn't be much to go on. Probably not any more than I already knew—at maybe three years old, I was left at a rest stop, a piece of paper with the name Ray on it safety-pinned to my shirt.

The gracious state of Florida gave me the birthday of January 1 and the last name of the first family I was placed with—the Quinns. After that, I bounced through sixteen different foster care homes before I graduated from high school and struck out on my own. I don't complain about those years; it doesn't get you anywhere.

The state never found out who my parents were, at least as far as I knew, or why they left me where they did. It was a different time then. People could just disappear.

Pam wanted me to find people who went to great lengths not to be found thirty-eight years ago. Not every case needed to be solved.

Pam had been telling me since we met that God had a purpose for my life and spared me for a reason. I did admit to her that solving her brother's case was an unusual set of circumstances and that after she prayed for me, the extreme guilt I felt for Trisha's death disappeared. I wasn't sure how that worked or if it was just a coincidence. But I still didn't know about any plan or purpose. If there was one, it was as cloudy to me as swamp water. I couldn't see it, not in my life anyway.

Maybe in Pam's. It was fine for Pam's life.

I put the folder back in the drawer and prepared to meet Megan.

19

THE PARKING LOT OF Jay Jay's was jam-packed, and the green neon lights pulsed like a giant traffic light. I'd not made a trip to a club that wasn't business related in a very long time, especially to meet a young lady. I found a spot, far away from the handicapped parking. I'd sooner drop dead hobbling through the lot than hang that little blue placard on my rearview mirror.

I paid the cover charge at the door and shuffled and pushed my way through the crowd, which was a bit tricky with the cane. I spotted Megan at the bar. She wore black slacks with a red shirt that showed off the contours of her willowy frame. She waved me over, drink already in hand.

"Glad you could make it," she yelled over the boisterous chatter and pounding music, a song I was sure I had never heard before. She appeared genuinely pleased to see me.

I got situated on the stool next to her. She'd chosen a terrible spot. We sat in the middle of the bar, and my back was to the crowd. I preferred a corner, dark, where I could keep watch on everyone around me, but I didn't want to make a big deal about it. I'd force myself to do this, to be normal again.

"What are you drinking?" she asked.

"Jim Beam and Coke." I patted my belly. "Diet Coke. Gotta watch my girlish figure."

She snorted when she laughed, then covered her nose. She waved down the bartender and ordered for me. Not shy by any means. Her business veneer as the face for Armon Mayer had been stripped away. She sized me up with untamed eyes.

We made some small talk until my drink arrived. It didn't last long. I waved at the bartender for another. I tried to focus on Megan, but with so many people around, I caught myself eyeing the area, checking the hands and waistbands of every person who passed by me. Checking every face for hostile intent.

My heart started to pound. The music was too loud. Why did I agree to this? I hit the fresh drink as soon as the bartender set it down.

"Are you okay, Ray?" Megan asked.

"Yeah, I'm fine," I said. "So what's it like working for Armon?" I tried to pay attention to her answer, but it wasn't working. There were just too many people around, pressing in on me. The department psychologist told me that someday I might be able to handle crowds again. Today didn't feel like "someday."

The guy standing next to me bumped me with his shoulder. I regarded him and couldn't seem to concentrate on Megan.

"I'm glad you're investigating Logan's case." She swirled her drink in her hand. "He didn't deserve that. He was a good guy."

"Yeah." I wiped my brow. "It's real tragic."

"Do you think you'll be able to get Armon's information back?"

"Working on it." The group next to us erupted in laughter, making me jump.

"Ray, you're sweating. Is something wrong? Are you sick?"

I was sick, all right. Sick in the head. Years of police work tortured my psyche. I wanted to tell her the truth—posttraumatic stress disorder ran my life. I hated crowds because I couldn't watch everyone. The constant fear of being ambushed again and helpless to stop the attack spiked at the worst times and made me feel like I was being pulled through a psychological blender. I just wanted a normal night out, to relax and feel human again. To be able to sit with a woman and talk without being a paranoid, neurotic ex-cop.

It wasn't going to happen. Mainly because I was still a paranoid, neurotic ex-cop.

I wanted to tell Megan all of these things but couldn't bring myself to even broach the subject.

I focused on her attractive face, but the world compressed until I could hardly breathe. My heartbeat pounded in my ears.

"Actually, I'm not feeling too well," I managed. I gulped down the rest of my drink and smacked the glass hard on the bar. "I'm sorry. Must be the flu or something. We'll have to do this another time."

I slapped a twenty on the bar, forced a smile, and hobbled my crazy self through the crowd, feeling stupid. I should have known it was a bad idea. I picked up speed as I pushed through the double doors. Once in the parking lot, I sucked in a deep lungful of precious air. I reached for my truck keys as I caned through the lot. My hand shook.

"Ray, wait." Megan jogged up behind me, her heels clacking on the pavement.

I stopped but only shuffled halfway around toward her.

"Was it something I said? I mean, you were barely here five minutes."

"No. No. It's not you at all." I waved the comment off. "It's been a long day, and I just don't feel good. We'll make it another time."

"Okay," she said. "I just wanted to make sure you were all right." She brushed her hair out of her face and smiled.

I took two steps and then stopped. "Why did you want to meet tonight, anyway?"

"I wanted to get to know you better." She closed the distance between us and rested her hand on my forearm. "I like cops. Always have. They're always interesting people, lots of fun stories. I just thought it would be good to talk with you for a while. And you did me a favor by giving Jack such a hard time. He's a real jerk and is always hitting on me. I figured I could buy you a drink for that alone. Logan used to give him a lot of grief too."

"I bet he did."

She stepped closer to me. "And when Jack got in your face, you had no fear in your eyes. You were ready to die for your cause. That intrigues me. I knew I had to get to know you better, see what made you tick. I'm just that way. Is that weird?"

"Yes," I said. "Very."

She snorted again. Must be her laugh.

Sure, she respected that I stood up to a jerk, even in my condition, and that I had an attitude. But would she still find me as interesting if she knew I had just fled a crowded room because of a serious mental glitch in the hardwiring of my brain? Probably not.

"Maybe we can try again later this week." I worked the keys in my hand. "Someplace a little quieter—much quieter, since I'm not much of a dancer."

"I think I can accommodate you, Private Investigator Ray Quinn."

She looked like she wanted to say more to me, but I climbed into my truck as fast as possible.

Maybe I needed more time before I started going out again. It had barely been a year and a half since Trisha was murdered. I didn't think all that baggage was still there, but I was wrong.

The ride home gave me time to settle down. I could never tell when the anxiety attacks were coming, but there was never a good time for them. Tonight was the worst.

I limped through the gate and to our apartment, my pride lagging far behind. I stopped before I opened the door and flipped open my phone, finding Pam's number. I almost dialed it but changed my mind. I returned my phone to its pouch.

I unlocked the door to our flat. Crevis snored on the couch, the TV still blaring, the credits for *Rio Lobo* rolling on the screen. Not a bad John Wayne flick.

I changed DVDs, putting in *The Sons of Katie Elder,* and saluted the Duke before I grabbed a bottle of Jim from beneath the sink. I brought the whole bottle into the living room with me; no need for a glass. Crevis didn't drink, and I didn't share this bottle with anyone, so I could lip it all I wanted.

John, Jim, and I hung out for several hours until I crashed in the chair. The last thing I remembered was Crevis tossing a blanket on me.

20

THUMP. THUMP. THUMP.

I knew the sound but didn't want to acknowledge it. Crevis was awake and pounding the heavy bag.

Thwamp.

And kicking it too.

"It's a little early for that." I patted the side of the chair, searching for my cane by Braille.

"Early? I've already run three miles and done my push-ups." Crevis shuffled to his right and fired three punches in rapid succession. He had his shirt off, and his lean, sweat-drenched physique was gaining in sinewy muscle. His dedication to his workouts was beginning to really pay off.

"Don't drop your hand when you retract your jab. You're leaving yourself open for a nasty cross. And don't hit that stupid thing so hard right now. I haven't had my coffee yet, and it's giving me a headache." I extracted my shell out of the chair and trudged into the kitchen to get the Joe going.

Crevis giggled and popped the bag twice more, following with two thunderous round kicks. Just to mess with me, I was sure.

I was running behind, so after a cup of stiff coffee, I showered, which washed away some of my night. Then another quick cup as I got dressed, and a third went into a travel cup.

Crevis washed up, but he didn't put on his normal suit and fedora. Instead, he wore blue jeans and a T-shirt.

"Why don't you have your suit on?" I asked.

"I don't want to get the smell of death on it," he said, his face turning ashen. "I'd have to toss it out then."

"Don't be so melodramatic," I said. "There's no better training ground for a cop than the M.E.'s office. Think of it as a field trip in school—anatomy class."

We arrived at the Orange County Medical Examiner's Office, a three-story red brick building at the corner of Copeland Drive and Lucerne Terrace, right next door to the Orlando Regional Medical Center. It wasn't far from our digs and took only ten minutes to get there through morning traffic.

Crevis chauffeured me as I nursed the Joe and gave the facade that I was unaffected by my late night with Jim and Megan. I wasn't sure Crevis bought it. He kept accelerating fast and then braking hard at every opportunity. His stupid grin hinted at his malevolent intent. Where was he learning that kind of belligerent behavior? I'd have to talk to him about that later.

We entered the front lobby of the medical examiner's office. I signed in at the log on the secretary's desk. The medical examiner's office was one of the few government offices open on the weekends. There were worse ways to spend a Saturday morning.

"Ray," Crevis said, almost in a whisper, "do I really have to do this?"

"Yes," I whispered back. "Now quit whining about it and sign in."

"Oh man." He released a dramatic exhale as he made his mark on the line. "I knew you were gonna say that."

"Ray," Greg Bowden called from behind me. He, Oscar, and Katie caught up to us. "Any more leads on your stolen stuff?"

"Not yet." I shrugged. "Still working on it. I'm probably gonna need a copy of the workup on Logan's cell phone, his last calls and all. We'll have to contact everyone on the list. It doesn't seem like Nikki is gonna be a lot of help."

"I'll get it to you as soon as I can," Bowden said.

We entered the autopsy room, and the acrid stench of bleach and cleaning fluids enveloped us. "Love Her Madly" by the Doors blared on a CD player.

Dr. Marek Podjaski hunched over a white male in his early sixties who sprawled on a metal gurney, his chest ripped open as if a wild beast had just burst out of his torso. The doctor was decked out in a light blue medical gown with a mask and a plastic visor, and he held a scalpel in one hand. Blood soaked his arms to the elbows.

"Ray Quinn, so good to see you. It's been too long. I would shake your hand, but...you understand." He raised his scarlet-stained gloves.

Crevis heaved twice and bolted for the door, smacking it against the wall. I made no attempt to stop him.

"Dr. Podjaski." I caned forward, the brass tip tapping the freshly mopped terrazzo floor. "Great to see you too. I don't think we have a hard one for you today."

Dr. Podjaski was in his midfifties and a little taller than me, maybe six-two. When he wasn't masked, he had gray hair as thick as his Polish accent and a bushy salt-and-pepper mustache. He had defected from Poland in the early eighties, when the commies still ran the place. He was fluent in five languages and loved hippie music. If it wasn't the Doors, it was Jimi Hendrix or Janis Joplin that echoed through the room. He was the only doc I knew who could make autopsies fun.

"I'm almost done with him." He pointed his scalpel at his compliant visitor. "Then I will get to your case, yes?"

He finished up with his current guy, and two lab techs in full scrubs—one a young black male, the other a middle-aged white female—unlocked the metal gurney from a sink attached to the wall. The gurney was set at a downward angle so the remnants of the good doctor's work could be washed into the huge bio sink. There were four sinks in the room, each with a docking station for the specially designed gurneys.

Dr. Podjaski was the only doctor working. Must have been a slow night. The techs rolled the man into the cooler, which was across the room, along the opposite wall.

While Dr. Podjaski changed gloves and gear and prepared for Logan's exam, we filled him in on the particulars of the case—how and where he was found and that we had a suspect in custody. Katie showed the doctor the photos of the knife and its dimensions, as well as some pictures from the scene. Autopsies weren't like what they showed on TV. The doc didn't take a blind look at the victim and then tell you how all the injuries occurred in great, precise detail. He needed a story and the facts of the case in order to see if the injuries were consistent. It was a good idea to develop a strong working relationship with the M.E. I'd learned a lot by pacing that floor.

The techs wheeled Logan's gurney out of the cooler. He was still zipped in the body bag, but just knowing it was him gave me pause. Katie worked with the techs to photograph the seals of the bag for the case file. The young black male held a placard with the case number on it over the bag while Katie snapped the photos. Logan's name wasn't on it; his life had been boiled down to a case number at the M.E.'s office.

They snipped the seal with scissors and zipped open the bag, revealing Logan's lifeless body. His face was considerably different than it was even two days before, the essence of Logan Ramsey disappearing quickly now, leaving only a waxy remnant of his former self.

His skin still held a pinker than normal tone. The wounds on his bare chest were more apparent—mere slits in the skin, with no blood at all coming from them. I'd never seen anything like that before. Stabbing homicides were notorious for the bloody scenes. Not this one, though.

Dr. Podjaski picked up his clipboard from the table so he could document his initial external assessment. He took his time walking around the gurney, carefully noting each wound and bruise. He sketched each injury on a human-body diagram on his clipboard. He probed the chest wounds with his finger, then measured the depth and breadth of each.

The Doors CD switched to Jefferson Airplane's "Somebody to Love." He swayed his hips and spun once to the music before he focused back on Logan. Dr. Podjaski was as bright as they came, but I worried about the man's sanity.

"If I die in this county," I said, "dress me in a tuxedo and drop me off at a bus stop over in Brevard County, preferably near the Cape. Somewhere well out of this district. I don't want you guys in here slicing, dicing, and poking me."

"Oh, Ray," Dr. Podjaski mumbled through his mask, wagging his scalpel at me. "We would take good care of you, trust me."

"That's what I'm afraid of, Doc."

"So this is how he ends." Oscar shoved his hands in his pants pockets and glowered at Logan's body. "Forty-eight years old. Too young to go out like that. And what did he have to show for it? Nothing. He wasted his life. He was a waste of life."

"Maybe the job finished him." I eased closer to Oscar. "He didn't start out like that. He was a good cop once, remember? He got too wrapped up in the undercover life. The job ruined him as much as anything."

"Are you defending him?"

"No, but I'm not throwing stones either." I held up my cane. "The job's ruined many a good cop."

"He made choices, and those choices ruined him." Oscar stabbed an angry finger toward Logan. "When he started dabbling in the dark side, he should have seen this coming. He made the choice to betray the badge. He made the choice to drink his life away and alienate everyone around him. He made the choice to steal from the Mayer people."

"Life's not always that simple, Oscar." I pointed to Logan with my chin. "Experiences can impact choices."

"Not buying it." Oscar grimaced. "I make the choice every day to go home, love my wife and kids, and chase all the crap from this job far away. I retire in a year and a half, and I'm walking away healthy and intact. Because I made that conscious choice years ago and have stuck to it. He should have too."

"That's great, Oscar, but not everyone is as lucky as you. Some of us carry this job around forever, whether we want to or not."

"Only by choice, Ray. Think about it."

Dr. Podjaski lifted his scalpel to Logan's chest and with the deft hand of Zorro, sliced a Y incision on Logan's well-muscled torso. Oscar, Bowden, Katie, and I all stepped closer to get a better look.

Dr. Podjaski placed his blade on the tray and raised a hawk-billed limb clipper—a mighty versatile piece of equipment in the good doctor's hand—and dug it into the first rib. A crunchy snip echoed throughout the room. Katie snapped photos along the way. A series of cracks and crunches followed until Dr. Podjaski had clipped a nice, clean circle through the rib cage. Even if Crevis had stayed longer, he never would have survived this. Doc Podjaski lifted the circle of bones, exposing the inner workings of what used to be Logan Ramsey.

"Look at this." Dr. Podjaski dug his hand through several organs.

I peered into the chest cavity. "What? I don't see anything."

"That's it," he said. "It's clean. There's very little blood in the chest cavity and abdomen. With that many stab wounds, the chest cavity should be full of blood."

"What's that mean?" Bowden said.

I sighed and rubbed my furrowed brow. "The wounds are post-mortem. Logan was dead before he was stabbed. That explains why the wounds look like they do."

"Nothing can be easy these days," Oscar said.

"What do you think, Doc?" I said.

Dr. Podjaski stepped back and shook his head. "Very odd, Ray. Very odd. He was dead long before he was stabbed. The knife wounds had nothing at all to do with his death. His heart was stopped already. That's why there wasn't much blood at the scene or here. I don't see any other trauma on him at all."

"Then what killed him?" Bowden said.

"We won't know until we get the toxicology results back," Dr. Podjaski said. "If I had to guess, I'd say someone slipped him a toxic cocktail, poisoning of some kind. I can see no other trauma to account for his death, and I don't like the skin color. A little too pink. This is more than lividity."

"Where does this leave us with Nikki?" Bowden asked.

"We have to call the state attorney's office and let them know about this," Oscar said. "They're not going to be happy, but it appears Nikki Bray didn't kill Logan after all."

21

AFTER A SHORT GAME of hide-and-seek, I found Crevis curled up in a bathroom stall. I coaxed him out with promises that he didn't have to go back into the autopsy room and I'd get him ice cream later for a John Wayne flick, maybe *Big Jake.* It was one of his favorites.

After splashing his face with water, Crevis drove me back to the office.

On the drive, I considered Oscar's comments about Logan, knowing he wasn't talking just about Logan. Life had been kind to Oscar, as it should have been. He was a great guy and a good friend to me when I had no one else.

But he didn't carry in him the things I carried in me. In some respects, I'd come to the place where I could think about Trisha and not be overwhelmed with waves of depression and misery. But there was much that still seemed out of control in my life, and I was helpless to do anything about it. My foray with Megan demonstrated that.

I was trying to fit the pieces of my life back together, but sometimes the pieces had changed and didn't fit where they used to. And some pieces were simply lost forever, never to be found again or replaced.

Logan's lifeless body stirred questions in my head that I had no answers for. I've never been a spiritual guy, but it was tough not to wonder what had become of Logan. Where was he now? Did he regret his life, his choices? If I were on Dr. Podjaski's gurney, would my life amount to more than a number on a placard? Would there be anyone to grieve my loss? What legacy was I leaving? Who would care if I were gone?

I flipped open my phone and pulled up Pam's information. Her picture was beside the contact number. She was smiling. I knew what she would say about such things, and the conversations would start something like, "The Bible says…" or "Jesus says…" But she never judged me or let me get away with being, well, me. I respected that about her.

Before I could dial her number, I closed the phone. I had too much going on right now to consider such things, and I had a case to solve.

"Why would Nikki stab someone who's already dead?" Crevis said, drawing me back. "That doesn't make any sense."

"You get a hefty pay raise if you figure that one out." I thumbed through my case file, a nervous habit that popped up when I needed inspiration or had to get my head back in the game. I couldn't afford to be thrown off by my personal issues right now. I'd tend to them later. "Nikki already had her first court appearance this morning and would have been given an attorney, so now we have to go through her attorney to meet with her. And no attorney in their right mind will let us talk with her again without a deal on the table—immunity or something. But we need to do that right away. This whole thing is getting strange, or stranger. Not to mention a little embarrassing."

We were at the office in about fifteen minutes, and I studied the flow chart I had made for Logan's frenzied life. "Nikki Bray confessed to stabbing and killing him, but he was already dead. Did she know he was dead and this is all an elaborate setup to throw us off the track of the real killer? Or is it possible she just thought he was sleeping when she stabbed him, as she said? Or is there something else we're missing, some connection we've not made yet?"

Crevis scratched his head. "Is it illegal to stab an already-dead guy?"

"I'm not sure. I should check on that. I thought I had seen it all, until now. Nikki said she entered his unlocked hotel room and stabbed him while he was asleep. Maybe she did it after the real killer had already finished him."

"If she didn't kill him, how did he die?"

"That's another problem. Doc Podjaski didn't find an immediate cause of death, so I'm not sure what we're looking at. Logan was too large and strong to have been suffocated, and there was no sign of a struggle in the room, so the only thing I can think of that would kill him and leave no immediate sign is poison."

"What now?"

"We back up and interview suspects we haven't talked with yet." I tapped the whiteboard with my cane.

"Who do you have in mind?"

"A gallery of rogues who had every reason to bump off Logan for putting them in prison—the Rebel Soldiers. We've not approached them yet. The whole drama with Nikki threw us off track for a bit. No matter what, these guys need to be scrutinized—and hard."

I did a little research on outlaw motorcycle gangs through the afternoon. Most motorcycle clubs were just that—like-minded people who enjoyed riding their Harleys and getting out on the open road. They were decent, hardworking people from all walks of life. But there was an element of the biker culture that wasn't so benign, the tiny population of motorcycle clubs that were in fact criminal organizations—like the Rebel Soldiers.

I learned these gangs often had a code of ethics much like that of police officers and private investigators, albeit from a totally different perspective. The rules were important to the clubs and those who dealt with them, and the etiquette was taken quite seriously.

In light of this newfound knowledge, I decided I would violate every one of these rules—until I got the answers I desired.

22

THE SUN HAD JUST set when Crevis and I stopped at the end of the quarter-mile driveway to the Rebel Soldiers' clubhouse in East Orange County. A No Trespassing sign hung on an open gate. I was sure it wasn't meant for us. The older Florida home, built in the '40s or '50s on several acres of property, provided the cover a group like this would need to keep their deeds secret.

We eased up the driveway, our headlights off, until we were about two hundred feet from the house. I killed the engine and waited. No movement from the house. Crevis and I exited the van and eased the doors shut, so as not to announce our presence too early.

"Watch your back here." I adjusted my Glock in its waistband holster. "Most of these guys have done Fed time, so follow my lead and don't give them an inch."

"Got it." He pulled his fedora down tight on his head and adjusted the pistol on his hip. He was ready for business. I hoped.

A string of eight Harley-Davidsons were corralled along the driveway, along with a beat-up brown Ford pickup. Laughter and music rumbled from the clubhouse at our approach. We stopped at the front door, and Crevis went to knock. I grabbed his arm and stopped him, then pointed to my ear. We listened to the goings-on for a few moments until I heard a voice yell, "Hey, Mongrel, next game's yours."

I tried the doorknob. It was unlocked, which meant an open invitation to the party, as far as I was concerned. I nodded to Crevis and drew a deep breath. I twisted the knob as I rapped on the door with my cane, and we invited ourselves in.

"Hello," I said. "Anyone home?"

Crevis slipped in behind me, and we hurried into the living room area, which took me a bit by surprise. The inside was more like a bar than a house. A large couch ran along the wall to our right, the Rebel Soldiers crest pinned above it—a flaming skull on a Harley. A pool table occupied the middle of the room, and a full-length bar, complete with stools, covered the far wall. A small darkened hallway ran off toward the rear of the house.

The gaggle of Rebel Soldiers, two of them with pool cues in their hands, froze and glared at us. At least four lady Soldiers were among them, an eclectic collection of women united in fondness for the Soldiers.

"I'd like to speak with Myron Dotson." I posted both hands on my cane. Crevis stood at the ready.

"Who are you and what do you think you're doing in our clubhouse?"

The befuddled mass of leather, tattoos, and noxious body odor oozed around us in a hasty semicircle. The thick cloud of pot smoke in the room would have been the envy of any reggae band.

"Which one of you is Myron?" I scanned the crowd with a pointed finger.

"Who?" a Rebel Soldier asked.

"Mongrel," the tallest and most antisocial-looking biker said. He stepped toward us and clenched his fist. "You don't just walk into our clubhouse and start askin' for people. You've got two seconds to leave before you get taken by ambulance."

Considerably taller than me, my new friend towered at about six-four with biceps resembling footballs covered in colorful artwork. One of the tattoos depicted an enormous crazed wolf biting the head off a helpless victim. Nice.

"That means now." Gigantous reached out his hand to poke me in the chest.

Crevis pushed his arm out of the way just before he touched me and fired an openhanded strike into Gigantous's Adam's apple.

The biker clutched his neck with both hands and staggered back, coughing and gasping for air. Crevis drew a Taser from his belt and popped both probes into Gigantous's chest, the arc of electricity sparking throughout the room. Gigantous shrieked like a little girl and collapsed to the ground in a fifty-thousand-volt seizure, kicking and flailing.

My Glock came eye level, and I panned the stunned crowd. "Back off and don't do anything stupid. Now I'm asking again, which one of you is Myron?"

The motley group raised their hands and gave us a much wider berth. A wild-eyed redhead in a Rebel Soldiers vest was still behind the bar. She had one hand on the bar's surface, but her right hand rested on something just underneath.

My pistol veered in her direction. "Lady, I don't know what your hand is tickling down there, but you better get both hands up where I can see them. I'd hate for us to have a situation here."

After a couple seconds of steely stare, she complied.

Gigantous attempted to stand.

"Stay down, big fella." My pistol alternated between targets in the room. "Or you'll get another ride. Where's Myron?"

"I'm Mongrel," a voice behind the crowd growled. "Who's askin'?"

A bear of a man emerged from the hallway as he closed a door behind him. My height with double the girth, Myron "Mongrel" Dotson was a bloated version of his last booking photo. Apparently he'd downed a large number of Happy Meals since his release. The reddish-brown mange on his acne-scarred face vaguely resembled a light beard.

He'd been out of federal custody for nine months after serving almost a dozen years on Logan's weapons charges and Racketeer Influenced and Corrupt Organizations Act charges, a nifty federal statute designed to take down mob bosses and gangs.

"Detective Ray Quinn," I said. "We need to talk. In private."

Mongrel paused, looking at Gigantous still on the floor, Taser wires hanging from his chest. Crevis, Taser in one hand and pistol in the other, had the room covered. He grinned in a manner that concerned me.

"What do you want?" Mongrel said.

The crowd parted as I caned through it to meet Mongrel. I holstered my pistol and stepped past him into the hallway, where we could have a little more privacy but I could still keep an eye on Crevis. I caught a whiff of chemicals mixed with the pot smoke, a smell I wasn't able to identify.

"When was the last time you saw Logan Ramsey, Myron?" I said.

"It's Mongrel to you."

"Yeah, whatever, Myron. When was the last time you saw him?"

"You came into my clubhouse to talk about that pig?" He squared up to me. "You got a lot of guts, boy. Now, you and your partner haul your butts out of here right now."

"No problem." I unclipped my cell phone and shot a quick video of Mongrel, and then I panned the room, lingering on the alcohol and marijuana in plain view on the table. "You don't have to talk with me. Maybe you should call 911 right now and have us removed. What are the conditions of your parole?" I tapped my chin. "If you can't remember, I'll remind you. You're not supposed to associate with any known felons, drink alcohol, or use any illegal narcotics. Wow. You've done all three tonight. But you don't have to tell me a thing, Myron. I'll just sit down with your parole officer this week and discuss what I've seen here, show him the video, and tell him how cooperative you've been in this investigation. Your mongrel butt will be back in the pound by the end of the week."

He squinted at me as his hands trembled. "You got two minutes;

then you better be far away from us. Because you just signed your own death warrant by coming in here like this."

"Sure, Myron," I said. "When was the last time you saw Logan?"

"At the federal courthouse in Orlando, twelve years ago, when I was sentenced to federal prison."

"It sounds like you're still a little miffed at Logan."

"Miffed? That snitch put me in federal custody and stole twelve years of my life. He got almost everyone in this room some time in prison. I don't think 'miffed' quite covers what I feel for that traitorous, no-good, filthy, lowlife narc cop, snitch, piece of sewage."

"Did you know he was murdered three nights ago?" I asked.

The smile took a second to cross his face, but when it did, it was large and long. "Couldn't have happened to a nicer guy."

"Where were you?"

"Right here with my brothers," he said, loud enough for everyone to hear.

"Are you sure? It was Wednesday night, Thursday morning."

He jabbed his finger in my face. "Whenever that pig was slaughtered, I was right here, with plenty of witnesses to verify it. Isn't that right, boys?"

The rest of the Rebel Soldiers chuckled.

"You know, Myron, Logan was only able to infiltrate you because you were just a bunch of Hells Angels wannabes, not even settled enough to sniff out an undercover cop. So you've got no business holding a grudge against him."

"If you're not outta here in thirty seconds, you're a dead man."

Mongrel's corpulent body vibrated and jiggled as he struggled to suppress the desire to knock me into tomorrow.

"Better men have tried, Myron." I lifted my chin, giving him a good first shot, as I adjusted my hands on my cane, preparing to smash the brass handle into his big, fat mouth. We locked eyes, and his hesitation told me everything I needed to know about him: Mongrel's bark was truly worse than his bite.

"I'll get your DNA; then I'm through with you."

"It's on file already," he said. "They took a sample when I got out. Get it from them. Leave now, while you still can."

"I'll be in touch," I said. "We're gonna need to talk some more later."

"Come here again, and you and Logan will be buried together, Quinn," Mongrel said.

I tipped my head to Crevis as I caned by. He let loose with another burst from the Taser on Gigantous, who flopped around on his free ride.

"Oops." Crevis flashed a snaggle-toothed grin. "Sorry. It slipped." He dropped the cartridge on the floor, the wires and probes attached, as a souvenir. We backed out of the house.

"Your name's Myron?" one of the bikers asked as we closed the door.

"Okay, Crevis," I said as we stepped out to my truck, "you've earned that raise."

23

SINCE WE'D HAD ABOUT as full a day as investigators could, I had Crevis steer us back toward the office so we could put the information we'd gathered into some kind of order.

I called Cassy Ramsey along the way and updated her on the progress and lack of progress of the case. She wasn't my client, but I figured I owed her the call. She shouldn't find out from the local news about Nikki being released, especially with no explanation as to why.

Then I called Wykoff, Esquire, and filled him in. He responded with the same prosaic questions and responses, displaying all the imagination and personality of a tree slug. At least he was consistent.

I wasn't sure we'd learned a lot from our visit to the Rebel Soldiers' lovely chalet, but at least we'd made ourselves known to Mongrel and his crew. We did discover that they were all associating again and trying to reconstitute the club, to venture back to their glory days of menace and mayhem. I would get a sample of Mongrel's DNA from the Feds and have it shipped to the lab as soon as possible. Maybe the lab could put him at the scene and close the case. He was one dog I'd like to see muzzled again.

Just as we were about to pull into the office, Crevis got a call.

"Mom?" He turned to me and shrugged. "Okay…I'll hurry. Don't say anything to him. You know how he gets. Just stay away from him till we get there." He hung up and sighed. "We need to get to my folks' house, quick."

"What's up?"

"Dad's at it again." He slapped the steering wheel. "Mom's locked in her room, and he's tearing up the house."

We popped a U-turn and hurried up Highway 50 all the way to Crevis's hometown of Bithlo, a small community on the extreme east side of Orange County, where there were more pickup trucks and pit bulls than people. About twenty miles out of downtown Orlando, Bithlo was also home of the Orlando Speedway.

His mother called twice more while we drove; Crevis's father's tirade blasted through the phone loud and clear. Crevis talked her out of calling 911 and assured her we'd handle it. The deputies who patrolled that area were more than familiar with the notorious drunk Dennis Creighton. So much for an easy night.

Just as we passed Bithlo's one and only traffic light, we turned off Highway 50 into a derelict subdivision older than me. Another right turn put us on Crevis's parents' street, and we skidded to a stop in the driveway. The sky blue residence had once been a dark blue, maybe back in the seventies, and the front door had jalousie windows down the center. Weeds and overgrowth encroached on every side of the house like invading armies. The interior lights of the house were on.

Crevis hopped out and was inside before I found the van's door handle. The screaming greeted me before I even entered the house— just like the domestics I used to respond to as a patrolman. I'd only met Crevis's father once before; I'd known kinder badgers.

Since the front door was wide open, I hurried in. Crevis stood between his mother and father. The elder Creighton, about three inches shorter than Crevis, swayed like he was standing on the bow of a ship in a hurricane. His bulbous nose shone like a radish underneath the living room lights, and his black T-shirt only covered part of his distended belly.

Crevis's mother held her arms tight across her faded flowery nightgown and remained mute. Her frizzed red hair was tossed about, and the lines on her gaunt face were more like war wounds from a lifetime of battle.

"Outta my way, boy," Mr. Creighton said, still searching for his balance. "And take that no-good, stinking cop with you. This is between your mama and me."

"You need to go to bed and sleep it off," Crevis said, hand out, nearly touching his father's chest.

"Don't talk to me like that in my own house, boy." He forced his chest against Crevis's hand and pressed into him. "And don't think you can mess with me just cause you...you're one of them detectives. Think you're Mister Big Britches now, don't ya? I know what you really are. So outta my way."

Crevis didn't budge. "Just go to bed, Dad. Sleep it off. Ain't nothing worth getting this mad about."

"Don't you try me, boy. Don't you dare try me in my own house."

He lunged toward Crevis and slapped at his head. Crevis dodged it with ease, and the elder Creighton's hand sailed past. He stumbled back, then launched a punch at Crevis's chin. Crevis parried the strike and sidestepped his father, who barreled past him and crashed belly first into the sofa and then rolled onto the floor.

"Ooh." He tried to stand but sprawled back onto the floor. "You got me good, boy." He lay there for several seconds and then closed his eyes and babbled something unintelligible. "You got me real good."

"Just let him sleep it off there," I said. "He'll be fine."

"I can't let him sleep on the floor like that." Crevis slipped an arm underneath his father's shoulders and lifted him into a sitting position.

"Why not?" I asked. "He's not gonna know the difference."

"I just can't." Crevis hoisted him to his feet. "He's my dad."

He and his mother shuffled Mr. Creighton toward the hallway, where they disappeared. Groans emanated from the elder Creighton, his cantankerous disposition tamed for now.

"You can go, Ray." Crevis poked his head out of the back bedroom. "I'm hanging here tonight."

I nodded and walked out of the house. He had things to straighten out, and I didn't want to get in his way any more than I already had.

I could have just headed home and tried to forget about the day, but I knew that wouldn't work. Cases, details, victims, and suspects pinged through my head with an unwelcome regularity. So instead I drove back to the office and moseyed up the stairs. I had a lot of computer work to do to figure out what my next move was.

Logan was still dead, and that wasn't likely to change. His Excellency's precious information was still on the loose, and I couldn't figure out what I was missing.

I studied Logan's flow chart as I booted up the computer and released Jim from his desk drawer. I think he missed me. He sloshed around the glass in a tea-colored wave before I emptied it in one shot. My eyes watered, my gut churned, my leg cheered. Some relief, finally.

I retrieved my dart gun from the bottom drawer and got some hasty practice on the murder mural. Once I ran out of darts—all of them striking suspiciously near Armon's picture—I stowed the gun back in its drawer. I was too tired or lazy to pull the darts off the whiteboard and reload.

When my background of the Duke appeared on the computer screen—as Sergeant Stryker in *Sands of Iwo Jima*—I checked my e-mail. The chime ushered in the latest response from my friends in South Africa:

Dearest Mrs. Simpkins,

Blessing and grace from South Africa. I hope the day finds you well. I have attached several website articles that express the dire economic situation my country and countrymen find ourselves in. My goal is to get our money into a stable economy, so at a later time I can use it to build orphanages and food banks to help the needy in my country. That is why I'm prepared to give you 10% of this money, because I know you are a woman who desires to help others. Our bank account number is 6660988 and is with the Regions International Bank. I have spoken personally with the President of the bank, and he, too, is eager to assist with the transaction and give his personal guarantee that the transaction can be done quickly and without issue, and you will get your money right away! Please give this as a good faith token to your son, so that he knows we are good men of honor. As soon as your son is satisfied, please send me your bank account information. Time is of the essence. I don't know how much longer I have.

    With great faith in you,

    Mr. Nomvete

I considered the magnanimous offer as I numbed my leg with another stiff drink. This guy was slick and didn't want to give up any information. The options were slim, but I needed something that would draw him in a little more, another tidbit to tempt him.

Dear. Mr. Nomvete,

    I do worry about you there in South Africa. I will present this information to my son, and I hope he will be satisfied. You're a good man doing a very good thing for your country. I wish my son was as concerned with others as you. He seems so reckless with our fortune, always buying cars and houses. I keep telling him that we don't need all that stuff and we should help others—like you—with our vast wealth, instead of wasting it on toys and frivolous spending sprees. I think I can talk him into helping, but I need a couple of days to do so.

Blessings,

Marion Simpkins

To keep this going, I had to convince those on the other end of the world—although I doubted they were really in South Africa—that she believed in their scam and had oodles of disposable cash to blow. If I could really convince them of that, they might slip up and let me spank them good. I'd have to be patient; the best cons are long and drawn out.

I chuckled as I pushed the Send button. Maybe I was enjoying the Mrs. Simpkins role a little too much.

24

I SPENT MOST of Sunday at home, getting caught up on my reports and putting together files on all the subjects involved, including criminal histories and personal information. Oscar and his team weren't working. When I was caught up, I spent the evening watching a private film festival of the Duke's movies, just Jim and me. Crevis didn't come home.

Early Monday morning, I drove out to meet Oscar at OPD. Crevis was still at his parents' house, so I wouldn't bug him until I needed him. I wanted to see if OPD had developed anything useful in the case.

Oscar, Bowden, and Rita were fixated on the flat-screen television in the bullpen. A news commentator flapped his gums about the case as video footage rolled of Nikki Bray being led from the 33rd Street Jail to Lakeview Mental Health for evaluation, her attorney right behind her.

Lakeview wasn't a bad place. I did a short stint there after Pam's case. Oscar had me committed on a Baker Act, a three-day mandatory evaluation. I'd had a mild breakdown at the end of the case in which I nearly sent our unarmed suspect into eternity. I rather enjoyed the rest and thanked him for it later.

"At least it's better than just letting her straight out." I joined the group. "Maybe they can keep her locked up and out of our hair for a while."

"Yeah, but we still shouldn't have made the arrest without positive cause of death," Oscar said. "We screwed up, and now it could come back to bite us."

"Oscar, she confessed to stabbing him to death, and he had a knife sticking out of his chest. Every cop I know would have made that call. So they knock the dust off of her and walk her to Mental Health where she belongs. No harm done. The case is still very redeemable."

"Maybe. But I'm still frustrated by this, and we're not any closer to wrapping this case up. It appears to be someone a lot more devious than we first thought," Oscar said. "I hate the clever ones. They make it tough."

"Where should we go now?" Bowden's tie dangled loose around his neck, and his sleeves were rolled up to the elbows. "Our best suspect just took a walk. Everything about this case is turned upside down."

"We need to start back at the basics." I posted both hands on the cane and rested my weight on it like the third leg of a tripod, a position that was growing more comfortable every day. "Nikki said she didn't check him into the motel room, and we still haven't found his car. I suggest going through his phone again and tracking down every phone call he made. Someone helped Logan hide for a while, and that someone either has information for us or is the same someone who helped him to an early grave."

"We're gonna need more detectives to log in the footwork," Oscar said. "I'll arrange for some others to drop what they're doing and help us out."

"This is a lot of work for a misdemeanor murder." Rita tossed a glance my way to ensure I heard her. "Whoever killed him should be given a medal, not an indictment."

"I guess I'm not putting you in charge of keeping contact with the family." Oscar scooped a stack of papers off the desk. "How about you check out these phone leads and see if you can get some current addresses for us?" He plopped the stack down next to Rita. She lifted the records and moved to her desk, grumbling the entire way.

"When is the toxicology going to be finished?" I asked.

"Dr. Podjaski has a rush on it," Bowden said. "Usually takes eight, nine weeks. If he pulls some strings, maybe a week or less, if we're lucky."

Bowden handed me copies of the phone logs for Logan's cell phone, which only held his last twenty calls or so, provided nothing had been deleted. We'd have to wait for the subpoenaed records from the service providers for a more thorough account. At least this was a start. I asked Bowden to send me all the records he had so far so I could add them to my database.

"We still have a Be On the Lookout Bulletin out for his car." Bowden lifted a picture of Logan's Jeep from the file. "I'll resend it today to keep information fresh with the patrol guys and everyone looking for it."

My cell vibrated and a number I didn't know showed up. I answered it.

"Detective Quinn."

"Hey, Quinn, this is Agent Tom Sloan with the FBI," a male voice said. "I understand you're looking into the murder of Logan Ramsey."

"You could say that." I knew of Tom Sloan but had never had any business with him. The law enforcement community in Orlando is small, so names tend to get around.

"Well, I think we need to get together," he said. "I have some information you might find interesting."

The Federal Building in downtown Orlando was just a couple of blocks away from the PD, so I decided to hoof it. The day was overcast with a forecast of rain in the afternoon, like just about every day in Florida. The traffic off of Hughey Street was constant and stirred up dust from the road.

I took a moment and scanned the Orlando skyline. Armon's penthouse office overlooked the entire city. I wondered if he was watching me at that moment. After my break, I walked as quickly as I could, but it was proving more of a jaunt than I was ready for.

The ten-minute security check at the door was about as pleasant and intimate as an over-forty doctor's exam. It didn't matter to the Feds that I was retired law enforcement, a PI, or anything else. I had to leave my phone with my pistols in a locker at the main desk and experience the magic wand and curious hands of security. As the wand beeped at my hip, I explained to the agents that I had metal screws there as well as plastic.

As I exited the elevator on the fourth floor, Agent Tom Sloan met me. About six-five with bushy blond hair and a basketball player's wiry build, he shook my hand and introduced himself. In his midforties, his eyes and demeanor were more street cop than Fed, more fighter than accountant. He wore a navy blue suit with a red power tie.

"Glad you could make it." He led me to his office and closed the door. The office was clean and neat with a bookshelf behind the desk. His view faced toward the OPD building. If I were him, I'd fight for an office with better scenery, but he didn't seem to mind. A degree in business from Florida State University hung on his office wall next to a picture of a much younger Sloan wearing a Tallahassee PD uniform and standing by a squad car. I'd pegged the cop thing right.

We exchanged some pleasantries before getting to the meat.

"What do you have on Logan?" I said.

"Logan and I go back a ways." He passed his hand over his tie as he took his chair.

"I've been hard-pressed to find anyone who doesn't have history with him—some good, some not so much," I said.

"I worked a few cases with him back in the day, when he was in Narcotics. I helped with the financial end of things." He pulled a pair of reading glasses from his shirt pocket, opened a file on his desk, and flipped to a page of handwritten notes. "We seized a lot of assets from dealers back then, and I was able to work up some cases for federal prosecution. Depending on the dynamics of the case, we could sometimes get the offenders more time in our system than with the state. We used it as leverage to get them to cooperate. It worked well. But I haven't heard from Logan since all the drama when he was fired. Never really knew what happened to him. To be honest, didn't much care. I figured after what he pulled, he got what was coming to him."

"I think most everyone forgot about him, or wanted to. He's made that a little difficult for me now." I eased back in the chair.

"Like I said, I forgot about him until about a week ago. He called me out of the blue and said he needed to meet with me. He had something very important to pass by me, needed my opinion. He was working something potentially large and within my realm—you know, financial."

"Did he say what it was?" I said.

"No." He laid the paper down and removed his readers. "He didn't elaborate. He just wanted to make sure I was still in the Orlando office and to find out if I was available to meet with him sometime. He kind of blindsided me. I told him I'd see what I could do, but with everything that happened, I was a little leery about meeting with him. Didn't know if he would lead me on some wild-goose chase or want back into law enforcement or if he was just sauced. Even though I was cautious, I would have met with him. But he never called back or contacted me again."

"Did he tell you anything else?"

"Nothing. Just that he was working something. I thought you should know."

I tapped my finger on my cane handle and paused. "So what's your gut tell you?"

He leaned back in his chair and swiveled in a half circle. "You have a dead ex-cop, murdered in a seedy hotel after reaching out to an FBI agent. I'd say he stumbled onto something and that something got to him before we did."

I nodded, not too disappointed with his assessment. Now we only had to get past the little issue of the who and why.

25

"Nothing?" I said, phone in one hand, steering wheel in the other. "That just doesn't seem likely."

"Sorry, Ray," Katie said. "I can't make this stuff just happen. I input the prints from the whiskey bottle and the glasses into the CODIS system, and there were no hits. I've checked our databases as well. Nothing. This person must not have been arrested before. Do you have any DNA results back yet?"

"No," I said. "I'll call the lab later and see what I can find out. This is aggravating."

I hung up with Katie and called Crevis to meet me for lunch. I told him it was to review some leads, but I really needed to see where his head was at. After the drama at his parents' house, I wasn't sure what was up with him.

We met at the City Diner on North Magnolia. Crevis swaggered in, dropped his hat on the table, and plopped down in his chair.

We got lunch, and I brought him up to speed on my chat with Agent Sloan while he did violence to a monster burger and fries. Armon's big paychecks were challenging my waistline, and since I wasn't likely to jog it off anymore, I ordered the grilled chicken salad. I gave Crevis a list of phone numbers from Logan's cell I wanted him to run through a program on his computer.

"How's your mom?" I asked.

"She's fine," he said, mauling the burger.

"You good?"

"Everything's okay, Ray." He rested the mortally wounded burger on his plate and wiped his mouth. "We've been dealing with him forever. One more bad night don't change nothin'. It is what it is."

"I just need to know that your head's in the game." I cut up my salad while focusing on him. "If you need time off, let me know. The last thing either of us needs is for you to be off in la-la land when you should be watching a suspect. That could get us both hurt."

"I'm good, Ray," he said as he continued his assault of the burger. "Pass the ketchup."

I handed it to him and watched him gobble down his french fries. As goofy as he was at times, he was tough to read on the personal stuff. I'd watch him a little closer in the next few days to be sure.

We parted ways, him with his assignment, and me with mine. The Mayer group was foremost on my mind.

———

The elevator door chimed as I arrived at the Mayer Holdings penthouse. The doors opened to Megan's perpetually pretty face. She grinned as I hobbled toward her.

"Private Detective Ray Quinn." She stood at my approach and

adjusted her black skirt with a tug and a wiggle of her hips. "I'm so very glad to see you."

"Administrative Assistant Megan Hansen." I stopped at her desk. "Also a pleasure."

She checked up and down the hallway and brushed her hair back. "How're you feeling?"

I was hooked. "Better. Must have been a bug. Maybe a twenty-four-hour thing."

"Well, you look much better. As a matter of fact, you look very handsome today."

It was a rare occasion in life when I didn't have a snappy response. This was one of them. After a few awkward seconds, I found my soul again.

"Maybe we could try again. How does nine thirty tonight look?"

"Works for me." She glanced down the hallway and put on her business face. "Just let me know where, and I'm there."

"Anything new, Quinn?" Jack Gordon said, stomping toward me.

"As a matter of fact, yes." I pulled my phone from its holder and held it out to him. "I got this really cool application from the Internet that allows me to watch movies and download videos on my phone. Is that not the neatest thing you've ever heard of?"

Jack growled. "I meant anything new about the case."

"Oh, sorry." I shrugged as I slipped my phone back in the holster. "You're gonna have to be more specific when you ask questions."

"Mr. Mayer will see you now," Megan said.

I winked as I passed. Her shoulders shook as she fought a valiant battle to contain her laugh.

Armon stood at the far end of the room. This time he wore blue jeans and a gray button-up shirt. His rings sparkled, brilliant as airport running lights. I guessed them to be pure gold. A long, distorted image of Armon Mayer reflected off the well-polished tabletop.

"How are things progressing, Detective?" he asked.

"We've had a lot of ups and downs," I said. "I'm sure Wykoff told you about our suspect being released to the mental health facility. I don't know what to think about her right now. We searched her house. Nothing related to your business. She doesn't appear to have the sophistication to pull off a theft like that, and she had no motive or known connection to your group."

"So you still do not have my client information?" He rested his hands on the back of a chair and scowled at me.

"No." I coughed twice, covering my mouth, and followed it with a deep sniffle. "But we are getting closer. I would like to see Logan's work station here. Since this girl Nikki is not the answer, there has to be some other connection. His work space might tell me that."

Armon released his grip on the chair and backed toward his sanitation station. His concentration on the case seemed to be broken, as I had hoped. I didn't want to be fired, but I also didn't want to be berated by him all day. Nothing like a little flu bug to shake him up. He pulled a sanitizing towelette from the dispenser and worked it around his hands with great speed. We were about done.

"We've already searched his computer and entire work space." Jack propped his hands on his hips, exposing the pistol at his side. "Why do you want to see it?"

"Because I do." I kept my gaze on Armon. I should have checked his work space when I was first there—a serious error on my part.

What other kind of information have you come across?" Armon asked.

"I've mainly been working on his cell phone contacts. I've talked with some people who knew him, and I'm trying to track down his last few days. He had to have contact with whoever killed him. It's just a matter of finding that person."

Armon paced a couple of chairs away and then returned to his position. "Jack, give Detective Quinn the access to Mr. Ramsey's work space that he desires. As well as anything else he needs."

"Yes sir," Jack said.

"And Detective Quinn," Armon said, "let's be perfectly clear— I'm a patient man, but if you don't have results in the next couple of days, I will be forced to replace you. Each day that slips by means more potential jeopardy for my clients. I cannot and will not risk that. Do we understand each other, Detective?"

"Loud and clear." I sniffled once more.

"Leave now and finish your job."

Jack smirked as he held the door for me.

26

LOGAN'S OFFICE WAS ONE floor down and right next to Jack's, so we took the stairs. Jack did it to mess with me. He walked a few steps down and then looked back at me with disgust as I held on to the rail and probed the next step with my cane.

The stairway opened to a corridor with offices on both sides. A secretary's desk stood at the far end from us, and Jack's office was the closest to the stairwell so he could be at the penthouse floor at a moment's notice, should His Highness summon him.

Logan's office was very small and unremarkable. No pictures on the wall. No awards. Just a cluttered, disorganized work space and a computer and in-box sitting on his metal desk. Papers were scattered about, a stapler on top of the mound to hold it all down.

"This is it." Jack held out his hand. "Satisfied now?"

"Not yet."

I sat at Logan's desk and opened the drawers—more mess. Files were laid on top of each other in no particular order, rather than filed neatly. A stack of *Law Officer* magazines filled one drawer alone.

I picked up an employee application off the desk and examined it.

"We've already been through all that." Jack took a step into the room. You're just wasting time and energy."

"It's my time and energy to waste. Besides, you might not have looked for the same things I am. You Army guys don't look for the same things that cops do."

"Marines, not the Army." He crossed his arms and rested against the doorframe.

"Yeah, same thing." I turned on Logan's computer as Jack grumbled behind me, his jarhead hackles raised. Logan's username and password were taped on the top of his monitor. The screen background was the same one that came with the computer, and nothing seemed personalized in the least. Logan wasn't the most computer-savvy guy.

I checked his e-mail and scrolled through the messages for anything that jumped out at me.

"What were Logan's responsibilities here?" I asked.

Jack sighed. "Mainly employee misconduct and such. He interviewed employees, dealt with potential issues here, and did background investigations. He could talk to people well enough, but he was lousy at reports and record keeping. I had to stay on him to get reports on time."

"Some things don't change." I checked his Word documents and started a hasty review. "If those were his only responsibilities, how did he get access to the client information? It seems that information would be rather difficult to access."

Jack folded his arms and paused. After a few silent seconds, he said, "I don't know."

"Then how do you know he had them at all?"

"Our IT people tracked a download of the client list to his computer—tons of personal and investment information, account numbers, spreadsheets," he said. "He was seen leaving the office right after the download was complete. Logan could have accessed those accounts and lived like a king, if someone hadn't stuck him like a pincushion first."

"Did Logan normally have access to that information?" I glanced over my shoulder toward Jack. "Would that have been part of his duties?"

"No," he said. "He hacked the system and got it. We're still not quite sure how. He covered his tracks well."

I attached a portable hard drive to Logan's computer and began copying his information so I could conduct a more detailed analysis later. Cover his tracks? He couldn't set up his own e-mail account, much less hack into the computer system. I should have checked his work space before; there was way more to this story. I was in over my head again.

As I finished copying the hard drive, I realized I had gained a lot of information on this visit, and very little of it came from Logan's office.

Armon's admonishment frosted me a bit as I drove home, so I stopped at a convenience store on Orange Blossom Trail and obtained DNA samples from two homeless men in the parking lot to send off to the lab—to be billed to Mayer Holdings. As far as I was concerned, they could just as easily be the killers as anyone else in Orlando.

If Armon made me really mad, I'd take samples from everyone at an Orlando Magic game.

27

THERE WAS A LOT to mull over, so I drove back to my apartment for a break. I dressed in some shorts and a T-shirt for a heavy bag workout. The leather bag hung between the living room and kitchen with just enough area to swing without hitting the kitchen table or the couch. Not exactly an interior decorator's dream, but Crevis and I appreciated it for its man appeal if nothing else.

I'd downloaded a training series off the Internet called "Cane Fu," in which a martial arts instructor taught a series of self-defense moves with a cane. I wasn't about to let Crevis see it, but the techniques appeared solid, especially for my situation. I practiced a series of strikes with the handle and tip on the bag, enough to get my heart rate up. With each smack of the bag, I ran the case through my head. I used to work through my cases when I ran or did bag work, but a couple of 9mm rounds put an end to that. Maybe in time I'd regain at least some of my prowess.

The cane moves were interesting and somewhat enjoyable, and as a martial artist, I appreciated them. I particularly enjoyed clubbing the bag with the heavy brass handle, swinging it like a baseball bat. A crude but effective technique.

I laid the cane to the side and slipped my bag gloves on my hands. I had to be careful here, because the shooting damaged not only the bones in my hip and legs but the nerves as well. My balance was suspect without the cane.

I loosened up my shoulders. To punch and kick with true power required digging in with a strong foundation from the legs. All the power started from the feet and ended as the knuckles crashed on target.

Since the shooting, I'd had to adjust my strikes. I couldn't push off with my legs anymore, so I'd started punching by whipping my shoulders around and creating momentum with my upper body, crashing my fist into the bag with a motion like a slap. While not nearly as powerful, it still provided some snap and could rock someone if it caught them on the chin. And it was better than relying on harsh language or a really nasty stare to stop an attacker.

The sound of chain rattling as I smacked the bag was nice, like a favorite old song you've not heard in years. I worked a series of two-minute rounds, flailing at the bag like a spastic kid. I lost my balance a couple of times but remained standing. At least I didn't fall on my face. Sweat lacquered my fatigued body.

The workout did its job. I was able to relax and try to arrange the pieces of this puzzle in a way that made sense. Logan Ramsey's world was more complex than I'd hoped. Possibilities swirled around. I toweled off, wiping my sweat and a little of the stress away.

After a quick shower, I met Oscar, Bowden, and Katie Pham at the homicide division's briefing room for an evidence review. The conference table had pictures of the scene laid out, as well as the property reports and some of the supplemental reports from the initial officers and other detectives.

"I've got all the evidence in." Katie slid a pack of freshly printed pictures from the motel room across the table. "We took a ton of DNA swabs and snapped a lot of pics. I'm not sure what we're looking for at this point."

We spread the photos out on the table and matched them with the evidence collected.

"The best theory I have now is that Logan was poisoned." Bowden held his chin as he spoke. "The doc said he didn't find any needle marks, so Logan must have ingested it somehow."

"If he was poisoned, there has to be some evidence of it from the room," I said. "We need to send every swab and piece of evidence off to be tested."

"I've called the lab every day, putting a rush on this." Oscar slid a picture of Logan on the bed away from the others and leaned down to examine it. "I've asked the chief to put a little pressure on them as well."

"First, I think we need to send off a sample of the whiskey in the Jack Daniel's bottle," I said. "I'd test it myself, but I don't feel like a canary today." I picked up the picture of the pizza box. Three slices gone. No crust left. Someone was hungry. "We need to test the pizza too."

"That might be a problem." Katie crossed her arms. "I kept the box but didn't keep the pizza. Sorry. I didn't see any reason to log it into evidence, especially with a knife sticking out of his chest. I didn't want it to go bad in the evidence room and stink it up. I really didn't know."

"That's okay. We'll make it work. Let's test the inside of the box." Bowden held up a picture of the pizza. "If there was any poison on the pizza, there's bound to be some residue left on the bottom. It's worth a shot."

Bowden's suggestion made sense. He was thinking more and more like a homicide cop every day, and he didn't let the hiccups in the case keep him down.

"We should test the outside of the box too," I said. "Someone had to carry it in. The cardboard should retain the touch DNA, especially on the bottom and the sides."

I examined a photo of the label on the pizza box that showed the customer's name: Mrs. Smith, no home address. Swell. It was a take-out order from the Antonio's Pizza at 1555 Colonial Drive, which wasn't far from the hotel.

"We need someone to go to the pizza place and get any surveillance tapes and interview the employees." Oscar checked his watch. "We're already four days behind. And Katie, you need to get this stuff off to the lab right away. This case is stalling. We don't even have a cause of death yet. We need to get ahead of this thing."

"Logan's car still hasn't been found," I said. "And I'm still missing the information he stole. I should talk to Nikki again. Something's just not right with how all this went down. She knows more than she's saying, or she's being used by someone. Either way, she's got to be interviewed again."

"You've got to go through her attorney now," Oscar said, "and no attorney in their right mind is going to let you talk with their client, especially if she's in mental lockup."

"O ye of little faith."

28

IT'S ALWAYS HARDER to ask for permission than it is to beg for forgiveness. A truism that worked in areas other than law enforcement. I hoped it continued to be accurate, especially since I'd called a friend at Lakeview and set up an appointment to talk with Nikki—without her lawyer's permission.

Lakeview provided Orange County with emergency mental health needs—such as the Baker Act for suicidal people. Like many things in life, I had one impression of the place—a lunatic asylum—until I actually spent time there myself. My attitude toned down a bit after that, since they helped me through some dark days.

An African American female orderly opened the door to the visitation room and held it for Nikki. She shuffled in wearing light blue scrubs, sandals, and bright red socks. A medical bracelet clearly identified her as a resident, not a guest. The kinks and knots had been combed out of her hair, and she didn't give me much attitude as she eased into the chair next to the couch I sat on.

"Call me when you're finished," the orderly said.

The soft glow of the lights and the feng shui of the room made it feel like I was doing an interview on Oprah's couch, but the mental health facility wasn't exactly decked out for police interviews. Maybe that was a good thing. The trauma we put her through in the interview room would still be fresh in her mind. A different environment would be good for this talk.

"Didn't think I'd see you again." She brushed her hair behind her ears and crossed her legs.

"I want to clarify some things." I kept my tone soft and monotone, like I imagined her counselor's would be. "Do you think you can talk to me?"

"My lawyer told me not to talk to the cops."

"I'm a private investigator." Swinging in and out of the cop thing could be useful at times. I used it to my advantage. "I just want to ask some more detailed questions. I believe you didn't kill Logan, but I think you might have seen or heard something while you were there that can help find who did."

"But I did kill him...at least I think I did. Now my lawyer and everyone else says I didn't." She spoke more slowly and softly than she had when I interviewed her last. "I don't understand. I told you and the other cops everything. Maybe I *am* crazy. It was all a blur."

The medication she was on must have been working, because she was more lucid than at our last visit. She'd had a couple of days to detox off of whatever street drugs she'd been taking too.

"I'm not reading you your rights," I said, "because I'm not going to use anything you tell me against you. I think you can help me figure out what happened to Logan that night."

She folded her arms and sat back, gazing at me for a few moments.

In this environment, she seemed almost normal, not a woman who'd done time for beating one boyfriend and stabbing another—albeit dead—boyfriend.

"What do you want to know?" she asked. "I'll tell you what I can remember."

"Walk me through that night again, slowly."

She sighed and leaned forward, resting her elbows on her knees. "Logan called me a few days before. He said we wouldn't be seeing each other anymore, like he was that special or something." The pitch of her voice grew with each syllable. She paused and controlled herself. The real Nikki was leaking out—the angry, bitter, and often psychotic woman.

"I called him a couple of times that day." She focused on her feet and wiggled them around. "He said we could meet and talk, but that was it. He had a lot going on, and he needed to get his life straight. He had something he had to do."

"Did he say what it was?"

"No. And I really don't…didn't care. I started drinking and got a little, you know, high. I went to the motel where he was. I waited for a while for him to come out and drive somewhere."

"His car was there?" I asked.

"Yeah." She met my eyes again. "It was parked right by his room. I waited to see if he would leave or drive away. I kept drinking."

"You're sure his car was there?"

"Yeah, that stupid Jeep," she said. "It was parked there."

"Then what?"

"His room door was open."

"Open or unlocked?"

"I think it was open a crack." She raised her hands as if pushing the door open. "I could see him there, sleeping. That's when I went in and…" Her voice cracked as she made a pathetic stabbing motion in the air.

"Do you remember a satchel in the room?" I showed her a picture of Logan carrying the brown satchel.

"I can't remember." She crumbled back into the chair. "I was really messed up."

"Did you take anything from the room?"

"No. I just did what I did, then left. I didn't take anything. I didn't know what I was doing, I swear. But I thought I killed him. I really did." She covered her mouth. "I loved him, but I killed him. I just don't know."

"He was long gone before you got to the motel, Nikki." I scooted forward as much as I could on the couch and made sure she looked at me. "You're sure his car was there?"

"Yeah, I know it was." She wiped the tears from her cheeks. "That much I know for sure."

Nikki had been pushed about as far as she could handle—and as far as I should go, given the circumstances. I made some small talk with her to ease the tension, not wanting to send her back to her ward looking disheveled or upset. It could make a return trip difficult with the administration at Lakeview. I had already bent the rules well past the breaking point.

I stepped out of the room and summoned her minder. After I gave Nikki a business card, I asked her to call me if she could think of anything else. The orderly escorted her from the room and down the hallway.

As I drove home, I considered everything we'd discussed. Nikki's interview had been helpful in a number of ways, but it also added to the stack of questions I had about this case. She seemed pretty sure about Logan's car being at the hotel. She had no reason to lie about that, which presented a couple of problems.

If Logan was already dead when Nikki arrived, then why was the car still there? Why was it missing when the police arrived? Did the killer come back to clean up? To look for something else? Either way, Logan's car disappeared long after he was murdered. And it was entirely possible that the only thing Nikki Bray killed that night was a little bit of time.

29

I ROLLED INTO the office parking lot at about 7:30 p.m. and ambled up to the office. The evening sun crawled behind the downtown Orlando skyline, Armon's colossal building slowly extinguishing its light. Another day was closing out, and I still didn't have my client's information or the identity of Logan's real killer.

I logged on to my computer and checked my e-mail, hoping for some good investment news from my friends across the globe. Nothing. Too bad. Anything could have lifted my spirits at that point.

Nikki was fully accounted for and would be under the watchful eye of the state for a while. I needed to concentrate on Logan's last contacts and work my way down the list. We were missing something, and this was as good a place to start as any.

The call log on his phone only retained the last twenty incoming or outgoing calls, dumping them after that to make room for the next ones. Numbers could be deleted from the list too, but it was the only thing I had to work with until we got the full record back from the service provider. I wished I could get his official records sooner, but the phone companies only worked on one

speed—their own. Our case wasn't the only one the companies were
working on. Tens of thousands of requests had to be processed
through the phone companies—all of them urgent, at least to those
investigating them.

As I scanned the list, Nikki's number appeared a few times, the
last being the night he died, consistent with the time line she gave
me. Another number occurred three times, once earlier the night of
his murder. The phone listed it as "ML."

I decided not to wait for the phone records and picked up my
recorded line, which showed on any caller ID as a telemarketing
business. I shot off a cold call. The automated operator said the number had been disconnected or was no longer in use. I'd have to wait
for the records.

My cell phone vibrated. Megan's number appeared and so did
my smile.

"Hello, Megan."

"Hey, Ray," she said. "I'm glad I caught you. Are we still on for
nine thirty? Where do you want to meet? That is if you're not chasing down some deranged killer. I'd hate to interfere with that."

"The deranged killer can wait," I said. "I could meet you in, say,
forty-five minutes at Burtons on Washington Street."

We said our good-byes and hung up. My mood lifted some. Burtons was considerably quieter, a place much less likely to throw me
into a paranoid cop tizzy. Plus I had some time to mentally prepare
as well as consult my buddy Jim.

I freed him from the purgatory of the desk drawer and downed
a shot to still my nerves. Going to the Rebel Soldiers' clubhouse

didn't scare me a bit. Meeting a beautiful woman at a crowded club—with people pressing in on me—gave me the willies. A psych student could write a doctoral thesis on my neurosis.

I took another swig before I checked my look in the mirror. I straightened my shirt and combed my hair. Since it was all I had to work with, it'd have to do.

The forty-five minutes was to give myself a head start, so I could beat Megan to the bar and pick the best spot for us to sit. It worked. I arrived before she did and checked the place out. Burtons was on Washington Street near Lake Eola. The parking lot had plenty of empty spaces, which wasn't surprising for a Monday night. As I entered the building, the bar was to my left with a mirror behind it and glasses stacked about two feet high. A half-dozen tables stood in the center, two of them occupied, and four booths ran the walls to my right. A pool table took center stage, and a dartboard hung on the back wall.

I settled into the farthest booth, where I had full view of everyone in the bar and my back to the wall. Maybe thirty people lingered in the entire place, and there was plenty of room to stand or move around. A boisterous group sat in another booth in the corner, but they seemed like college kids just having a few laughs, nothing to tilt my crazy meter.

I hadn't even ordered yet when Megan arrived. She stood at the door for a moment, scanning the room for me—a look I could get used to. Her nimble figure shifted her weight from one foot to the other. I was tempted to raise my hand but was rather enjoying the view. She saw me and power-walked my way in heels, a black skirt, and a beige top, clutching a red purse in her right hand.

"Is this better?" She slid into the booth and kept her purse at her side. "It has more of a PI feel to it. Dark and mysterious."

"I like it," I said. "It should give us a chance to talk more."

I ordered vodka on the rocks, stepping out on Jim for the night. I didn't think he would mind, and I desired a change. Megan ordered a Jack and Coke.

We made some small talk. She was from Missouri originally. She loved fried pickles and played saxophone in a jazz band through college. Graduated with a computer programming degree. Wanted to get a job at a high-tech firm, but no one was hiring. Bounced from job to job until she answered an ad for Mayer Holdings and had been there ever since, two and a half years now. Was overqualified for her job and hated it. Very much loved the pay. Mayer Holdings possessed all the loyalty that money could buy.

"How's Logan's case going?" she asked, teasing her drink with her lips. "Any ideas on where the information is or who killed him?"

"It's a bit more complex than I'd hoped. It seemed pretty easy at first, but now I just don't know." I wasn't sure how much I could reveal to Megan. The PI handbook forbade it, of course, but that wasn't the only reason I was cautious. She was Armon's assistant, a position of at least some trust in the group. Anything she heard could be on Armon's desk by morning, but I understood her curiosity, and she might be a good ally on the inside if I dealt with her correctly.

"So where did you grow up?" she asked.

"Around here, mostly."

"Did you play sports?"

"I dabbled," I said.

"How long were you a police officer?"

"Long enough to know better."

She sat back, crossed her arms, and arched her eyebrows. "Hey, you really make a girl work. I spilled my guts, and I still hardly know a thing about you."

I shrugged. "Not much to know, I guess. I catch bad guys. It's what I do."

"But it's not who you are." She leaned forward and rested her elbows on the table. "That's what I'm trying to find out."

"Good luck." I smirked. If there was an instrument on this planet that could get me to cough up information, it would be Megan Hansen's sassy smile and emerald eyes—eyes that reminded me a lot of Trisha's. I fought not to be hypnotized by them.

Megan pursed her lips and pouted. Another nice ploy to draw me out. As attractive as she was, that little cop voice inside me screamed to continue keeping my cards close, to take things slow for now. Even though I was a PI now and not a cop, my ethics and common sense also told me not to get too close to people in my cases. It could only end poorly.

That hadn't stopped me with Pam on the Hendricks case, but that was different. Pam was different. I never had that fear with her. My gut was right that time too.

"What's the story with your boss?" It was tough for me to leave business in the office. I left the question open-ended so she'd have to fill in the gaps and couldn't rely on a yes or no answer. I wanted her opinion first, then I might offer mine, though it would still be sanitized, like Armon's hands.

"Let's just say that working for Armon Mayer is not what I expected." She ran her fingers through her hair and shook it out. "He's nice enough and always formal with me, none of that harassment or creepy stuff. But he really doesn't have me do a lot, other than answer the phone and schedule appointments. I expected to be writing memos or typing minutes to meetings, having more interaction with him. But he doesn't work that way at all. When he's meeting with a client or other employees, I'm expected to stay at my desk. He's got some very high-profile people on his list, so he demands discretion. I had to sign a waiver when I got hired that I wouldn't disclose any information about the clients or the nature of their business. I never expected to sign a prenup for a secretary job."

"That's odd. Almost as strange as his clean-freak thing."

She was drinking when I said that and almost spewed Jack and Coke all over me. She grabbed a napkin and dabbed her mouth.

"Oh my gosh," she said. "He orders me to fill the hand-wipe containers every day, and I bet he's got stock in the antibacterial hand-gel companies. He's nuts with that stuff."

I probably shouldn't have been so hard on Armon's germ issues since I had baggage of my own, but there was crude entertainment value in mocking him, so I didn't feel too bad.

"So, since we're all about business now, what's Armon hiding?" I took a drink and peered over my glass to see if she caught the seriousness in my tone.

She paused, and even though her blood alcohol level was somewhere between tipsy and topped off, a glint of panic flashed in her eyes. "Did you ask me here just to liquor me up and interrogate me?"

"You called me, remember?" I said. "And, yes, this was all part of my diabolical plan."

She toyed with a lock of hair. "How long did you say you knew Logan?"

Her weak attempt at diversion concerned me, but she had said that Armon made her sign the company policy to keep all the inner workings at Mayer mum. For whatever reason, she didn't want to go there, and since I wanted to get to know her better personally, I wasn't inclined to push it. I relented and tossed her a morsel to chew on.

"About fifteen years. We worked together in Narcotics for a short time."

"He liked all that undercover stuff, huh?" She grinned like a woman who had just gotten her way—because she had. "Like being a spy, never knowing who your true loyalty belongs to."

"Something like that. Undercover can be a weird world to live in. I think he did it too long, and it sucked him into the slime of that life. He forgot who he really was. He forgot what the badge meant."

"A little insightful for someone who just catches bad guys, don't you think?" she said. "Maybe Logan never really knew which side he belonged on."

"He knew. He just forgot."

"You sound pretty sure of yourself."

"Maybe, maybe not. Just an observation."

"Logan was like a big kid sometimes," she said. "You remind me of him, always messing around."

"Could be a cop thing."

"That's why I've always liked cops." She spun her glass on the condensation of the table. After a few moments, she said, "Just do me a favor, Ray. Find the person who killed him. I don't care what everyone else says he did. He shouldn't have ended up like that, alone and dying without some…someone to be with him. It's just not right."

"'What everyone else says'? You don't believe he stole the information?"

She locked eyes with me. "Just find who did this. That's all I'm asking."

"I will. I have no doubt."

"How can you be so certain?"

"I have to be. Only the most committed win."

I had work to do in the morning and was wise enough to know that if I spent too much time with Megan, I might regret it. I paid our bill, left a tip, and listened to Megan's tipsy talk all the way out to the parking lot.

As we stopped at her car, she turned to me, and an awkward silence fell as she stood by her door. She had a way of smiling at me that made me feel stupid and anxious all at once, like a school kid on his first date. A thick gust of humid summer air swirled around my face. I swayed, more from bullets than booze.

Gazing into Megan's inviting eyes, I lost myself for a moment.

I was drawn back by a familiar look from Trisha—my fiancée, who died two feet away from me a year and a half before. Her fresh memory helped me realize I was more of a basket case than even I knew. I wasn't ready for this. I wasn't ready for a lot of things. As much as she might have reminded me of Trisha, Megan wasn't Trisha. My head needed to be straight before I waltzed down that road.

She stepped closer, almost on top of me. "You're an enigma, Private Detective Ray Quinn."

"I've been called much worse things than that."

She snorted and took my hand in hers. "Thanks for the drinks and the laughs."

"I really need to get going. I have an early morning."

She eyed me in the dangerous way that made me thankful I hadn't had one last drink.

"It's still pretty early. Maybe we could go back to my place," she said, "for another drink. Talk a little more."

"Maybe another time."

I hurried to my truck so as not to change my mind. I pulled out of the parking lot, fully convinced I was a hapless moron.

30

I KEPT THE RADIO OFF on the ride home for some silent contempla-tion. Megan was young, attractive, and intelligent, albeit a bit of a party girl. Yet she was making a pretty strong play for me. At least it seemed that way. I'd been out of the game for quite a while, so it was hard to tell. Maybe it was just the liquor talking in her.

I wasn't sure I'd gotten down to the real Megan Hansen, past the veneer she displayed. While she tried to portray the happy party girl, it felt like there was a part of her she held back. Maybe she was naturally cautious. Maybe it was something else altogether. A little more time and effort, and I should find out what it was. People could be complicated.

Logan was still causing turmoil even in death, possibly more than he'd stirred up in life. Would he even care about that now? I glanced in the rearview mirror; only a few lights were behind me.

I turned off Washington Street onto John Young Parkway. Nikki, the motel room, missing data, angry bikers, that crazy knife, and my phobic client competed in my mind for one theory that would weave all these threads into a tapestry for a first-degree murder indictment against…someone. We were a long way from that.

Logan's case and my personal issues shared some frightening similarities—both were chaotic and had no recognizable pattern to them, and neither looked like they'd be solved anytime soon, regardless of the puffery I gave Megan.

I went to bed at 2:00 a.m., to sleep around 4:00.

My morning routine felt like a slow-motion film with a couple of frames missing, but I managed to work through it and meet Oscar and Bowden at their shop before 10:00 a.m.

"We spoke with the manager of Antonio's Pizza." Bowden flipped a page on his legal pad. "We got a receipt from the transaction for the pizza in Logan's hotel room. We also interviewed the cashier who made the transaction. As best she could remember, a white female picked up the pizza. Paid cash for it."

"What about security tapes?" I took a seat at Bowden's desk. "Do they have the transaction on video?"

"The tapes are only of the last forty-eight hours, and then they recycle," Bowden said. "We lost any chance at getting them. The order was called in about 8:00 p.m. We do have the number used to call it in."

I shrugged. "At least it's a start."

"Not really," he said, flipping over a page. "It's from a pay phone about two blocks away. We've checked around the area for video. Nothing."

"If I were of a suspicious nature, I'd think someone tried to keep that pizza purchase as untraceable as possible."

"True," Oscar said. "We're still going to run a lineup with Nikki's picture in it past the cashier. See if she can pick anyone out. I don't know. They do a couple hundred pizzas a night, and it's been almost a week. The faces can blur together. I wouldn't hold out a lot of hope on her picking anyone out of a lineup."

"Well, I have some interesting news." I referred to the notes I'd made about my second talk with Nikki. "Logan's car was definitely at the motel that night."

"How'd you find that out?" Oscar said.

"I went to see Nikki." I smirked.

"Without her lawyer?" Oscar posted his hands on his hips, pushing his coat back, exposing his pistol and the badge clipped to his belt.

"Absolutely," I said. "I didn't read her her rights either. I don't think she's our main suspect, at least on the actual killing of Logan."

"I hope not, because you just two-stepped all over any chance her statement could be used against her in court." Oscar jabbed his finger at me and turned to Bowden. "Don't ever do anything he does. I had too many years of running interference for this guy. I don't need another like him."

Bowden dipped his head. He got it.

"My gut tells me Nikki's just a fly in the ointment," I said. "I need to figure out if she's there intentionally or by accident."

"In twenty-five years of law enforcement, I've never seen a case where someone stabbed an already dead man," Oscar said. "Doesn't speak well for Logan that he had at least two people who wanted him dead."

"But only one of them succeeded," I said.

"Yeah, but not from a lack of trying." Bowden leaned back in his chair and locked his hands behind his head. "Nikki gave it a good try. Six stab wounds in the chest. She gets an A for effort."

"Well, we've got to get on track and get the toxicology back from the lab." I flipped through the pictures of the motel room as we spoke. "We really need to know what killed him. We're kind of stuck until then."

Oscar's phone vibrated. "Yeah…really. Are you sure? Okay, we're on our way. Maybe twenty-five, thirty minutes." Oscar slapped his phone shut. "We might not be out of luck yet."

"Why's that?" I said.

"Because they just fished Logan's Jeep out of a lake."

31

LOGAN'S JEEP CHEROKEE spewed water from the doors and windows like a fountain as the wrecker hoisted it from the murky lake waters behind the Christmas RV Park.

Christmas, Florida, is a rustic village in a desolate area of east Orange County, where the second you step out of your car, you become part of the food chain—and not necessarily the top of the chain, either. Canals flanked both sides of the road, and swampland surrounded the area as far as I could see. The waterways served as tributaries to the St. Johns River. The lake was about a mile down the dirt road from the RV park, in Boonies Central.

Oscar, Bowden, and I watched from the bank as the spectacle unfolded before us. Katie Pham had parked her crime scene van on the side of the road. She stood closer to the water, snapping pictures as the Cherokee crawled out onto dry land.

Two deputies from the Orange County Sheriff's Office Dive Team, wearing full diver's gear and bodysuits, ascended from the dark waters like something from *Creature from the Black Lagoon*. Two other dive team members helped take off their masks and air tanks, dropping them on a staging area in the grass. They'd explored the area and hooked up the chain to the Jeep so the vehicle could be pulled out. They'd checked for a body too. Thankfully, there was none. That would have seriously complicated an already convoluted case.

Another deputy in the sheriff's office green uniform stood on the bank with a scoped .308 sniper rifle, providing gator watch for the guys in the water. If he spotted one in the area, he'd dispatch it to gator heaven before it got anywhere near the divers. No cop I'd ever known wanted "Eaten by a gator" written on their headstone. There were plenty of better ways to die.

"What are the odds that Logan ditched his own car here, then hiked back to the motel and poisoned himself, and then had Nikki stab him?" Bowden said, eyeing Oscar. "Is there any way we can just rule this thing a suicide and go home?"

"Nice try." Oscar paced the grass. "This thing just keeps getting deeper."

"Well, the car answers one question." I stepped off the grass and back onto the road. The easement was a bit squishy and had a significant pitch downward. The last thing I wanted to do was to tumble the length into the water. I'd never live that down, and chances were good Katie would get it on tape. "But it raises a few others. Now we just have to figure out how it got here. How'd they come across the car?"

"A fisherman and his son were back here chasing bass, and they saw it submerged," Bowden said. "Only the top was visible. He called it in."

I surveyed the area. A lone country road in east Orange County. No homes to visit; the RV park was a good mile away. Sparse traffic at best. Someone could dump the car and be gone in a minute.

I hobbled back down the grassy side of the canal with great care, my cane sinking deep into the soggy bank. A set of vehicle tracks creased the embankment just off the road, leading into the canal. Apparently our suspects aimed it from the roadway, and it hit the water at an angle, sinking there. No other tracks stood out on the hard-packed dirt road. The suspects probably kept the second car on the roadway while they dumped the Cherokee. It was the rainy season, so the water levels were up. The Jeep was probably sucked into the canal and hidden from sight within seconds. There were more reeds, gators, and snakes than answers at this scene.

"There's some good news about finding the car so far out here." I swatted a host of bugs buzzing around my head.

"What's that?" Bowden asked.

"Odds are really good that our suspect didn't act alone," I said. "He would have needed someone to pick him up. And that's very good news."

"Why?" Bowden scrunched his face. "It's still two people out of a million right now."

"True." I held up my index finger. "But there's an old adage in homicide: how do two criminals keep a secret?"

Bowden shrugged.

"One of them dies."

———

Logan's Jeep was loaded on a flatbed wrecker and hauled to the evidence garage at OPD's impound lot. The wrecker driver backed into position, slowly raised the front of the bed at an angle, then lowered the platform to the ground. The Cherokee was eased into place in the bay. Shelves lined the walls of the garage with bags, gloves, and tools of every kind to examine any area of a vehicle. A hoist in the middle of the floor allowed a view underneath if needed. Gasoline fumes hung in the air and were strong enough to stick to my clothes.

Katie, fully geared up, snapped a photo of the entire vehicle, then moved forward to capture sections for closer examination.

"Not much to do right now since everything's still wet." She opened each door with care and photographed the inside of the vehicle. "I'll get the dehumidifier going, and we'll start a more thorough search when it's dry."

"Do you mind if I take a peek?" I said.

"Go ahead," Katie said. "Just don't rummage through anything, mess up my scene. I know how you like to finger everything you see."

"Everyone's an expert now." I left my case file on a shelf and leaned my cane against it. "I'll be careful."

I worked a pair of rubber gloves onto my hands and opened the passenger-side door. Nothing noteworthy in the front seat. The glove box contained a mishmash of damp papers and unidentified mush. The inside of the Jeep held an abundance of fast-food wrappers, cups, and empty soda cans, all displaced by the water rushing in and then out of the car. The raw pungent stench, though already nasty, was nothing like it would be in a couple of days after the mildew set in. I did a light search of the front seat area, the backseat, and the trunk. No satchel, no computer info or hard drives.

Why had the suspects gone through all the trouble of dumping the Jeep in the middle of nowhere? But more importantly, where was Logan's satchel? Had he hidden it somewhere to protect his investments, or had someone relieved him of it, after relieving him of his life?

Either way, my current client wasn't going to be happy.

32

I PICKED CREVIS UP at our place and hit a drive-through on the way back to the office so he didn't start gnawing at my arm with his large, uneven chompers. If I didn't feed the kid every couple of hours, he got a dangerous kind of hungry.

The evening darkness was chased away by the headlights of the cars streaming into the Amway Arena parking lot for some event there. I peeled out of the traffic and into our lot and hobbled up the steps with my legal pad for the case in tow. Crevis scampered ahead of me and already had the lights on and the alarm off when I arrived at the door.

The office sprang to life as we booted up the computers. The light blinked on the answering machine, so I checked the messages. Nikki's lawyer had left a terse and rather threatening voice mail, something about suing me and my never talking to his client again and taking me before the judge and blah, blah, blah. I deleted it.

I caned over to the whiteboard, which needed some serious updating. Logan's driver's-license picture occupied the middle of the board with lines jetting out in all directions. I drew another line to the location of his vehicle in Christmas. I hoped it would prove to be a good present. I'd tape a picture of it there later.

I slid another line to FBI Agent Tom Sloan. Savannah Breeze had yet to be identified. The picture of Armon was next to Logan's. The spider had morphed into a mutant beast with more legs than it needed. Many legs, many leads, few answers.

"Any good evidence from Logan's car?" Crevis asked.

"Probably not," I said. "Unless we find some surprises, the water probably destroyed any fingerprints or DNA. But the car does raise some interesting questions. Why was it taken? Why was it dumped? At least two people would have been involved to drive there, dump it, and drive back."

Crevis tossed his feet on his desk and kicked back. "Why would someone kill Logan at the motel, then take his car and dump it way out there? Seems kinda stupid to me."

"Real dumb," I said. "Unless they had evidence they wanted to get rid of or delay us finding Logan. But to delay us, they would have to know someone was looking for him, other than them."

Crevis removed his fedora and scratched his orange scalp. "Say that again?"

"Never mind. We could spend hours speculating, but it doesn't mean a thing until we have some evidence."

I grabbed the black marker from the tray, drew a scar on Armon's cheek, and blackened out one of his teeth. While it did nothing for the case, it gave me a bit of pleasure and satisfaction.

Footsteps shuffled up the stairs toward our office. We were the only business open in the building at that time of night, so we had to have a visitor.

I checked my watch. "Is Pam coming this late?"

"I don't think so," Crevis said.

I grabbed my cane and took two steps toward the door.

Pop. Pop.

The door's glass window shattered as the rounds tore into the drywall to my left.

I dropped to the floor. "Get down!"

Crevis launched out of his chair and rolled on the ground, drawing his pistol and firing a furious flurry of rounds toward the door.

"Stop shooting! Crevis, stop!"

Crevis's 9mm was locked back and out of ammo. He dropped the magazine and reloaded as he scrambled to his feet.

"Only shoot if you can see something!"

A motorcycle rumbled to life in the parking lot.

I rolled to my side. "Get me up, quick!"

Crevis righted me in seconds, and we sprinted toward the door. The motorcycle hopped the curb and hit full-throttle, weaving through the line of cars turning into the arena.

Crevis raised his pistol for another salvo. I smacked his hand with my cane. "There's too many people around. Let's go after him."

I hopped down the stairs on my good leg, lost it on the third-to-last step, and belly-flopped on the asphalt. Crevis bounded past me, then came back and scooped me up again. He slid an arm underneath mine and bull-rushed me to the van, then tossed me in the passenger's seat. Seconds later, he mirrored the shooter's path over the curb and into oncoming traffic on Colonial Drive. The jolt smacked my head on the roof.

"Catch him, catch him, now!"

33

OUR VAN SWERVED across the median and into the right lane of traffic. Crevis locked up the brakes, skidding to a stop in the roadway just short of the slow-moving car in front of us.

"Go around! Hit the median again."

Crevis veered into the median and floored it. The motorcycle, a chopper, weaved effortlessly in and out of the cars well in front of us, like a child on a swing set. I smacked the dashboard twice.

"Get up there." I pointed toward our suspect. "Get him!"

"I told you we needed a better car, but no, you said the minivan was the greatest PI surveillance vehicle ever made. And now when we need a faster car, you're yelling at me!"

"Shut up and drive," I said.

Our suspect dipped into a turn as he veered off Colonial onto Rio Grande Street. He gunned it, popping a wheelie, then leaned forward and pulled away from us again. Our van listed left as we lagged behind him.

A car changed lanes in front of the motorcycle. The suspect skidded, his back tire wobbling, before he laid the bike down on its side, sliding to a stop.

Crevis punched it, and we finally gained ground. The guy jumped to his feet, lifted the bike, straddled it, and was off again just as we caught up to him. He was white, which was about all I could tell. He had a head covering of some sort, maybe a helmet, maybe not.

I dialed OPD's direct number and waited for a dispatcher. The driver zigged left onto a darkened side street. My camera, laptop, and recording equipment slammed into the side of the van as Crevis attempted to match the suspect turn for turn. We turned just in time to see his taillight take a right. We were losing him.

"Orlando Police Department, what is your emergency?" the dispatcher said.

"This is Ray Quinn," I barked. "We're chasing a suspect that just shot at us. We're on…I don't know what street we're on now, but it's off Colonial. We had shots fired."

The suspect turned onto Ventura Avenue, where the street sign read Dead End.

"We're on Ventura," I managed, then dropped the phone on the floor.

The suspect hit the cul-de-sac and slowed to turn.

Crevis headed for him and accelerated hard. Our headlights lit him up. He wore a black leather jacket with no markings and a bandana over his face and head. A white guy for sure.

Crevis jammed on the brakes, but the van slid toward the biker, whose eyes widened into hubcaps. He lifted his leg just as the front of the van crunched into the side of the bike, tossing him off. He barrel-rolled twice into the middle of the cul-de-sac.

I opened my door and swung my legs around, trying to get my left foot on the ground to support me. I held onto the door with my left hand and drew my pistol with my right.

The scumbag wobbled to his feet and staggered backward.

"Stop!" I swung the pistol toward him. "Get on the ground!"

He drew a pistol from his waistband. The muzzle flash was followed by a sharp *crack*. Crevis dived back into the driver's seat, his head down, as the windshield splintered.

Steadying myself with the door, I popped three quick rounds at the suspect as he sprinted into the darkness between two houses.

———

The searchlights from the Orange County Sheriff's helicopters traversed over us like two sabers crossing in a galactic battle overhead. Lieutenant Figueroa was the night commander, and he had over twenty units scouring the area for our attacker.

A solid six feet tall with a torso as thick as a mountain gorilla's, Figueroa—or Fig as he liked to be called—had a shaved and shiny head like a bullet, which reflected the red and blue lights around us. Fig stood by the open door of his patrol car and studied a map of the area on his mounted laptop. He hooked his thumbs in his gun belt.

Oscar arrived in his navy blue Suburban, his dash-mounted lights blending in with the dazzle of the others. He adjusted his tie as he approached us. I sat on the bumper of one of the patrol cars; Crevis stood next to me.

"Wreaking havoc on the city again, Ray?"

"If it matters, we're both going to be okay," I said.

"They found anyone yet?" Oscar rotated in a semicircle, checking out the area.

"Nope. No blood trail either. I don't think I hit him."

"Losing your touch, Ray? It's not like you to miss."

"It was an awkward shot. The situation was a little…dynamic."

"Any ideas who this guy is?"

"A couple."

"Anything you wanna share?"

"Nothing I can prove." I planted both hands on my cane handle and boosted myself to my feet. "We didn't get a good look at the guy, and the motorcycle, a Harley-Davidson as coincidence would have it, was stolen two days ago, according to Lieutenant Figueroa. So nothing solid. But I can't help thinking that our buddies from the Rebel Soldiers might have had their hand in this. They weren't too happy when we showed up at their clubhouse."

"Our shop is gonna take this case, since you're working with us and all. I sent Bowden and Stockton over to your office to make sure Crime Scene is collecting everything."

A male crime scene tech I had never met before focused a stationary floodlight on my van, the motorcycle crushed in its grill, illuminating the roadway scene. Numbered yellow markers covered each shell casing on the roadway—one from his .45, three from my 9mm.

I was a little perturbed I hadn't dropped the guy, but I'd been still trying to extricate myself from the van, holding on to the door, and firing with one hand at a moving target twenty-five yards away. I supposed I was lucky to get any shots off at all. My ego was wounded, but it had survived worse. I just hoped the department wouldn't recall my Expert Marksman badge.

34

CREVIS AND I GAVE a preliminary statement to Oscar on scene. There wasn't much to it, but it had to be part of the record. Oscar used his pocket digital recorder to tape them. Crevis got too chatty on his statement, providing much more information than necessary. He needed to answer the question as presented and not offer anything else. Not that we did anything wrong, but the more you information offer on a statement, the more chance an attorney down the road could misuse what was said—especially after an adrenaline dump like we just experienced.

Since our van was evidence now, Oscar gave us a ride back to the office. As we pulled into the parking lot, Katie stood on the walkway in front of my storefront, snapping pictures. The glass window of my front door with the cool logo was gone, only a few slivers of glass still hanging from the top like icicles. Two shell casings were marked below in the parking lot, just beneath my door. Bowden and Stockton walked the parking lot with their flashlights, checking for more casings or evidence.

"Looks like your suspect shot from the parking lot up to the office," Oscar said.

"Or he shot from the walkway and the casings ejected down to the parking lot." I pointed to the walkway. "The rounds impacted close to me, where I stood by my desk. The angle should tell us where he stood. And right before the shots, someone was walking up the stairs."

"That makes sense." Oscar called to Katie, "Can we go in?"

"Yeah." She fumbled with her camera. "Aren't you getting tired of people trying to kill you, Ray?"

"Not really." I wiggled my finger at her. "Each person has their own personal touch that's unique and keeps it interesting."

She rolled her eyes. "You're strange."

"You're just now figuring that out?"

Katie had nailed the truth more than I was ready to admit. I'd been nearly shot—again—and having been through that once before, I was in no hurry for a replay. The adrenaline was wearing off, and my body quaked. I tried not to let everyone see it. The tumble down the stairs and Crevis's wild ride had bruised me up good too, especially since I was still healing from Keith Wagner's beating. I was glad I had good insurance.

I stepped through what used to be my front door, glass crunching under my feet. The wall next to the door was peppered with rounds meant for the suspect—Crevis's rounds. As he stepped in the door, I pointed at the chaotic pattern. "First, you need more range time. You're all over the place. Second, you have to know what you're shooting at. You can't fire blind."

"I saw a flash or something." He ran his fingers around one of the holes. "I couldn't just let him shoot in here like that."

"I get it," I said, "but you have to be sure where your rounds are going. Fortunately, it looks like most of your rounds hit the drywall in the office. But look through the door. What do you see?"

Crevis's head hung. "The road."

"Not just the road." I pointed across the street. "The parking lot to the arena itself, for goodness' sake. Bullets don't know the difference—good guy, bad guy, innocent civilian. A bullet doesn't care. It tears through whatever it hits."

"Sorry, Boss." He shrugged. "I got amped up."

"Just watch it in the future," I said. "The last thing we need is some civilian suing our butts off for catching one of our rounds."

Crevis wanted to do the right thing. His instincts were good, but he needed to be reined in a bit. At least he jumped into the fight right away and didn't cower under the desk like some frightened kid. When I was a cop, you never knew how a new guy was going to react when a call went bad. That was why most cops didn't trust the rookies until they had proven themselves under fire. No one wanted somebody watching their back who wouldn't do the right thing when the time came. Crevis didn't have that problem. If he could get on the force, he'd be okay.

I stepped to my desk. "I better make sure the most important thing in this office wasn't damaged."

"Your laptop?" Crevis asked.

"Nope." I opened the bottom desk drawer and retrieved the bottle of Jim. I held it up.

Oscar shook his head. "You're crazy, Ray."

After returning the bottle to its resting place, I examined the wall behind my desk. The bullet holes were about a foot from where I'd been standing, perfectly circular, which meant they'd probably been fired straight on.

"The suspect must have stepped in front of the door and let loose," I said. "He was definitely on the walkway, not shooting from the parking lot."

I probed the hole with my finger. Crevis and Oscar stepped closer and studied it as well. "Katie, are you going to dig these out?"

"I was planning on it," she said. "We'll match the rounds and the casings to the gun, if we ever find it."

"Hopefully we won't give you any more evidence to collect."

Oscar, Katie, Stockton, and Bowden closed up the scene at about midnight. Crevis took my truck to Wal-Mart and got some wood to board up the door.

As I was sweeping the broken glass into piles, Pam's car turned into the parking lot, and she parked right next to the stairs. She wore blue jeans and a white shirt, and she hurried from the parking lot up the stairs.

"Looks like you had a rough night, Ray," she said, stopping just outside the door.

"Let me guess, you just happened to be in the neighborhood and wanted to stop by." I leaned the broom against the wall next to the door. "In other words, Crevis called you."

"Actually, he texted me." She folded her arms across her chest and gave me a genuine look of concern. "I just wanted to make sure neither of you needed anything."

"We're good." I sensed there was more on her mind. There usually was. "Do you want to come in?"

She stepped through the door and zigzagged through the debris on the floor. Then she hugged me, catching me off guard. She was a serial hugger, but I didn't see this one coming. She was trembling.

"I'm glad you're okay," she said. "I prayed as soon as I heard, and I knew I should come up here and check on you both."

"Wow. That's a personal speed record. You normally don't get to me until I'm in the hospital."

"Let's hope it doesn't come to that this time." She inspected the newest murder mural. "You tend to push the envelope, Ray. I get the feeling my prayer life is going to improve a lot because of this case."

"Is that a bad thing for you Christian folk?"

I didn't mind her prayers—for the case, anyway. I could take care of myself, but I needed leads. I'd twirl a dead chicken over my head and hop on one foot if I thought it would bring me some solid information on the case. Pam's praying seemed fine with me. If there was a God, He'd listen to her. Prayers weren't coming off my lips anytime soon.

"Where's Crevis?" she asked.

"He went to the store to get some wood so we can board the place up."

She shuffled her feet. "Can I ask you something serious, Ray?"

"If I said no, would it stop you?"

Her smile chased the melancholy away from her, at least for the moment. "Probably not."

I rolled my hands. "Get on with it. Ask away."

"What if... If you'd been killed tonight, what would happen to you, Ray? What would happen to your soul?"

"Crevis would probably sell it at a garage sale or on eBay, along with my shoes." I turned my hip and showed her my pistol. "I know he could get a good price for the gun."

"I'm serious," she said. "Can you be too for one minute? Where would you go? Really, I want to know."

"I've had a long day, Pam. I appreciate your concern, but the midnight ride to save my soul isn't helping right now."

She closed the distance between us. "I just want you to think about it. And I'm glad you're okay. Tonight really scared me. I'm afraid one of these days I'm going to get a call and it's going to be too late."

"I'll think about thinking about it." I smirked.

I wasn't angry with her for going God on me. I wouldn't expect anything less, and she'd earned the right with me. At least she cared enough to show up. But her question did cause a bit of angst for me, because I didn't know the answer.

I knew what she believed. Since we'd first met some six months before, she'd articulated the tenets of her faith to me no less than a dozen times, always hoping I'd jump on her Jesus bandwagon and be healed of my multitude of dysfunctions. It hadn't happened yet.

My big problem now was that I didn't know what I believed. I used to be a comfortable agnostic, perfectly happy not worrying about God, and I figured He had better things to do than worry about me. But after three days in a coma, more days in intensive care after my shooting, an attempt on my life during Pam's case, and now another, the facade of invulnerability was long stripped away. Whether I liked it or not, at some point I was going combat prone, stiff on a gurney like Logan Ramsey. There was no way out of it.

I didn't know where Logan was now, and I had no idea where I'd be had the shots hit their mark. I didn't like that.

35

AFTER CREVIS RETURNED with the plywood and supplies, we boarded up the door. Pam stayed with us until we finished, helping sweep and clean up the place. It was well after 2:00 a.m. when we finally got home.

Despite all my joking around at the scene, I was more than unnerved about being attacked. I couldn't let Crevis know that, though. He watched how I reacted to situations. He couldn't lose his mind at every crazy situation when he became a cop, so I wasn't going to start him down that road now.

I kept a cautious eye on our surroundings as we got out of my truck and ambled to the apartment. My pistol-toting friend was still out there, and if he knew where my office was, it wouldn't be too hard to find out where I lived. The computer age made available, at the click of a mouse, information that used to be difficult, if not impossible, to get. The scumbag had struck at me in a place where I was comfortable, where I let my guard down. A well-thought-out move. I wasn't going to let it happen again, even if it meant letting my paranoid psychosis go unfettered around the house.

I was so exhausted that I didn't need a round of Jim on ice to sleep, but I tipped one back anyway, lest dear Jim get lonely without me.

Crevis and I got moving at the crack of noon—another benefit of working for myself. I dropped Crevis off at the rental car office to get us another van and headed to our office.

I logged into my computer and found an e-mail from Bowden with "Logan's Phone Tolls" in the subject line. He'd attached a spreadsheet of the last month of Logan's phone calls—number called, time, date, and duration. It also listed the cell tower location for the calls. Each cell tower served only a small radius, sliced into three or sometimes six pie-shaped quadrants. A call registered off a certain quadrant, giving an approximate location for the person making the call. New technology changed how police work was done almost on a daily basis. I saved everything to my hard drive.

I called Armon's office, and Megan picked up after the first ring. It was good to hear her voice. "Megan, I need to speak with Armon, to update him on the latest."

"I'm sorry, Ray. I can't put you through directly to him. He'll have my head. All calls go through Richard. I don't make the rules, but if I don't follow them, I'm unemployed. He's weird like that."

"No problem," I said. "I'll chat with Wykoff then."

"I had a great time the other night. Call me later."

She put me through to the ever-boring Richard Wykoff, and I filled him in. His labored breathing on the other end made it sound as if my description of the chase and shootout was more than he could handle.

"I'll let Armon know the details," he said, "but he's not going to be satisfied that you haven't found the information yet."

"Well, let him know that the important thing is that Crevis and I are okay."

Wykoff paused before he answered, almost as if he perceived that I was messing with him.

I hung up, and not even a minute later, I got a text message from Megan.

Why didn't u tell me u were shot at?

Fill u in later, I messaged back to her.

U better! she wrote.

I started typing out the particulars from the night before. I'd learned through the years that if I didn't get it down in a narrative soon after the event, I would lose information.

My cell phone vibrated again. I expected it to be another text from Megan, but it was an incoming call from the medical examiner's office. I had set the picture for the M.E.'s office to be a skull and crossbones. It seemed to fit.

"Ray, Dr. Podjaski here."

"What's up, Doc?"

"Like I haven't heard that one before, Ray," he said as Grace Slick crooned "White Rabbit" in the background. "But to answer your question, quite a bit is 'up.' We got the preliminary tox screen back from Mr. Ramsey's blood."

"Any surprises?"

"Of course. Why else would I call you? This is a particularly interesting surprise—cyanide. And lots of it. His toxic level could have killed two or three men his size. That accounts for the pinkish hue of his skin too."

"Didn't see that coming. I didn't think cyanide was big anymore," I said. "I've only seen it in the movies. Never had a case with it."

"It's making a comeback," he said. "It was used in the past to clean precious metals, gold and silver, but now it's mostly found as a by-product of crystal meth. A lot of the meth labs that have been busted lately had some form of cyanide in them. It's a bad exposure risk for the agents. So it's not as uncommon as it sounds."

"By coincidence, I'm sure, I just happen to know a group of people busted for crystal meth who didn't like Logan very much. The Rebel Soldiers are climbing to the top of the suspect list. Just for curiosity's sake, what was his blood alcohol level?"

Doc Podjaski paused for a moment, and I could hear papers shuffling. "Nothing. He didn't have any alcohol in his system."

"That's strange. For Logan anyway."

"He was clean except for the cyanide."

"Interesting."

I hung up with the doc and started putting Logan's phone information into my Threads program, software that linked each suspect or witness with their appropriate phone and address records. The program then correlated any connections, like calls or contacts, and kept everything in order. Each person's driver's-license photo served as the icon for all of their information. It was enough to make a geek like me all giggly and sure made my life easier, especially with a case like this with so many people and records running together. I could only do so much linking analysis on my whiteboard or by using markers to color-code numbers on paper printouts.

As much as the Rebel Soldiers were back on the screen—I was formulating a plan for them—I also needed to identify Savannah Breeze. Threads would assist with that too. I checked the phone records for the time Logan checked into the motel. I assessed his favorite numbers and would have Bowden send subpoenas to the providers for their information. I had the numbers but needed to know who owned the phones, put some names with the numbers. More precious time would be wasted waiting for the paper chase.

Several of the numbers jumped out at me right away. The number for Logan's daughter, Cassy, was sporadic. I attached her name to the number, which meant Threads would flag the number in any other records we received. I also flagged all the numbers I knew were associated with Mayer Holdings. It sure beat the old method of sorting through reams of paper records for one phone contact. I searched back a few weeks and noted the call to Agent Tom Sloan.

I called a friend at the Orange County Sheriff's Office and pulled some favors. We'd meet later.

Someone knocked at the door. "Hello." Pam's familiar voice echoed through the office. "Is Crevis around?"

"No. He's out getting us another van. He'll be back in a while. Is he going to get a detention for missing class?"

"I think he has an excused absence today." She perused the bullet holes around the door and shook her head. "Were you able to get any sleep?"

"About the same as usual, which is not nearly enough." I got up and walked around my desk to meet her. "But isn't that why God made coffee?"

"At least your theology is sound there, Detective Quinn." She laid her purse and briefcase on Crevis's desk. "You're starting to come around."

"Don't get your hopes up."

She regarded Logan's murder wall and crossed her arms. "I'm sorry about your friend. That's got to be tough."

"I'll survive, but it is a little odd, since I knew Logan. You never anticipate seeing someone you know end up like that. Not the most enjoyable case I've ever worked."

She rested a hand on my shoulder as we took in Logan's photo together. As much as I wasn't having fun, I was sure it was worse for Logan. I decided to switch the conversation, so as not to get too melancholy.

"How's Crevis doing? Do you think he's going to pass the test this time?"

"I don't know," she said. "He's had a lot to overcome. It's not just the learning disabilities. He's so far behind in the basics. I'm doing everything I can to get him caught up, but I don't know if we're going to have enough time. The test is just days away. He really wants this, though. That helps. He has the desire."

I sat on the edge of my desk. Pam had put in a good effort with Crevis, no matter what happened. It was one of the many things I respected about her.

"Ray," a female voice called from the door. With a faint knock, Megan Hansen sashayed into the office. She wore a short tan skirt with stilettos and a white long-sleeved silk shirt. "Oh, I hope I'm not interrupting something."

"Not at all." I hustled to my feet and straightened my shirt. "Megan, this is…a friend of mine, Pam. Pam Winters."

They shook hands, and Megan brushed back her hair. An awkward silence filled the office as the two women faced each other. Pam was one of my best friends, one of the few people in my life I trusted without question, and Megan was, well, someone I was trying to know better. Our relationships weren't any more complicated than that, but it still felt weird.

Both ladies—about as similar as mint julep tea and tequila—turned their attention to me. I checked my watch. It was getting late—late for what I wasn't sure, but I would find something.

Megan crossed her arms as she scowled at me. "Since I had to hear from Jack Gordon that you were shot at, I figured I'd come down here and get some answers."

"It's my job." I shrugged. "Sometimes people try to kill me. What can I say?"

"I should be going." Pam grabbed her purse and briefcase. "Crevis and I can do this another time."

"No, it's okay. I'm leaving now anyway." I looked at my watch again, thankful for the exit strategy. "I've got a meeting with the sheriff's narcotics unit. We have a rendezvous with some old friends."

"I'll walk you down." Megan glanced toward Pam, who hurried toward the door with her briefcase. "You can fill me in on who in the world would want to kill you."

"The list is long and distinguished."

36

THE FRONT-PORCH LIGHT illuminated the shadowy front yard of the Rebel Soldiers' clubhouse, and a herd of steel Hogs lined the driveway, as if the whole leather rodeo had just roared into town. Our rented van eased to the edge of the dirt extension road, blacked out.

"Nobody's movin' outside," Crevis said.

I scanned the front of the house again with my binoculars. "If our intel is right, they should be having their meeting about now. To discuss the philanthropic interest of the club, I'm sure."

Crevis lowered his binos and arched an eyebrow at me. "What?"

"I'm getting you a dictionary for Christmas this year. Just keep a lookout."

I checked my watch. It was time.

A man in camouflage emerged from the wood line to the north of the house, a rifle down at the low ready. Another crept behind him, followed by another. The number of armed men rose to a dozen as they hurried toward the Rebel Soldiers' front door, weapons trained at the house.

"This should get interesting very soon." I zoomed in closer.

The team eased past the corral of motorcycles and gathered on the porch. An officer with a ram stepped in front of the door and bashed it once, knocking it open. A flash of light and a clap like thunder rocked the evening air. The Orange County Sheriff's Office S.W.A.T. team breached the door to the Rebel Soldiers' clubhouse with a controlled fury and poured inside.

Even as far away as we were, I could still hear them screaming, "Get down! Get on the ground!" Two more flash-bangs exploded in rapid succession, followed by an unnerving silence.

After several tense moments, my phone vibrated.

"Okay, it's clear," Oscar said. "The house is secure, and we can move up."

I started the van and followed the trail of unmarked police cars heading down the driveway. Oscar's Suburban was in front of us, two Orange County SUVs in front of him. The Orange County Crime Scene van was behind us. Bowden, Steve Stockton, and the ever-gracious Rita Jiminez were chasing down a lead in the city.

The Rebel Soldiers had superior parking, and all the vehicles fit nicely in front of the residence, almost as if it were designed for a multiagency assault. Two S.W.A.T. team members stood guard on the porch, weapons slung at the ready. The front door of the house no longer existed, having been knocked clean off its hinges. Smoke billowed out the doorway, and another S.W.A.T. guy stood just inside, covering a load of Rebel Soldiers lying prostrate on the floor.

"Went off without a hitch," Agent Brent Young with the Orange County Narcotics Unit said. He was quite a bit shorter than me, about five-six, but with a fireplug build that suggested he could bench-press a Cadillac. His brown hair was tied back in a ponytail, and he had a goatee and a piercing on his right eyebrow. "No one hurt. Lots of dope in plain view. Looks like your intel was good, Ray."

"Did you doubt me?" I said.

He shrugged.

Several S.W.A.T. members wearing green ballistic Kevlar helmets strutted out of the residence while four more agents wearing masks to hide their identities formed at the door. I let them go in first. They gathered everyone in the main room, and Agent Young read the search warrant to Mongrel and the rest of the mutts while another agent recorded it on video. My sworn statement about what I observed during my first visit gave Young the probable cause he needed for the search warrant. It was time to tune up the Rebel Soldiers.

"We're just minding our own business," Mongrel said, sitting on the floor with his legs crossed Indian-style and his hands cuffed behind him. "Why're you cops harassing us? You've got no right."

In law enforcement, like just about everything else in life, it was all about the timing. And now was the time. I caned my way into the clubhouse.

"Ray Quinn!" Mongrel growled. "I should have known this came from you."

"I was just in the neighborhood and thought I would stop by." I pointed my cane at some of the cops in the room. "Seems like you already have company. I hope I'm not interrupting something."

He mumbled a litany of unprintables under his breath. Handcuffed Rebel Soldiers littered the floor and the couch, about a dozen in all. The redhead was on the floor, cuddled next to Mongrel and well restrained. Her glare made me glad she was handcuffed.

Gigantous lay on the floor as well, Taser probes extending from his chest again—just like our last visit. Evidently, he didn't get on the ground fast enough for the S.W.A.T. guys. Some people never learned.

I studied Gigantous's build, hoping to make a positive ID on the suspect who shot at us. His real name was Scott Long—like his rap sheet—but Gigantous worked for me. He certainly had the right frame and biker garb, but I couldn't be sure. His criminal history was the envy of the Rebel Soldiers—aggravated assault, battery, robbery, cruelty to animals, and a heinous illegal dumping charge, just to name a few. We'd interview him later and see what he had to say.

A masked agent exited the back room and called for Agent Young and me. I hurried over.

"Don't go in there." The agent held up both hands. "It's a meth lab. The chemicals are toxic. We need to get everyone out of here, pronto. Lots of meth out on the table as well. Good call, Quinn."

"We need a good sweep from the evidence techs," I said. "The meth will get them in prison, but if we can show cyanide, it will go a long way toward the murder charge."

Agent Young got everyone out of the house and secured it for the crime scene techs, who would need to work with masks and ventilators because of the noxious mix of fumes.

We paraded the Rebel Soldiers out to their spacious front lawn and waited for the jail van to take them to the station. Club Rebel Soldiers was in full lockdown.

37

THE ORANGE COUNTY SHERIFF'S Office substation was jam-packed with unmarked cars of all kinds, including some OPD vehicles. The interview rooms were on the ground floor. Mongrel, Gigantous, and the redhead were taken there immediately. We didn't want them getting too comfortable in the cells or having time to come up with a story together.

Oscar chatted with some of the agents gathered in their offices. They gave him a rundown on their interview rooms and recording equipment.

"Crevis, just stay quiet and watch." I pulled out a chair and pointed to it. "You don't get training like this at the academy or from a book. And try not to touch anything. We're guests."

His head rotated like an owl as he gawked at the area, his mouth wide open. He nodded like he understood me, but I wasn't convinced he wouldn't start fingering all the cop paraphernalia in the office—raid vests, clip badges, and pictures of major busts. It was a cornucopia for a cop wannabe.

"My charges are solid, Ray." Agent Young tossed his file on the desk. "I've got them producing meth and at least a trafficking amount at the scene, and we haven't even dug deep yet. Since Myron's on federal parole, I can't flip him to use as an informant. Talking to him is useless to me. You can do what you want with him on your charges. Our Crime Scene people will finish searching the clubhouse, and I'll let you know if we find anything interesting."

Agent Young bore the cocky swagger of most narc cops I'd known. He was even a bit reminiscent of Logan. The world is different when you become a narc agent. One minute you were in uniform, hopping from call to call, foot pursuits, fights, or worse. Then you were stuck undercover, growing your hair and beard out, working on your lingo and attitude. You started trolling the bars and the streets, getting snuggly with the very same people who would spit on you in uniform.

If there was an area in police work where you could get in real trouble, it was the narcotics unit. Logan found that out too late. Agent Young seemed pretty squared away. I just hoped he stayed that way.

"Appreciate the help," I said. "I'm not so concerned about them taking potshots at us—if it was them—but if we can make the charge stick, maybe one of them will flip on Logan's murder."

"Want to interview them with me?" Oscar rose to his toes, then sank back down, ready for a fight.

Mongrel was in full view of the monitor. His shoulders were rolled forward, his features sagged, the years of hard living worn on him like a crusty, stretched-out leather vest.

Oscar and I entered the room. Mongrel sat up and threw his

shoulders back, resting both hands on the table. "You're wasting your time, Quinn."

"It's not my time that's wasting." I remained standing to loom over him. The dynamics needed to change from our last talk. "And from the looks of things, there's a lot of time fixing to be wasted. Yours. The parole violations alone are going to keep you in Club Fed for a very long time. The meth lab, and whatever else we find, is gonna add years to your sentence. You're gonna be a very old dog before you ever breathe free air again…Myron."

"Tell me something I don't know." He flipped a hand in the air. "Read me my rights, and let's get on with it."

I was surprised Mongrel didn't lawyer-up right away. Oscar read him his rights to provide a little distance from me. Oscar walked him through the Miranda warning, and Mongrel agreed with each stipulation.

"Knowing these rights, do you wish to speak with me without an attorney present?" Oscar asked.

"Sure, I'll speak to you."

"Good. Sign here." Oscar pointed to a line on the form.

Mongrel signed it and then crossed his arms. "I have a statement I'd like to make," he said.

"Go ahead."

"You both can pound sand." He sat tall and smiled. "Now I want my attorney. I've made the only statement you're gonna get from me today."

I slammed the door as we exited. We'd let the deputies take him back to the booking area. Right now we needed to press the redhead.

As we entered her room, we were greeted with the same loving eyes she'd shared with me before—like she wanted to chain me to her Harley and drag me for a couple miles.

"How's things going, Savannah?" I said as I hobbled into the room.

"The name's Judy." She'd left the Rebel Soldiers vest somewhere, probably the booking area. She wore a black sleeveless T-shirt and well-worn blue jeans. In her midthirties, she had sharp cheekbones and an athletic build that might have been attractive if not for the biker apparel and lethal leers. The whole angry-chick thing didn't work for me.

The Savannah jab was just a hunch, but she'd given no reaction that suggested I'd struck gold with it.

"I guess you're here to get me to snitch on my men," she said.

"We're here to get you to help yourself." I sat down carefully and tried to mend the rift a little. Tried not to come off as the authority figure and just lay out her options. "You don't have a long criminal history, and you weren't with the club when Logan infiltrated it and brought everyone down the first time. So you're in a position to help yourself. We want to know who killed Logan, who shot at us, and where Logan's property is."

"How does it feel to want?" she asked, smiling for the first time. "I don't have anything to say."

Neither Oscar nor I was surprised when Gigantous refused our kind offers to chat. The Rebel Soldiers were united in their silence. Not what I was hoping for, but not a huge surprise either. The true outlaw bikers had a strict code about giving the police information on the club or other members. Anyone who violated that code had a lot more to worry about than just being excommunicated.

Since none of the Rebel Soldiers felt like keeping us company, I collected Crevis, and we followed Oscar and Agent Young back to the clubhouse. Two more crime scene techs had showed up since we left, and they wore Scott packs to breathe with. The poisonous fumes from meth labs had cut more than one police career—and life— short. Dismantling such an operation had to be done with great care.

"We'll send everything off to the lab for testing," Agent Young said. "Maybe we'll find some cyanide and you can put your case to rest."

"It could put his case to rest." I pointed to Oscar. "I still have other items to find. I'm looking for an external hard drive and a satchel belonging to Logan. The satchel might have other items in it. If you run across either, let me know." I gave Agent Young photos and descriptions of the items.

"I'll drop you a line if we run across any of these," he said.

I didn't hold out a lot of hope that Rebel Soldiers were behind the theft too, but I had to check.

38

As Crevis and I drove home, I detoured to the Sand Dollar Motel one more time. I was getting off track with the pace of the investigation. Stopping by the scene from time to time helped keep me in the fight and the proper mind-set. The last few days had been a whirlwind, like the beginning of most homicide investigations. If I wasn't very careful, I could get overwhelmed by the information.

Most of the parking spots were empty, and the moon lit the shadowy areas the broken streetlights forgot. I chose a spot close to the room where Logan was killed, and Crevis and I got out.

Two white guys stood a few spaces away, next to a derelict car. One had a dark hooded sweatshirt. The other wore an Orlando Magic jersey and had enough ink on his arms to fill two comic books. They did a less-than-concealed hand-to-hand deal, probably crack, while keeping suspicious eyes on us.

Crevis and I walked toward the room as the two dirtbags watched us. I unclipped my badge from my belt and held it up for them to see.

"Nice night for a felony arrest, don't you think?" I said.

The male with the jersey tossed a small white pebble across the parking lot and sprinted toward Colonial Drive. The other guy scurried in the opposite direction, sneakers smacking off the pavement at a frantic pace. Crevis took a step to run after them. I hooked his arm with my cane handle.

"Let 'em go. We ruined any chance they'll have tonight to enjoy their high." I slid the cane back to the pavement. "Besides, you have to appreciate the little things in life, Crevis."

I hobbled up onto the walkway in front of room 107. It was dark, but the curtains on the large window over the air conditioner were open. Using a miniflashlight from my pocket, I lit up the room. The sheets had been stripped off the bed, and I visualized Logan's body lying there—the knife planted firmly in his barrel chest, the pizza box on the nightstand next to him, the bottle of Jack Daniel's and glasses on the floor. What were we missing? Who could have done this?

"So, do you think we got Logan's killers?" Crevis pressed his face against the glass.

"Hard to tell. I have concerns. Do the Rebel Soldiers strike you as a sophisticated group?"

Crevis scrunched his face with an expression I knew all too well from him.

"In other words, do they strike you as real smart people who would take time to plan a murder and season a pizza with pepperoni and cyanide?"

He shrugged.

"If you're going to be a cop, you need to start thinking like one."

I tapped my temple. "I'm not saying they didn't kill Logan, but let's look at the crime. Whoever did this is more devious than tough. Poisoning is a particularly strange crime, often done by people with latent anger, or someone who is weak and unable to commit the crime any other way. Does that sound like the Rebel Soldiers?"

"No. They seem like they'd just shoot you or beat the crap out of you."

"Now you're thinking. We need to sift through the evidence on this. We can't rule them out yet, but we can't get giddy like we've caught our killers either. I'm not sure what this all means, but it feels like we're missing something."

Crevis drove home, and I stretched my leg out in the passenger's side and massaged my hip as best I could. The day had been long, and the leg could only take so much. I dreamed of a day when I would be pain free and not reminded of the shooting with every step.

"Your leg hurt?" Crevis said.

"No, it feels great. I'm limbering up because I'm thinking about going back into kick-boxing." I hissed and continued to work the leg. "Just get us home."

"You don't have to be such a grump. I was just asking."

In ten minutes, we were back at the apartment complex, and I staggered into our place. I slapped *Brannigan* into the DVD player and brought Jim into the living room with me to enjoy the show.

Brannigan was a real departure from the Duke's usual Western roles, but he captured the essence of detective work, and his performance was stellar—as usual. I needed inspiration, and if I couldn't get it from John Wayne, I couldn't get it from anyone.

I settled into my recliner, and Crevis flopped on the couch. We didn't talk much as the movie started. It was one of Crevis's favorites and much easier than apologizing.

Jim tried hard to console me, but he only served to numb me for the show. I was out halfway through the movie.

39

SLEEPING IN THE LIVING room chair did have its benefits. When I was reclined, it kept my leg at a good angle that hurt considerably less than when I lay flat on my back. The downfall of the chair was that I couldn't get out of it quickly.

"Come on in," Crevis said to Pam as she broached the doorway. She wore a pair of black jeans and a nice button-up green shirt. She shouldered her briefcase strap, and the case itself appeared stuffed with Crevis's materials. Her hair was brushed back, and her jovial smile greeted me.

I had to fake my smile as I hurried to get the footrest down and myself up. I straightened my T-shirt and grabbed my cane.

"Sorry," Pam said. "It's almost noon, and I thought you guys would be awake."

"We're up," I said, moving the nearly empty Jim Beam bottle from the top of the stand to a shelf underneath. "What are you doing here?"

"Crevis's test is next week, so we don't have much time. We have more work to do." She lowered the bag to the floor. "Crevis said it would be okay to do it here. Is it okay with you?"

"That's fine." I aimed my cane at Crevis. "But I don't want you using this as an excuse to slough off. I'm gonna need you later."

"I know, I know." Crevis snatched some folded clothes from the coffee table, hustled to the bathroom then closed the door.

"We're a little cramped in here," I said to Pam. "When I'm done with this case, I'll move us into a two-bedroom. So excuse the mess."

"I understand. I haven't been here since David's case." She glanced around. This time the whiteboard displayed Logan's information, not her brother's. That file had been packed away and wrapped up nicely with a solid arrest. The dirtbag had gotten what was coming to him, and I promised myself I would be there when the death penalty was carried out. But knowing how the court system worked, we were a long way from that.

Pam hadn't mentioned her brother's killer or the pending trial since shortly after his arrest. I didn't know how she felt about all of it.

"Do you think you're ready for the trial?" I asked. "Those can be tough."

"I'm ready." She clasped her hands in front of her. "Nothing could be as hard as those weeks of wondering whether David was murdered or…killed himself and Jamie. Had you not taken the case, I'd be a wreck right now."

"We've already been down this road." I shuffled my feet. "It's my job. It's what I do."

"You did it for free." She smirked. "Wouldn't let me pay you. So that doesn't qualify as a job, Raymond Quinn."

"Whatever," I said. "And it's just Ray, not Raymond. You know that."

"Have you had any time to look at your foster care file?" she said.

"You've really been on my case about my case," I said.

"I'll be happy to help when you're ready. I just want to do something for you, Ray."

"I've got a lot more cases to solve before I get to that one."

"There's always going to be other cases," she said. "And it's not just about you, Ray. Your mother is out there somewhere. She would want to know you, your life, and what you've become. She'd want a chance to reconcile, maybe explain why she left you like she did. A mother wants that chance, Ray. Trust me, I know."

"What do you know about it, Pam? She left me at a rest stop on the interstate with the name Ray written on a piece of paper pinned to my shirt. What more do I really need to know? That alone tells me everything about her and the situation. You're a preacher's kid, grew up in a *Leave It to Beaver* land. Believe me, you don't know anything about this."

"I know more than you think." Her arms crossed her stomach, and she shuffled back a couple of steps. "I think you should at least look at the file. That's all I'm saying."

Crevis came out of the bathroom dressed in jeans and a nicer-than-usual shirt. He looked ready to tackle the day—like a good little pupil. Pam walked over and rested her briefcase on the kitchen table. Our apartment didn't have a discernable dining area. It was one all-purpose room, but it worked for us.

Pam and I made eye contact again, and she smiled, a peace gesture I reciprocated. We both had other things to do. Pam meant well, and I cut her more slack than anyone else in my life. I didn't get why she was pushing so hard on this. It was my life and my childhood. Pam's heart was in the right place, though. That made it easier to swallow.

I worked around them as I brewed my coffee and got ready for the day. Pam laid the workbooks out for Crevis, and they dug into his first lesson.

I said my good-byes and headed out to meet with Oscar and Bowden. My phone vibrated, and Katie Pham was on the other end.

"Hey, Ray, guess what the lab found on the bottom of the pizza box."

"Cyanide."

"You should be on *Jeopardy*. You were dead on, pardon the pun, about the pizza being tainted. Good call."

"Well, to be honest, I already spoke to Doc Podjaski, and he told me about the cyanide in Logan's tox screen. The poison in the pizza made the most sense," I said. "It was unlikely anyone held Logan down and poured it down his throat. And he didn't have any alcohol in his system, so that narrows it down a bit."

"Sounds like we're heading in the right direction. I've already told Oscar and Bowden, so I thought I would let you know."

"I'm going to their office to meet with them now. This just confirms what we already knew, but at least we're on the right trail."

I toyed with the extra toppings on the pizza on my ride in. Did Logan send someone, possibly Savannah Breeze, to pick up the pizza?

We knew a female called in the order, but how did she get it to him? Was she with him? Just as a few questions were answered, more questions sprang up like mushrooms in a cow pasture.

I entered the homicide unit from the back stairwell and bowed my head to Trisha as I passed her picture. Bowden and Oscar were waiting for me.

Bowden's tie was loose, and he tipped his chair back and forth, gazing at the ceiling as if in a trance. I knew the look. When a homicide wasn't solved right away, the pressure swelled up inside you like a runaway boiler ready to explode. Upper administrators wanted answers; other officers questioned what was going on; families kept calling, demanding results. After running straight on a case for days, it wore on you in a way few other things in life could. Bowden was being baptized into Homicide the hard way, with a crazy, unresolved case that had more legs than a millipede. But if the case broke well and we got to arrest our suspect, there was no high like it in the world, and it made all the long hours and frustrating moments worth it. Once you worked Homicide—with its extreme highs and lows— you couldn't go back to anything else. It ruined you that way.

Rita Jiminez and Steve Stockton walked down the hall toward us, both with file folders in their hands, probably heading out to shake some folks up.

"Hi, Rita. How's our little ray of sunshine?" I flashed a full-toothed smile and gave her a small wave. "Might I say that you look mighty chipper today?"

"Drop dead, Quinn," she said, not even turning her head as they passed.

"Why do you tempt fate like that, Ray?" Oscar rubbed his forehead. "You're like a little kid, always seeing how far you can push things. Don't mess with Rita. She'll cut your hamstring and leave you to suffer. I mean that literally, Ray."

Bowden awoke from his stupor with a snicker. "I've got an inventory from Agent Young on everything taken from the Rebel Soldiers' clubhouse, if you're interested."

"Anything look promising?" I said.

He rolled his chair closer to his desk and lifted a piece of paper. "Lots of chemicals for the meth, some pot, lots of pipes and other paraphernalia. The nicest part is the sawed-off 12-gauge shotgun they found under the bar and a 9mm pistol in the back bedroom. The Feds should be interested in picking up the case. With the combination of drugs and guns, Mongrel is never gonna see the light of day again."

"Was there a .45 caliber?" I shuffled over to gawk at the list. "Still looking for the gun that shot at Crevis and me."

"Nope," he said. "Nothing here."

"They probably got rid of it after the shooting," Oscar said. "They knew they would be hot after that, so they dumped it in a lake somewhere. Not hard to find a dumping spot in Florida."

"Maybe," I said. "I had my money set on the infamous Mr. Scott Long being our shooter. Figured we could squeeze him with the charge. Maybe we can turn it up on the others come time for trial."

"I'd be surprised if that happened now," Oscar said. "They seem pretty loyal to each other."

"Any kind of satchel or hard drives taken in?" I said.

Bowden didn't even have to look at the paper to answer me. "No. Nothing like that at all. Sorry, Ray."

Of course Armon's information wasn't in the inventory. That would be way too easy, and nothing in this case was coming easily.

40

THE PLYWOOD COVERING the office door was uninviting and unprofessional—not the image I wanted for my business. As soon as I settled in at my desk, I contacted a glass-replacement business about the door and made an appointment to fix the damage from our malevolent visitor. Armon Mayer's recent paychecks had increased my cash flow, so the price didn't sting as much when they told me. The two holes in the drywall behind my desk served as a reminder to be vigilant in all things. I would keep them until the case wrapped up, so as not to lose my edge.

I checked my e-mail, and a note from my South African friends appeared to brighten a rather dull day.

Dear Mrs. Simpkins,

Blessing to you! I have not heard from you for several days. Do you have the account numbers we need to send the money? I fear that our time is short in this matter. And we have so much money to send. We desperately need your help. Please contact me as soon as possible.

Your friend,

Mr. Nomvete

Mr. Nomvete was getting impatient. Good. He was right where I wanted him, but the next part of the plan was the most difficult—switching the dynamic between us.

Dear Mr. Nomvete,

I've not made any progress with my son. He's so stubborn and insistent on more proof and verification. I think if he could meet with you or a representative of your organization, he would be much more open to releasing funds and making the transaction needed.

Or there is another way I can bypass my son altogether. If someone could come here, to the U.S., and help me get to my bank and conduct the transactions myself, my son might not have to know anything about it. I have no one here who can help me do this. He's isolated me from everyone. Please let me know if this is possible. I pray that it is. I hope to hear from you soon.

God bless,

Marion

I really hoped Pam wouldn't find out about this, especially the religious touches. She'd give me what-for about it. But it was necessary to reel in this scumbag. Scammers often prey on religious people and use spiritual language to entice them by making them think they're helping someone. They rely on either the greed of the victim or their good nature. I was feigning good nature and ignorance. I'd see what their next move would be.

Still, the less Pam knew, the better. She didn't need much provocation to go God on me. I wouldn't give her any more than necessary.

I did a cursory search of the computer files I'd copied from Logan's office. Not much there. Some internal memos, poorly written reports on employee investigations. The best I could tell, Logan didn't use his computer for more than the basic word-processing functions.

I did find the date and time he supposedly entered the mainframe computer and downloaded the client information. I couldn't tell how he did it, but it did happen. I found it odd that Logan could have pulled that off, given what I'd assessed about his computer skills and knowledge. That would be no small feat for him—not only how he did it, but why.

Until I knew the "why," I wasn't convinced I'd ever discover the "how." Logan had lived fast and loose, but his behavior was mostly hedonistic and self-destructive. Even when he'd given information to Nikki back in his police days, it was pillow talk, not for financial gain. He got drunk and stupid and ran his mouth. Now he'd supposedly stolen personal client banking and investment money? What would a guy like Logan do with it anyway? He lacked the technical know-how needed to pull off any kind of serious fraud or even tap the accounts. It didn't make sense.

Then a nagging thought occurred to me—maybe it wasn't supposed to.

I searched for Armon Mayer in some news and financial data-bases. Very little appeared beyond the usual press releases and media packages, which, for a man of his position, I found odd. He was definitely media shy. I guessed the majority of his business was by word of mouth through the halls of the powerful and extremely wealthy. You didn't just walk into the doors of Mayer Holdings and drop some cash for an investment.

I did locate an interview with an Orlando-based actor who was one of Armon's clients. A tidbit buried in the article grabbed my attention. The actor, nobody I'd ever heard of, mentioned Armon and Mayer Holdings as his financial advisor and money manager and said he was guaranteed ten to fifteen percent on his returns. The "guaranteed" quote bothered me. In college, I majored in criminal justice with a minor in English. I took a few film critique classes to further appreciate the Duke's brilliance, but math and finance were far from me. I wasn't a numbers guy, which explained why I was playing catch-up keeping my business afloat. But I didn't have to be a financier to understand there was no such thing as a guaranteed return. All investments were risks. Some investments produced well, but "guaranteed" translated into a red flag for me.

There were only a few pictures of Armon available on the Net, each with his haughty mug and half smile. I didn't understand a lot about what Mayer Holdings did or was involved in, but I'd learn more. Whatever personality glitches I might have had, I was a good student.

My e-mail alarm chimed. I checked it, half expecting the desperate-yet-persistent South Africans to have answered Mrs. Simpkins. I was wrong. Bowden had forwarded the latest round of phone records: Jason Santos, Nikki Bray, and Mongrel. He said he'd forward more as he got them.

Maybe Armon was right that my having connections with OPD was a good thing for this case. I doubted any other PI in the city could gain access to this kind of info so quickly. I didn't feel too bad about that. It was the one thing that separated me from a sea of others in a very competitive market. Besides, I'd paid my dues with years on the streets—and was still paying.

It took about fifteen minutes to convert the files and enter them into my Threads system, which produced a readout with graphs and charts to show the correlations.

As I scrolled through the records, the system flagged an important contact for me—Nikki Bray had called Jason Santos two nights before Logan's murder, contradicting Jason's earlier statement to me.

I fired off a text message to Crevis: *Picking u up in 10 minutes. Be ready!*

41

"DON'T SAY ANYTHING," I said. "Just stand there and look crazy and angry."

"Got it." Crevis fixed his fedora in the side mirror and dangled his arms at his sides, like he was prepping for a scrap.

I parked our van two houses away from Jason's and hiked up to Santos's sidewalk, the assortment of toys still amassed on the lawn. As we stepped onto the porch, I listened at the door; the television was on. I knocked once, and Cindy Santos opened the door quicker than expected.

If her eyes had been lasers, they would have cut me in half. I'd had that effect on women recently. Maybe it was my cologne?

"I knew you'd be back," she said in a low tone that trailed off into a hiss. "Jason didn't believe me, but I knew. You cops always come back and dig and dig. You can't leave things or people alone."

"It's a pleasure to see you again." I tipped my head in her direction. Crevis didn't speak. "Could you please have Jason come to the door so we may converse?"

"I didn't realize the first time you came by just how famous—

or infamous—you are." She leaned against the doorframe and crossed her arms. "Ex-homicide detective with Orlando PD, before you got shot. Impressive. It's a shame about your shooting and your partner getting killed right in front of you like that. I'm sure you did everything you could to protect her, like a good little police officer is supposed to do."

When I used to kick-box, if an opponent scored a hit that rattled me, I smiled and acted like it had no effect. I couldn't afford to let him know where I was vulnerable or hurt. As Cindy Santos's sadistic smirk crossed her face, I was reminded of that strategy and employed it.

"I'm glad to see you can use the Internet," I said. "Could you please summon Jason for us?"

"Her memorial page was interesting, although very sad. She looked like a nice girl. Too bad she had to die in such an awful, tragic way…with you right by her side."

My fight strategy faltered as I envisioned the handle of my cane ricocheting off Cindy's forehead. She'd found my weak point and nailed it like a pro; I had to give her that. She was more on the ball than anticipated. A few seconds passed before my blood pressure lowered.

"I assume he's preoccupied with work in his shop," I said. "Would you be kind enough to let him know we need to speak with him, please, ma'am?"

Her purposed stare sharpened to a fine point. She apparently didn't appreciate that I wasn't fazed by her digs at the shooting and Trisha—at least on the outside—or that I was killing her with kindness. My acting skills were improving.

"This is the last time you disturb our home," she said, eyeing me from head to toe before closing the door hard.

Crevis hadn't moved, and he had a ridiculous snarl on his face, his eyebrows hiked up his forehead. He looked like something out of a horror flick. I smacked him in the shin with the cane.

"I said look 'angry and crazy,' not deranged."

"Sorry," he said. "I'm just trying to do what you tell me."

"Try angry and intense."

"Okay." He changed his features to a range closer to normal. "Do you think she's coming back?"

"Don't know." I rested both hands on my cane. "We'll just have to wait here and find out."

It took less than a minute to get the answer. Jason was visible through the window next to the door; he and Cindy were arguing, rather passionately. He finally opened the door, and Cindy rounded the corner out of our sight.

"I thought you said you wouldn't be coming back." He shut the door behind him and puffed out his chest.

"I thought you said you would tell us the truth," I fired back. Crevis breathed hard and heavy. Not a bad touch.

Jason lifted a pair of goggles off his head and rubbed his hands on his stained smock. He paused before he answered. "What are you talking about?"

"When was the last time you saw Nikki Bray? The truth would be really good right about now."

He swallowed hard and alternated his attention between me and Crevis, who remained agitated and mute.

"Okay, okay. I didn't want Cindy to know." He glanced over his shoulder and through the windows next to the door. "She'd be extremely angry, and you see what I have to deal with."

"Let me get this straight. You perjured yourself on my statement as well as the one with Detective Greg Bowden so you wouldn't have an irritated wife?"

"I wouldn't say it like that." He leaned back against the door. "I just left things out."

"You lied on a formal statement in a homicide investigation. How do you think your probation officer is gonna treat that, especially when we all stand up at your hearing and describe how you hindered this investigation? Lifetime probation means you're eligible to go back to prison—for life—for any violation. Do you want to keep playing games? You'll lose, I promise. And the happy Santos home will be ripped apart forever."

"Please." His hands extended, goggles dangling. "Please don't do that. I wasn't trying to hinder anything. I was just trying to help Nikki without my wife finding out. That's it. It has nothing to do with Logan or this case."

"Tell me about it." He'd been tuned up enough for now. I wasn't in the mood for more games, especially since his loving wife had just twisted a knife in my heart. "For real this time."

"She called me a couple of days before Logan was murdered." His head dropped. "I don't know how she found my number, but she did, and she called."

"Go on."

"She said she was out of money and needed help. Really, that was all. She just needed some money. She does that every few years or so, just appears out of the blue, then disappears again. I've always felt sorry for her, so I try to help. If Cindy ever found out, she'd make me pay for sure. She knows about our history, but it's just that— history. I wanted to help an old friend."

"What did you do?"

"I met her at a convenience store about two miles from here and gave her a hundred and fifty dollars," he said. "She looked like she needed a good meal. We talked for maybe ten minutes, and then I came home."

"What did you talk about?"

"Just life stuff, how she was doing. No big deal."

"Did you talk about Logan?"

He drew a breath. "She mentioned they were seeing each other again, but he was starting to act weird and not return her calls."

"Did she seem to be taking that well?"

"No. She didn't take stuff like that well. I told her to forget Logan and move on and get herself straight, but she just kept talking. I don't think she listened to me, but I did want her to look into rehab or something."

"Did she talk about killing Logan?"

"Of course not."

"Did you ask her to kill Logan to keep him away from you?" I still didn't know the connection between Nikki stabbing Logan and the poisoning. I wasn't going to mention either mode of death, so if he told me how it happened, I'd know if I was getting the truth or not.

"That's crazy. I didn't do anything like that. I was just helping a friend."

"Why am I supposed to believe that? Based on your track record and your honest testimony in this case already?"

"It's the truth. I did lie to you. I'm sorry. But that's all. I just didn't want the drama from all this in my home."

"Is there anything else I should know? And you better not lie to me again."

"That's it, I swear."

"It better be, or the next time you see me it will be with your probation officer and a warrant for your arrest."

"That's not necessary. You won't have any problems from me. Cindy said you were going to be back to make life miserable for us. I didn't believe her."

I aimed my cane at him. "If I find out you lied to me again, I'll prove her right in ways you never imagined."

42

I WASN'T SURE WHERE I stood with Santos, since he still had some problems with the truth. I didn't tell Jason I had his cell tower information, which showed that he, or at least his phone, didn't leave his house the night Logan was murdered. I still didn't know if Nikki's psychotic attack on Logan was an oddly timed coincidence or purposefully sent to throw off the investigation. Her lawyer had ensured that I wouldn't get to ask her any more questions.

Since Jason's lie and his charming wife had gotten my blood stirring, now was a good time to see my client and prod some answers from him as well. I found myself in the conflicted position of trying to determine who I detested more—the Rebel Soldiers, Nikki and Jason, or my client. Although Armon cleaned up better, like window dressing at a sausage factory, I still couldn't clear the stench of corruption from my nose. His arrogance offended me too.

The fifteen-minute drive through downtown Orlando gave me time to settle down and ease out of full-on attack mode. Armon was a different animal on many levels and needed to be approached that way.

Crevis and I exited the elevator and were greeted by Megan, which was refreshing, especially since most of the women I'd visited lately would just as soon cut me into small pieces and toss me into the river. My tough-guy persona cracked a little as she smiled at me, taking me off my game.

"What a pleasant surprise," she said. "Private Investigator Raymond Quinn."

"It's just Ray." I caned to the desk. "Never Raymond."

"Should I let Armon know you're here, or are you visiting me?"

"Yes to both."

"Glad to hear that." She glanced up and down the hallway. "I'm supposed to call Jack Gordon anytime you show up. I thought I'd let you know."

"That's okay. He should be here too. I'm in the mood for all takers."

Megan made a series of calls, announcing our presence.

"This is a really nice place," Crevis said. "Not like most of the other places you take me."

"It's clean and manicured, but keep your eyes and ears open," I said. "That doesn't mean it can't be just as dangerous, maybe more."

"Mr. Mayer will see you now," Megan said.

"We'll talk soon." I passed her desk and walked into Armon's lair.

Armon lingered at the end of the boardroom with Wykoff at his side. A few seconds after we arrived, Jack Gordon strode in. He passed me without offering his hand.

I caned quickly toward Armon, and he stepped to the other side of the room to keep his distance from me and the table between us. Good move on his part, because I'd been about to wipe my nose and then reach for his hand. Maybe it was best I stayed out of arm's reach in order to remain employed.

After our ring-around-the-rosy game, I finally took a seat next to Crevis. Armon and Wykoff sat across the table from me, Gordon in the last seat, nearest the door.

"Hopefully you are here to update me on your progress, with good news this time," Armon said.

"Actually, I'm here to apologize." I thumped a rhythm with my fingers on the smooth tabletop.

Armon's head tilted back, and he regarded Wykoff, then settled his gaze on me. "Apologize for what, Detective?"

"I'm really new at this whole PI thing, and I've made some assumptions that were a little off base." I twisted the tip of my cane into the carpet. "My approach on cases still needs to be honed and adjusted to the new rules of private investigation. For example, I took it for granted that when I take a case, the person hiring me is telling me the truth and simply looking for my assistance, not jerking me around." The calmness I sought on the way in had evaporated as I spoke.

"You think I have lied to you, Detective?"

"There's a much larger story here that you're not telling me, and it's getting old."

"Please, indulge me." Armon spread his arms wide. "Tell me what is missing."

"First, I should have checked Logan's computer and office when

I took this case. Do you really think he hacked into your system and stole all this information on his own?"

Armon regarded Jack Gordon, who straightened his tie and assailed me. "Quinn, your job is to find what Logan stole and return it—period. Not to come in here and make accusations."

"Your job was to prevent these types of thefts in the first place," I said, "so I don't want to hear a lecture from you. But since we're on the subject, how did Logan pull this off? He didn't have the know-how to hack your computer system, and he certainly didn't know what to do with that information once he had it."

"What are you saying?" Gordon bent forward like he was about to crawl across the table after me.

"He had to have had help. Or he didn't steal anything at all and was framed, making this whole investigation a dog-and-pony show to cover the real issue."

"That's crazy," Gordon said. "We've got the track to his computer with his login information when he was working. We've got him on security tape, leaving the building and never coming back. He then fell off the face of the planet. He was going to sell that information to the highest bidder to bring down Mayer Holdings."

"I want access to the information that was taken." I almost let it slip about Logan's call to the FBI in my tirade but fortunately stopped short. I'd keep that tidbit to myself. "I want to see it and ana-lyze it. There could be something in the documentation that can help me."

"That is not possible, Detective Quinn." Armon shuffled to the window closest to him and peered out. "Nor is it necessary. My client information is extremely confidential and will not assist you in this case at all. I understand your frustration, and in spite of the obstacles, I am convinced that with all your connections, you're still the right person for this job."

"Then I want what you're not telling me. From the beginning you've been hiding information and floating me different stories. I can't do my job if I don't know the truth and what, exactly, I'm looking for."

"You're looking for an external hard drive with valuable information on it," Armon said. "My information. That's all you need to know. Find it, and you will be rewarded. I'll add a bonus that you should find quite satisfactory."

"We will find your information and solve this case, that much I'm sure of." I rose from my chair and Crevis followed my lead. "And you can pay anything you like, bonus and all. But when this case is finished and you and I are all squared up, I'm gonna slap you in your arrogant mouth."

Wykoff looked like he was going to faint.

Jack Gordon rose to his feet. "Quinn, you're out of line!"

"We'll see about that, Detective Quinn." Armon smirked, baring his polished white teeth. "Find that hard drive. Then we'll talk about the slapping."

43

"You're gonna get us fired, Ray," Crevis said as we entered the elevator.

"Shut up until we're out of this building," I said.

The Muzak entertained us with a spry tune from the Captain and Tennille, something about a muskrat in love, until we hit the lobby floor.

"Don't say anything in this place." I hoofed it outside as best I could. "You don't know if someone is listening or not."

"I can't believe you threatened to slap him." Crevis raised his hat and slicked his crimson mane down flat. "He's really rich and owns all sorts of stuff. Some days I think you're just plain crazy. I can't figure you out."

"Why didn't he fire us right away?" I stopped and faced him. "Why?"

"I don't know." Crevis posted his hands on his hips. "Maybe he didn't want to hire another PI and start all over."

"You're close," I said. "I was testing him. He wants to keep me close and pay me off because I know something is going on. He thinks he can use me to find his information and then pay me off like he does everyone else in his life. If he fired me, I'd be disgruntled and dig deeper. He's smart enough to know that. Besides, I really do want to slap him."

"I don't know, Ray." Crevis rubbed his chin. "Seems like a lot of guessing to come up with that. I wouldn't push it with him. He's our only client right now."

"Suddenly you're a business expert," I said. "Maybe I'll put you in charge of client relations."

"No, but you told me when we started that we were in this together. I'm part of the business too, so I get my say."

"Fair enough, Crevis. I'll try to keep a lid on it. But as you do this job and learn to understand people, you'll see that there are some you can slap down and some you can't. It's knowing the difference that keeps you out of trouble."

My phone vibrated with a text message from Megan. *Have u lost your mind?*

I tipped the phone up so Crevis could read it. "I guess they're talking about us now."

Call me later, I texted back. Having someone on the inside would be helpful now, as I bet we were missing something big with Armon and his crew. Maybe it didn't have anything to do with Logan's death and the theft, and maybe it had everything to do with it. I hated not knowing, and I wondered if the reason Armon wasn't more candid with me was because he sensed it and used it to keep me in my place. Hard to tell.

I'd catch up with Megan later at a bar of my choice and debrief her over a bottle of whiskey.

Crevis and I left the Mayer Temple and found ourselves in Cassy Ramsey's neighborhood. I wanted to see if she was home. I had a few items I wanted to discuss with her, keep her in the loop.

We arrived as she was carrying two armfuls of groceries from her car into the house. She wore brown dress slacks and a white button-up shirt. It appeared she was just getting home from work.

"Can we help?" I said.

"Sure, if it's not too much to ask."

"Get the bags, Crevis." I pointed to Crevis, then the bags. There were times it was good to be the boss. "I was hoping we'd catch you at home. Can we come inside to talk?"

"Just give me a minute." She unlocked the front door and opened it for us. We followed her inside. "Put those on the kitchen counter, please."

Crevis set the groceries on the counter.

"Thank you," she said. "Is there any more news?"

"A little," I said. "We've been doing a lot of digging and talking with suspects, but we're still not close to catching the person who killed your father."

"Okay. Then why are you here?"

"I got the medical examiner's report on your dad's case," I said. "The toxicology results showed there was no alcohol in his system. He was clean. I just thought you should know that."

The air rushed from her lungs, and she leaned against the kitchen counter. "So he was sober?"

"That's what the tox says," I said.

She shook her head. "All those years he was drunk with my mom and me, all the hell he put us through, and when he finally gets himself killed, he's sober. That's just terrific. He couldn't meet anyone's expectations even in death."

Not how I hoped she'd respond, but grief had strange effects on people. "Maybe he was trying to stay sober and do the right thing."

She hissed. "Yeah, then he stole stuff from the company he was working for. Doesn't sound like he was trying too hard."

I had the picture with me that Logan had in his coat pocket, of him and Cassy when she was young. I almost gave it to her but then thought better of it. She wasn't taking the news of her father's sober ending too well. No need to stoke the fire.

"Sorry for bringing it up. I just felt you should know, and I didn't want to tell you over the phone."

"It's okay." She rested against the counter. "I didn't mean to vent on you. I just—he put us, especially my mom, through so much. It's hard to think of him like most people think of their fathers. I can forgive him for not being there for me, but how he treated Mom, I'm still working through that. She deserved better."

"Police work can be tough on everyone involved, especially families," I said.

She turned away, giving her attention to the window facing her backyard, and didn't answer me.

"We'll be going now." I tipped my head to Crevis. "You have my number if you need anything."

"I appreciate it, Detective Quinn," she said, wiping her eyes.

44

AFTER DROPPING CREVIS OFF at the apartment, I headed back to the office. I toyed around with my Threads program for a couple of hours, updating some of the information. Then I took a break and checked my e-mail. I got one from the lab. They had extracted DNA from the bottom and sides of the pizza box—a female's profile that wasn't in the system. That was good news and some much-needed potential evidence. Now we just needed a suspect to match to the DNA. A little easier said than done at this point.

I checked my pseudonym e-mail account, and an interesting message appeared for Mrs. Simpkins.

Dearest Marion,

It is not possible for any of us to leave the country right now, because our situation is so very dire. Plead with your son to help us with our plight. I fear that there is no time left. He MUST open the accounts so that we may send the money to you. Our very survival depends on you, Marion. Please do not abandon us in our time of need!

Mr. Nomvete

My South African buddy was getting desperate. That was good; it could make him stupid—and ripe for the harvest. I poured myself a glass of Jim and formulated my response to my greedy—yet persistent—friend.

Dear Mr. Nomvete,

I don't think my son will ever give me any information on our fortune. He's just so controlling. The only way I'll ever be able to release the account is if someone could assist me here with the process. My name is still on the accounts, and I could access them without delay. You must come here and help me get access to my fortune. I'm counting on you.

Marion

The lust for the easy buck was what made cons work, but if it was turned around on them, it could lure the suspects in as well. Marion Simpkins and her millions dangled in front of my South African friends like a basted turkey over a pit of starving dogs. Given the chance, they'd tear each other to pieces just to get to her. The thought of a susceptible old woman sitting on a mountain of cash just might make them take the risk.

Since it was officially playtime, I texted Megan to see if she was interested in a night on the town. Maybe I could talk her into meeting me again, and we could tip a few down, talk a little. I could find out more about Armon's reaction and what was really going on in Mayer Holdings, all while enjoying the company of an attractive young woman. Not a bad way to end the day.

My phone vibrated in my hand. I opened the message, hoping Megan had beaten me to the punch. No such luck. It was from a number I didn't know.

Call this number. I know where Armon Mayer's information is. Don't play games.

So much for an easy night.

Since I didn't recognize the number, I pulled my digital recorder out of my shirt pocket and found the microphone cord in my top desk drawer. I connected the two and turned on the recorder. I took a breath and dialed the number.

"DETECTIVE QUINN," a computer-generated voice said. "YOU ARE VERY PROMPT."

"Who am I talking to?"

"THE PERSON WHO HAS WHAT YOU ARE LOOKING FOR."

"How do I know you're not just jerking me around or playing a game?"

After a long pause, the voice said, "LOGAN RAMSEY STOLE DAMAGING INFORMATION FROM MAYER HOLDINGS. HE KEPT THE HARD DRIVE IN A BROWN SATCHEL. IT'S IN MY POSSESSION NOW."

"Anyone could say that. A dozen people originally knew about the theft, which means a whole lot more could know now. I'm not convinced. You're gonna have to do better than that." I wasn't sure what he meant by "damaging," but I was sure I'd find out.

Several more seconds ticked past. The person was probably typing responses that the computer translated into speech. Whoever he was, he was definitely shrewd.

"LOGAN WAS STABBED IN THE CHEST WITH A KNIFE WITH A SKULL

ON THE HANDLE. HE WAS WEARING A T-SHIRT AND BLUE JEANS. NEED ANY MORE PROOF, OR ARE YOU READY FOR BUSINESS NOW?"

No one but the cops at the scene and Logan's killer knew that information. I was communicating with the real deal, the guy who had Armon's property and had possibly murdered Logan. I had to move slow and smart.

"What do you have to tell me?" I asked.

"I WANT TEN MILLION DOLLARS FOR THE RETURN OF THE HARD DRIVE. THIS SHOULDN'T BE DIFFICULT FOR MAYER HOLDINGS. IF YOU CONTACT YOUR POLICE FRIENDS, I WILL KNOW, AND THE DEAL WILL BE OFF FOREVER, AND THE INFORMATION WILL BE TURNED OVER TO THOSE WHO CAN CRUSH ARMON. HE WILL KNOW WHAT THAT MEANS."

"Why don't you tell me what that means so I can make sure he understands?" Maybe my new friend would tell me what Armon and his minions would not.

"DELIVER THE MESSAGE. ARMON WILL PAY WHAT IS REQUESTED. DON'T TRY ANYTHING, OR YOU, YOUR PARTNER, AND YOUR FRIENDS WILL LOSE BIG."

"Well, we can't have that, now can we?" I checked the recorder; it was working perfectly. I didn't want to miss a word. The computer-generated voice was clever but aggravating. At least this guy could have added a female voice or something. "Do you want me to call you back at this number?"

"I'LL CALL YOU WITH INSTRUCTIONS AT NOON TOMORROW. PREPARE FOR AN ELECTRONIC TRANSFER. NOW DO AS YOU'RE TOLD."

He hung up, and I switched off my recorder. As grating as the caller's voice had been, it was refreshing to get an actual lead.

I went to dial Oscar but then held off. Would this guy know if I called Oscar or Bowden? Our suspect was at least a little technically savvy. What if he was able to scan my phone calls? It wasn't out of the realm of possibility, so I had to play it safe. I texted Crevis and told him to get to the office. We had some business to attend to.

I hurried to my metal file cabinet against the wall, worked the combination, and opened the top drawer. A box of electronic equipment, more recorders and microphones, was stashed there. Sorting through the junk, I found the spare cell phone I kept for emergencies. It was a pay-as-you-go and wasn't registered to me, so it should be safe to use. I dialed Oscar.

"Sergeant Yancey," he said after the third ring.

"Oscar, it's Ray. Got a great lead tonight. I need you to get an emergency order on a phone number for me." I spent the next five minutes filling him in on the situation.

Fearing I would spill some Jim on my laptop if I tried to pour him back in the bottle, I downed the remnant and relocated the bottle and glass to the bottom drawer. Playtime was over.

After wiping my mouth with my sleeve, I was ready for work.

I fired another call off to Wykoff and set up a morning meeting with him and Armon. If I was up working this, everyone was up working this.

45

CREVIS BURST THROUGH the door about twenty minutes after I sent him the message. He was dressed in blue jeans and a black T-shirt; he hadn't even stopped to put on his Bogey suit. The kid had his challenges, but when I told him to come, like a well-trained attack dog, he came. Now if I could only get him to sit and heel.

"What's up, boss?" he asked.

"Our case just got ramped up a notch."

I'd removed several plastic storage containers from the closet and riffled through them, seeking the proper accessories to make this deal happen. I had no idea how Armon the Magnificent would respond to extortion; he was a tough read on anything. Ten million dollars seemed over the top for client information, but, again, finance and business weren't my strong suit. Still, it seemed like a lot to me, and I had no idea what "damaging"' meant to the suspect and Armon. Maybe I had what I needed now to drag the truth from him. I wasn't holding my breath, though.

I placed some possible accoutrements on my desk as I briefed Crevis on the robo-caller. I let him hear the recording and then downloaded it onto my laptop in the electronic folder I'd created for this case.

Oscar called me back on the pay-as-you-go phone. He had contacted his team, and they were on their way into the office to start a track on the number that called me. It would take a few hours to get everything in place.

I was so caught up in getting ready to catch our bad guy that I'd not given much thought as to who it could be. It had to be someone who knew I was on the case, had intimate knowledge of the scene, and bumped off Logan to get the goods. Financial crimes were more dangerous than I thought.

The Rebel Soldiers were locked up, for the most part, and I was still waiting for lab evidence to come back on other suspects. Another three or four investigators would be helpful with this case. I was fortunate to have Oscar's unit doing a lot of the heavy lifting for me. Homicide cops could get information a lot faster than I could. That bothered me in my new role, but I'd have to get used to it.

"So what are we gonna do about this, Ray?" Crevis asked, bouncing up and down in front of my desk like a circus monkey.

"Give me a minute," I said. "We've got to come up with a plan."

Crevis sniffed the air twice and then frowned at me. "You been drinking?"

"What does it matter to you, Little Miss Carrie Nation?" I said. "I had a couple before the call came in. I've got it under control."

"We've got to run on this tonight, and I just wanna make sure you're up for it."

I eased my cane off the floor and aimed it at him. "Don't push it, Crevis. I decide if either of us is up for anything."

"Yeah, whatever." He looked down and sighed. "What do you need me to do?"

My cane lowered but my angst didn't. Crevis needed a reminder about who ran the Night Watchman Detective Agency and who was an employee. He was getting cocky and was in desperate need of a smack down. He'd been a private investigator for a whopping six months, and I'd been a police officer for almost twenty years, with multiple jobs under my belt. I knew when I couldn't function and when I could. So I'd had a little buzz going earlier. I was fine now…or mostly fine. I'd be perfect by the time we got to Armon and our suspect. I knew my limits.

"I'm not sure what Armon will want us to do." I grabbed a gym bag from the closet and started filling it. "A lot will depend on that. I'm formulating plans for the many ways Armon could play this thing. Even if he doesn't want to pay this person, I think we still need to do something to help Oscar and Bowden solve Logan's homicide. But we've got to be smart about it. The guy who contacted us has some know-how, so don't talk about this case on your phone. I'll get you another one."

"You think he can tap our phones?" Crevis lifted his phone from his pouch and examined it. "Too weird."

"If the cops can do it, the bad guys can do it too. You need to remember that. Just because someone is a criminal, it doesn't mean they're stupid. So no matter which direction our plan goes, watch what you say on the phone."

"Got it." He lifted his crooked thumb in the air and gave me a jagged-toothed grin like a boated trout. "How 'bout I get you a cup of coffee?"

"Sure, Mother Hubbard." I finished packing our bag and zipped it closed. "That would be fine. Just make it a slap-in-the-face kind of strong. We've got an all-nighter ahead of us."

I relaxed in my chair and swiveled around, contemplating my next move. Oscar would get his crew together and acquire a phone ping with the location as soon as possible. He'd move on the homicide portion of the investigation. I'd work the extortion angle. If what I was planning was going to work, we'd need some serious coordination and uncommonly good luck. And I was going to need some help.

I trusted only one person enough to call in the middle of the night and ask for help. I dialed her number.

Pam's semiconscious voice answered.

46

THE RISING SUN at my back pursued me as I rounded the corner of Rosalind Avenue and Washington Street into downtown. The gleaming reflection off Mayer's building shimmered like a pillar of light reaching toward the heavens, temporarily blinding me as I plunged into the darkened underbelly of Armon's empire.

I flipped on my headlights and found a spot next to Armon's black Lamborghini. The temptation to carve a canyon-sized scratch in it with my key as I passed nearly overwhelmed me, but I resisted. There would be time for fun later. It was business now.

I'd sent Crevis on an errand, which meant I had to take care of this alone. The elevator chimed a lovely tune as it whisked me to the glorious Mayer penthouse. Jack Gordon met me at the door with his usual enthusiasm.

"Armon will see us in the office." Gordon aimed a finger at me. "Just to let you know, he's not happy."

"With me or the situation?"

"Both."

Megan's desk was empty, and I guessed they hadn't called her in early for this. The fewer people who knew the details, the better. As she had told me, she wasn't part of his inner sanctum. It would have been good to see a friendly face, though. Where I was about to go, there would be none.

Jack pushed the door open, and I had a hard time keeping up with his pace. Armon posed next to the row of immense windows, the sky on fire behind him. Wykoff lingered next to him.

"Who is this person and what does he want?" Armon said.

"Don't know who he is," I said, "but he wants ten million. Whoever he is, he seems pretty confident you'll pay it."

"Had you captured this person already, he would not be in the position to blackmail me."

"Had you given me all the information, I might be holding your precious hard drive right now and this guy wouldn't be sticking it to you."

"What is it you want to know?"

"The truth would be a great start."

Armon laughed and ran his jewel-studded fingers through his graying beard as he paced in front of the windows. His anguished expression almost made me feel sorry for him.

"I think it says in the Bible somewhere that the truth will set you free. But that's not exactly accurate, is it, Detective? Rarely does the truth free anyone. You should understand that better than most."

"We have little time for esoteric babblings, Mr. Mayer. No matter what else has happened, you're still my client, and I'm going to do everything I can to guide you through this. This guy said he had 'damaging' information. Sounds like more than just client and banking stuff to me. He's gonna hammer you if you don't get to him first. Tell me what he has on you, and maybe we can figure out who he is and nail him."

Armon regarded Wykoff, then Gordon. "Have you contacted any of your police associates?"

I hesitated before I lied. "No."

The entire plan would crumble if Armon picked up on my deception. And whether it was successful or not, I realized that the flood of disposable income I had experienced lately was evaporating with each word we spoke.

"Make the arrangements and use whatever means necessary to close the deal," Armon said.

"I'll handle this however you want, but I disagree with paying this guy. Do you understand, Armon, that just because you bought the information back once, that doesn't mean it's over? This guy could have copied that hard drive a thousand times by now, and you'll pay for it again and again. He will own you and this corporation if you give in."

Armon nodded as if for this moment, however fleeting, he thought I made sense. "What do you suggest, then?"

"Let's trap him." I shuffled closer to him. "We need to smoke him out and catch him at his own game."

"I don't like it at all, sir." Jack Gordon held up both hands. "If Quinn's plan doesn't work, this guy could get away and exploit all of the clients' information, among other things. It would cost a whole lot more than ten million to clean up that mess. I think you should pay the money and move on, with no police involvement. You can't risk any of this getting out. You have your clients to think about, sir."

Armon stared down at the city for several quiet moments before he made a pit stop at his sanitizer dispenser, working the cloth around his hands in a frenzied scrub. He tossed the soiled wipe in the trash.

He stepped back to the table and adjusted his coat. "We will pay this person. Then I will have you track him down at a later time, Detective. But first we will make this go away, no matter what it costs."

"You're the boss," I said, not terribly surprised by his answer. "He's supposed to contact me at noon to discuss the particulars. Judging from my first contact with him, he'll be on time. I'll be here so as to get your approval right away. You need to make whatever financial arrangements you have to for a payoff this large via an electronic transfer."

"Do as you see fit." Armon flicked a dismissive—and clean—hand at me. "But nothing that happens today will be discussed anywhere else. We must contain this. And I want no police involvement whatsoever."

"I understand. I've got a lot of things to take care of before all this goes down." I headed for the door. "We'll be back here about eleven o'clock. We need to set up communications for the pickup. If we don't do this right, you could pay ten million dollars for little more than a chat with a computer."

"Everything is riding on this, Detective. Don't fail me."

47

MY TRUCK BOTTOMED OUT on the street as I tore out of the Mayer Holdings parking garage. The morning rush-hour traffic had begun. I fired off a call to Oscar.

"Are you up on the phone?" I asked as soon as he picked up.

"Good morning to you too," Oscar said.

"I don't do friendly when I'm in the zone, Oscar. Are you up on the phone?"

"We got everything in place about an hour ago," Oscar said. "Bowden wrote the order and got it signed by the judge. We've got two tactical teams, both ready to track the phone with Triggerfish when it's turned on. With two units, we should be able to triangulate his position quicker. I've pulled in some of the narc guys for surveillance too. We're throwing everything at this."

"Any signal yet?"

"Nothing. The phone must be turned off."

"He'll probably keep it off until he's ready to use it again, so we need the teams ready to roll right away."

Triggerfish was a handy piece of technology that let us pinpoint the signal coming from a particular phone. We could only use it with a court order, but that wasn't too difficult to get, especially with a murder involved. The nifty gadget triangulated signals off the cell towers to the phone, but it sometimes took awhile to get a strong fix on the position. I'd have to keep the blackmailer talking as long as possible.

"We'll be ready, Ray," Oscar said, "but this is risky. The potential for things to go wrong is high here."

"I know." I held the phone with my shoulder as I flipped the visor down to keep the sun from blinding me. "But do you have any better leads in Logan's murder?"

"No. That's why everyone's out here. We're gonna finish this thing today."

"I've got my reasons too," I said. My very job and limited reputation as a private investigator in this town was at stake. "I'll let you know when we're ready to step off."

As I hung up with Oscar, the nagging question of Armon's veiled agenda gnawed at my psyche. I was walking into this whole setup with only part of the story—still. Not a comforting consideration since I had no idea what I faced from within, much less without. I'd have to play this thing very carefully. I didn't trust my client, didn't like his staff—save Megan—and wasn't overly thrilled with Logan, though I shared some similarities with him. The job had wrecked both of our lives and taken something from us that couldn't be found again.

Now I was brokering a deal for information I wasn't sure of, from a person unknown to me, for a truth-challenged client. When all this was finished, the PI career might need some thoughtful deliberation.

If true friends could be measured by how they react to a call for assistance in the middle of the night, Pam was first-rate. She and I arrived in my office parking lot at the same time. I didn't have underground parking like Armon, but at least I had some room to work with our new rental van. She parked next to me and sauntered over.

"Sorry I woke you up last night." I shifted around to set my legs on solid ground and get steady. "I really need your help. Again."

"I assume this is going to be something crazy and mildly dangerous."

"You assume correctly."

Her warm smile threatened to overturn my lousy, harried morning.

"That's a hard offer for a woman to turn down," she said.

"I'll pay you for your hours."

"You're already paying me to tutor Crevis. You don't have to pay me for this."

I checked over my shoulder to make sure Crevis wasn't in earshot. "He's never, ever to know that," I said with an emphasis she would understand. "That was part of our deal."

"I would have done that for free, you know. But your secret is safe with me, Ray. No one will ever know you're a nice guy. I promise." She rested against the van. "So what do you need me to do?"

I filled her in on the case so far. She had a good grasp of technology and software, so I would make use of that. Crevis was okay with the computer, as far as e-mail and checking his social networking sites were concerned, but he had other responsibilities in this. I needed him to watch my back. Pam could run my equipment with ease, and she was willing.

"Is this where you want it?" Pam said.

"Yeah, right there."

"Is your friend Megan helping you with this too?"

I sensed more to the question than the obvious. "Why do you ask?"

"Answering a question with a question? You always pull that detective stuff with me."

"She might. Hard to tell right now. Back to my question—why do you ask?"

"Truth?"

"Would you tell me anything else?"

"I'm not sure I trust her."

"You met her for all of two minutes. I thought *I* didn't trust anyone. You're getting worse than me."

"I'm just looking out for you. There was something about her that I didn't like. I can't put my finger on it, but something about her didn't sit well with me."

Megan was attractive, spirited, and intelligent. A bit of jealousy had possibly crept into Pam's assessment. Not that Pam wasn't all of those things too, although in completely different ways. I took her warning with a healthy dose of skepticism.

"Well, I appreciate you vetting her for me, but I think I've got this one under control."

Pam and I spent the next two hours making sure the van was set up with a laptop and a camera for our mobile unit. Then I networked her laptop to mine by wireless air cards and tested my system a couple of times. I downed two large, nasty cups of sludge impersonating coffee. The up-all-night thing was taking a toll on my mind. Years ago I could work a couple of days straight and bounce back in a day. Now I'd be down for three or four days. If I solved this case, I'd take a much-deserved vacation.

Crevis arrived back at the office, and I dispensed last-minute directions to him and Pam.

"I've witnessed you putting together some crazy schemes before, but this is by far your masterpiece," Pam said.

"It's the crazy stuff that keeps life interesting," I said. "Make sure your cell phones and laptops are fully charged. We're only gonna get one shot at this."

———

The three of us strolled off the elevator and into Armon's office at 10:58. Not a bad run.

Armon, Jack Gordon, and Wykoff waited for us in their seats in the conference room, as if they'd never left. I held a briefcase with my laptop and recording equipment. I'd attended a hostage-negotiations workshop back in my police days and hoped the information I learned there might be useful, since I'd never brokered a deal like this before. I had no idea how this might play out. Like much of my life, I was making it up as I went along.

I set up the laptop on Armon's table with the Web cam and my recording equipment. I tested them both. I couldn't be too careful. If my equipment failed, the entire operation would fail.

I split the screens so I could see Pam's screen and still work with mine, which was already up and running in the van. I liked to see what was going on, especially since I was leaving Pam alone with Armon and his buddies. I wasn't going to be caught short on this. The Web cam and microphone gave me the added dimension of listening to every word out of Armon's wooly mouth in real time.

"Pam will stay here with you so we can stay in constant communication." I pointed to her with my chin. "Crevis and I will pick up the hard drive."

Jack Gordon stood and rushed to my side. "I'm going with you."

"We've got it covered. Everything is in place."

"Jack will go with you," Armon said. "He can assist with anything you should need."

Jack smirked as he unbuttoned his coat.

"Swell," I grumbled. "This should be lots of fun."

48

At 11:59 A.M., according to my watch, a phone number one digit off from the blackmailer's first call appeared on my screen.

Our van was parked two blocks from Mayer's building so we could respond anywhere if needed as fast as possible. The middle seat of the van had been removed, and I sat in the back as Crevis drove. My laptop and recording devices were secured on the table in front of me. Mad Jack Gordon had parked his rump in the front passenger's seat. I wanted him as far away as possible from me so I could send messages to Oscar without tipping my hand. Also, the guy's presence stoked my desire for violence. I'd delouse the van later.

I slipped the recording earpiece into my ear. Pam's face appeared on the Web cam screen. She sat next to Wykoff in the conference room. I winked at her; she smirked and rolled her eyes. Oscar was set to receive my e-mails to his BlackBerry. We were ready.

I texted the new number to Oscar—a glitch I hadn't anticipated—so he could recalibrate Triggerfish. I switched the recorder on before I answered my phone to the same computer-generated voice.

"DETECTIVE QUINN. COPY THIS NUMBER DOWN." He gave me

a sixteen-digit number with a letter at the end. "THIS IS AN ACCOUNT WITH THE INTERNATIONAL BANK OF CAYMAN. WHEN I SEE TEN MILLION DOLLARS DEPOSITED IN THE ACCOUNT, I WILL TELL YOU WHERE THE HARD DRIVE IS LOCATED."

"How do I know you'll keep your word and we'll get our hard drive and *all* information back—for good?" He needed to keep talking to get a track on the phone. Since he'd called from a different number, I wasn't sure Oscar and his team could adjust Triggerfish, get the signal, and hone in on it in time.

"YOU DON'T REALLY HAVE A CHOICE, DO YOU? DO AS YOU HAVE BEEN INSTRUCTED IF YOU WANT YOUR HARD DRIVE."

"I have a better idea," I said. "Why don't you tell me where it is, we'll pick it up, and then we'll think about paying you."

"Are you out of your mind?" Jack Gordon twisted around like he was about to pounce on me. "What are you doing?"

"Excuse me for a moment," I said to our extorter as I covered the receiver with my hand. I aimed my cane at Crevis. "If he speaks again, silence him. I don't care how you do it." I swung the tip toward Gordon's chiseled face. Crevis grinned and unbuckled his seat belt.

I put the phone back up to my ear.

"DON'T PLAY GAMES, DETECTIVE QUINN. TELL ARMON TO PAY NOW OR THAT INFORMATION GOES TO LAW ENFORCEMENT."

That caught me off guard.

"YOU HAVE TEN MINUTES." The suspect hung up.

I typed a message to Oscar's phone. *Sequenced cell numbers. Must have bought them at the same time, from the same place. Set up on the next number up. He'll call back soon.*

Armon stepped into the Web cam's view, the radiance of the noon sun in the conference room exposing deep furrows along his forehead like crags on a crumbling statue. "Pay the amount. Make the deal."

"Not a good idea." I leaned in as close as I could to the camera. "At least pay only half until you have the information in hand. We have no confirmation or guarantee this guy will keep his word. We have to do something to hold him to his end of the bargain."

"We can't risk…" Armon fumbled with his hands. "We need to close this deal right now. Do as I have instructed. Tell him the money will be there momentarily." Armon turned away from the camera and said, "Richard, make the transaction. Do it now."

"I have everything arranged," Wykoff said. "It will be completed momentarily, Mr. Mayer."

"I don't like this, Armon," I said. "Whoever did this knows you and your business very well. They're not going to stop here. It will be just the beginning."

"That's really not your business, Quinn," Jack chimed in, eyeing Crevis. "Your job is to do what you're told—without question."

"My job is to look out for my client." I faced the camera and turned up the gain on my microphone to ensure that every word resonated throughout the conference room. "Even if he's jerking me around!"

Armon's face was in full view of my Web cam, nearly forcing Pam out of the way. He appeared to be studying my setup. I couldn't risk him figuring out what I was doing.

I texted Pam on her cell phone and watched her jump as it vibrated on her hip.

Cough loud now. Don't cover your mouth.

She raised one eyebrow. I sent another message, the phone still in her hand.

Do it now!

She coughed without expression, then followed it up with a deep hack. Not bad. Armon disappeared from the camera view with record speed. Pam and I traded smiles.

My phone rang. It was a number up from the one that called me last.

"I DON'T SEE THE MONEY IN THE ACCOUNT YET."

"Patience is a virtue. We're working on getting the accounts transferred. Is there anything we can do to make it faster?" I searched for more to say to keep him on the line longer.

"It's been sent," Wykoff said in the background.

"It should show up in your account momentarily," I told our extorter. "Hold on so we can make sure."

Several tense, silent moments passed.

"VERY SMART, DETECTIVE QUINN. THE TRANSACTION HAS BEEN CONFIRMED."

"Now your end," I said. "We've kept our word."

"THE SATCHEL IS IN THE BLUE TRASH CAN IN THE PARK BY THE CHAMBER OF COMMERCE ON IVANHOE STREET. IT'S BEEN A PLEAS-URE DOING BUSINESS WITH YOU."

"Stay on the line until I have our property," I said.

"GOOD-BYE, DETECTIVE QUINN."

He hung up.

49

"GET THERE NOW, CREVIS." I typed the last conversation to Oscar while Crevis pulled into traffic. Pam waited patiently for me to finish. "We're heading to the park to retrieve the hard drive now. I'll let you know when we find it."

Armon called from the background that he understood. I doubted that he would get anywhere near Pam now.

Jack checked his watch. "Let's wrap this up."

We were less than a mile from the park and just north of downtown. Crevis hurried down North Orange Avenue, turned on to Ivanhoe, and cruised along the outskirts of the park. I surveyed the area as well as the bystanders and the cars parked along Ivanhoe, which was right next to the I-4 underpass and Lake Ivanhoe itself.

The caller could be anywhere, but he was somewhere close, to watch his handiwork come to fruition. He'd been thorough and well planned, but he had made a mistake with the sequenced phone numbers—one I hoped we'd exploit.

"Slow down a little." I scanned every passerby. Of course, the park was bustling: joggers, walkers, two women pushing baby carriages and talking. No one stood out as a possible suspect.

"Don't slow down." Jack waved frantically. "Go. Go. We need to get there."

My e-mail chimed. Oscar.

We're close. The signal is right at the park. Call the number again. One more call should put us on him.

I called the number back, and to my surprise, it rang. He should have turned the phone off. Another bad mistake.

"What's taking so long?" Mad Jack said. "Let's pick this up before we lose it."

"Patience," I said. "First things first."

Oscar's blue Suburban shot past us like a rocket. Two more dark SUVs followed.

"They're onto something," Crevis said, pulling in behind the caravan.

"Who's onto something?" Gordon's head swiveled between Crevis and me. "Who's doing what? Talk to me, Quinn."

"Nothing," I said, sharing a nasty scowl with Crevis, who still needed to learn when to keep his mouth shut. "Crevis just can't stand serial traffic violators. They're a menace to the roadways."

"What are you up to, Quinn?" Gordon said.

"Solving this case," I said.

Oscar's Suburban roared into the parking lot of the Dr. Phillips Performing Arts Center, which had a clear view of the park, and skidded to a stop in front of a black Ford Focus with tinted windows.

One SUV blocked the back of the car; the other took the front. A flood of tactical officers poured from the SUVs, submachine guns trained on the vehicle.

Crevis stopped the van just behind Oscar's Suburban.

"You're ruining everything, Quinn," Gordon said. "We need to get the hard drive."

A white guy in his midtwenties stepped from the vehicle with his hands held high in the air, complying fully with the myriad of officers' demands. He wore blue jeans and a dark green shirt. He had brown hair and a chalky complexion barely touched by sunlight, made all the more pallid by the dozen automatic weapons trained on him.

Derek Strickland. Armon's computer guy.

With hands still in the air, Derek sank to one knee, then the other. An officer was kind enough to assist him to a rather firm face plant into the pavement by the scruff of his neck. A deep groan loosed from Derek as two hulking officers buried their knees in his back and finished handcuffing him.

The front door of the Ford was open, and a computer and several cell phones were scattered on the front seat. Water bottles and fast-food debris littered the car as well. He'd established his mobile command center like I had mine. But he didn't have OPD assisting him. Too bad.

I climbed out of the van. Crevis and Jack followed.

"Hey, Derek," I said. "Remember me?"

Derek was hoisted to his feet, and I put my hand on his shoulder. "We're going to have a long talk when we get to the station."

He dummied up. That would change soon.

"Who is this guy?" Oscar asked.

"He's Derek Strickland." Jack Gordon shook his head. "He works in our IT department. We brought him in to track Logan's computer usage after the theft. Would never have figured him to be in on it."

"Load him up," Oscar said. "We'll talk to him at our office."

Derek Strickland stared at Jack and me as the burly tack officer ushered him to the waiting SUV. He sported a physique more suited for computer games and social networking than extortion and murder. He could be a poisoner, though. It fit his weasely, soft countenance.

The most wonderful part of the entire situation was the abject fear in Derek's eyes. The kid was scared. Answers came a whole lot quicker that way.

"Crevis, go check the location for the hard drive," I said.

Crevis hopped back in the van, backed it up, and flipped a U-turn on Ivanhoe.

"Quinn, I'm fed up with you and your games," Jack Gordon said, squaring off on me. "You've placed Armon's reputation and company security at risk by doing this. You were simply supposed to bargain for the hard drive and be done with it. But no, you had to do it your own way."

"Yes, I know," I said. "But now I've recovered the hard drive and found the person responsible and possibly solved Logan's murder all in one shot. I can see how Armon's going to be really upset about that."

Jack wagged his finger in my face. "I'm going to make sure he doesn't pay you another cent for what you've pulled here."

"If you two ladies can stop squawking for a minute, we're taking the suspect to our office for an interview." Oscar opened his Suburban door. "You're welcome to sit in, if you can behave yourselves long enough."

"Fine," I said, eyeing Mad Jack.

"We have to find the hard drive first," Jack said.

My cell phone rang, and Crevis's number appeared on the screen. I'd assigned a picture of Bart Simpson as his ID.

I answered, and Crevis shared his news.

"Hold on. I'm going to put this on speaker." I switched on the speaker function and held the phone close to Jack. "Now say that again, very loudly, so Jack can hear you."

"I found the hard drive and Logan's satchel right where he said it would be, jerk."

I really needed to give Crevis a raise. He was earning his keep and learning the precious gift of irritating the right people at the right time.

I thanked Crevis and hung up. "Now, let's go to the homicide office and listen to Mr. Strickland confess."

"When the time comes, Quinn, you and I are going to have it out," Jack said. "We're not finished yet."

"Make an appointment," I said. "There are plenty ahead of you."

50

THE SECOND FLOOR of police headquarters bustled with the activity of a case resurrected from the dead. Greg Bowden prepared with Oscar on the finer points of the case. The large monitor in the bullpen glowed with the image of Derek Strickland sitting in the interview room, waiting to be interrogated on extortion and murder charges. He rested his elbows on his knees and slumped forward, his head drooping. The interview wouldn't be difficult; he was already defeated. His car had been towed into the station and was being processed by Katie Pham. Rita Jiminez and Steve Stockton loitered around, waiting for Bowden to do his work.

"Hi, Rita," I said as I caned past her. "Lovely day, isn't it?"

Her eyes reflected the bloody crime scene in which she envisioned me, something torturous and excruciating, I was sure.

Jack and I had shared a silent, tense ride to the station with Oscar. He'd called Wykoff and whined about me going off the reservation and drawing the police into the investigation. An earful was coming my way later from Armon. The last check I'd received from Mayer Holdings was probably the last check I would ever receive.

I had a long way to go before I truly understood the PI gig. I had an obligation to my client—my handbook told me so—but I had a difficult time ignoring the truth and what was right. They often seemed to be in conflict with the job.

My phone vibrated. A picture of Eeyore popped up, my icon for Wykoff. I didn't answer it. Too much going on to listen to his complaints, so I let it go to voice mail.

"This guy's not going to talk," Jack said. "I'd bet on it."

I reached in my wallet and drew out a twenty, waving it in his face. "He'll talk in less than ten minutes."

Jack rolled his eyes. "Not going to happen."

"If you're so confident, then put some cash on it."

He waved me off.

"I wonder why a geek like Strickland would try to blackmail Armon," I said. "And did he kill Logan? I don't really see it. You never know with people, but I don't see this kid pulling that off. I bet he's got a story to tell."

Crevis marched down the hallway with the infamous brown satchel in his hand.

Jack reached for it. "I'll take that."

Crevis sidestepped his grab and kept his distance.

"That's Mayer Holdings' property." Jack jabbed his finger at the satchel. "Turn it over now. Your job is finished."

"I'd like to check and make sure everything is there," I said.

"I'll do that," Jack said. "Hand it over, Red, before there's a problem."

I nodded to Crevis, who handed the satchel to Jack while baring his crooked teeth.

"Once I get this back to Armon, I'm sure you can consider yourself fired," Jack said. "I can't believe you disregarded Armon's clear instructions. That's why I can't stand working with cops. You can't even follow simple orders."

I shook my head as if throwing off a trance. "I'm sorry. I wasn't paying attention to you. You said something?"

Jack growled. I shared a grin with Crevis.

"You've got the hard drive, thanks to Crevis and me," I said. "You can go back to Armon now, suck up to him, and maybe keep your job. Blame everything on me if you like. I'm fed up with the whole Mayer operation anyway."

"I'm staying to see what Derek has to say." Jack swung the satchel in front of him and held the handle with both hands. "Then I'll fill Armon in on your shenanigans today."

"Do what you like," I said. "Just don't leave out any of the juicy details."

Oscar and Bowden entered the interview room. Strickland looked up but dropped his head right away. They stayed silent for a few moments, a psychological move to rock his comfort level all the more.

Bowden asked some questions about his employment and where he lived. Strickland answered them freely. Bowden read him his Miranda rights, and he agreed to talk.

After some light questions, Bowden stabbed at the meat. "It's obvious that you're not a good criminal. You were busted with everything in your car, so I don't need to ask *if* you committed the crime. I only need to ask you *why.*"

"I want immunity or something." Derek alternated his gaze from Bowden to Oscar as if looking for a friend. There were none in the room. "Isn't that what it's called? I'll tell you what happened, but I want some kind of help."

"Why should we do that?" Oscar rested his elbows on his knees. "We've got you in the vehicle with all the evidence we need. You had the briefcase stolen from a murder victim. Please tell me why we have to bargain with you for anything. We'll just lock you up, move on to the next case, and forget about you."

"I know what you're thinking, but I didn't kill anyone, I swear." He held out his hands, palms up. "None of this was my idea. I'm just helping someone. That's it."

"This kid is full of it." Jack shifted his weight back and forth on his heels. "He's just trying to divert attention from himself. I've seen enough."

"So far, it makes sense." I crossed my arms and focused back on the screen. "By the way, you owe me twenty bucks. He's singing like Madonna in there."

Jack shook his head and hurried toward the exit. "I need to get this back to Armon."

"Who's idea was it?" Bowden asked.

"Jack Gordon set this whole thing up," Derek said.

The revelation ripped through the bullpen.

Jack brushed back his coat and reached for his side arm, but my pistol raised first. Jack's ugly head appeared at the end of my sights. His hand fondled his .45, but he had yet to remove it from the holster.

"Don't move," I said. Several leather holsters unsnapped behind me—all pointing at Mad Jack Gordon.

"I'm not going to prison." He froze in defiance, his eyes and mine locked in a stare across my sights.

"I can arrange that." I narrowed my target to the middle of his forehead, exhaled, and took up the slack in the trigger. "Just lift your pistol a little higher out of the holster, and I'll make sure you never reach a prison cell."

Jack panned the room, taking in the contingent of pistols all squared on him. Oscar left the interview room and joined the firing line.

"That kid is lying," Jack said, like a death-row inmate pleading his case to anyone who would listen.

"Really? The phones used to extort Armon are still in the car," I said. "When we check the surveillance tapes from the store where they were purchased, who are they going to show buying them? Whose fingerprints are going to be on them? I think we both know the answers to those questions. So what's it going to be, Jack? I'm waiting."

He focused on me, and for all his bluster, all his bravado, when it came time to test his moxie, he blinked. His right hand released the pistol handle and reached for the ceiling.

Crevis bounded toward him and crashed a right cross on Jack's well-dimpled chin with a bone crushing smack. Jack's limp body collapsed and bounced as he hit the floor.

"Was that necessary?" Oscar asked, holstering his pistol and reaching for his cuffs.

"Absolutely," I said. "Nice shot, Crevis!"

51

JACK DID A BOBBLE-HEAD-DOLL imitation as he scanned the interview room, the fog imposed by Crevis's well-placed right hand still apparent in his eyes. His suit-coat collar was flipped up, and his tie was wrenched to the side. Oscar and I were doing his interview.

Derek Strickland had provided an alibi to Bowden—he was at home with his wife during the time of the homicide—and said Jack had called him with the plan after he found Logan in the hotel room early Thursday morning. He helped Jack dump Logan's Jeep to throw off the investigation. Bowden took Derek on a field trip to verify his alibi and his story. He was doing the smart thing and cooperating.

Jack's .45 was secure. Probably not a coincidence that it was the same caliber of pistol fired at Crevis and me a few days before. After the tussle in the bullpen, we ran Jack through the computer and found he had a motorcycle endorsement on his driver's license. Also not a random event. We would submit his pistol to the lab to compare against the shell casings from the shooting at our office.

Oscar walked Jack through his Miranda warning. He might have fully understood, but the goofy expression on his face betrayed that possibility.

"We didn't kill Logan." Jack attempted to tuck in his shirt and regain a little of his dignity.

"I'm having a hard time believing that one," I said. "Why'd you blackmail Armon?"

"I found out Logan was staying at the motel," he said. "He was dead long before I got there. The satchel lay on the floor, so I took it. After all this, Armon will phase me out, or do away with my position or something. I know how the man works. I needed a little cash to take care of myself. I busted my tail for that man for years. I deserved that money as much as anyone else."

"You say you didn't murder Logan," I said. "Where were you that Wednesday night?"

He smiled, the residue from Crevis's love-tap lifting from his brain. "I was with Armon in Atlanta. We didn't return until about 2:00 a.m. We landed at Orlando Executive Airport. I have a dozen witnesses. I didn't kill Logan."

"Well, you're going to do some serious time for extortion," I said, "so it would be good if your memory improved on Logan's murder. If you didn't do it, you had some hand in it."

"I didn't kill Logan, and I don't know anything about it. And I'm not going to be prosecuted for the extortion or theft." He leaned back in his chair, his pitted chin swollen. "Once you let Armon know I'm involved, he won't press charges. I can promise you that."

"What makes you so sure?" I asked. "You tried to squeeze him for ten million bucks. He'll want to put you away for a long time."

"I know Armon," he said. "And better than that, I have insurance."

"What kind of insurance?" I knew exactly what he meant, but I wanted to get specific.

"Enough to know that Armon will not press charges once he knows that I've seen *all* the data." His smugness returned and irked me all the more. It was hard not to call Crevis in to tune him up again.

"What's that supposed to mean?" I said.

"Just let Armon know that I know. He'll take care of the rest. I might just be a security guy, but I know the value of the cards I'm holding."

I checked my notes and probed a little more. "If you were in Atlanta until 2:00 a.m., how did you find Logan? You couldn't have been out looking for him."

He just smirked.

"You're too stupid to have found him yourself," I said, "so I'm going to guess that you got a tip."

"Guess all you like," he said. "I didn't have anything to do with Logan's death. You have nothing else on me. Call Armon and let him know what's happened."

"Not yet," I said. "The casings from your pistol are being compared to the ones from the shooting at my office. I'm betting they will match. You're still facing attempted murder for Crevis and me."

"Maybe they will, maybe they won't." He shifted. "If I really wanted to murder you, you would be dead. Do what you have to do with the pistol, but either way, Armon is never going to press charges. I think we're finished here, gentlemen."

My major regret at that point was that Crevis hadn't broken his jaw with the punch, because I still had to hear that haughtiness in Jack's voice. I wanted to dismiss what he said about Armon, but he was way too confident. He was close to Armon; he wasn't bluffing.

I left the interview room, letting Oscar clean up the details. I passed Crevis and the rest of the homicide squad as I hobbled to the hallway. I dialed Wykoff, who answered on the first ring.

"Give me Armon," I said, not waiting for his greeting.

Armon took the phone.

"We've arrested Jack Gordon and Derek Strickland from your company as the people extorting you. We suspect them in Logan's murder." I stopped and waited for his reply; he needed to fill in the blanks on this.

Armon paused several moments before answering me. "The police were not supposed to be involved. How did that happen?"

"It's a long story that I'll tell you later, but Gordon and Strickland are neck deep in this. They were going to bleed you for everything they could."

"So Jack arranged all of this?"

"Yes, he did. But he didn't get away with it," I said. "We have a great case on him, and he confessed. We're going to book him now."

Another pause. "What did he tell you?"

"He's been rather chatty." I paused as I considered whether to deliver the message. Fatigue weakened my resolve to squeeze the truth from Armon. "He wanted me to tell you that he's seen all the data."

The line was silent for several seconds. "You have the hard drive in your possession?"

"Yes."

"Then I don't wish to pursue charges against either of them," he said. "I will arrange for an attorney to bail them out of jail and give them legal representation. Now bring me the hard drive immediately so we can settle up our account."

"You're going to pay for the attorney for the men who attempted to extort you?"

"That is not a matter for your concern," he said. "Just bring me the information as soon as possible."

I slammed my phone shut. Oscar met me in the hallway.

"Did you contact your guy?" Oscar said.

"Yeah," I said. "And Jack called it right. He must have some real dirt on Armon, something he can't afford to have come out."

"So what do you want to do with these two?" He pointed to the interview room with his thumb.

"Let's book them on the extortion charges anyway," I said. "At least they'll spend a few hours in jail. Not only does Armon not want to press charges, he's sending a lawyer to bond them both out."

"You've got yourself wrapped up with some rotten folks." Oscar rubbed his face. "Something's really not right with them. Watch yourself, Ray."

I texted Pam to pack her things and get out of there and to let Armon know I would be there soon, but I had some things to take care of.

Crevis picked up the satchel as we headed toward the parking lot. I took it from him once we made it to the van. I pulled out the elusive hard drive and held it in my hand, wondering what secrets that small storage unit contained and how it played into the murder of Logan Ramsey.

"You drive." I tossed Crevis my keys and placed my laptop with me in the front seat. "Take the long way to the Mayer building."

"The long way?" Crevis asked.

"Stall." I logged in and pounded on the keys to boot the system. "Give me some time to look at this hard drive."

After attaching the hard drive to my laptop, I started reviewing the files. Nothing overly complicated, but extensive financial information. Not my forte. Names and numbers scrolled down the screen like rain in a monsoon. I copied all the files to my computer so I could make a closer audit later. It took several minutes.

One of the spreadsheets caught my attention. Deposits were going into Mayer Holdings, and within a couple of weeks, larger payouts came back out to the same clients. A substantial return in a very short amount of time. As best I could tell, it seemed to be a cycle. I rubbed my eyes. I wanted to know what Jack was talking about, but I was way too tired to be delving into all this right now.

Crevis guided me on a sightseeing tour of downtown Orlando as I finished up the download. We looped around Armon's building three times before descending into the labyrinth underneath.

I'd done what I was hired to do, which should have made me giddy but didn't. Logan's death remained a mystery. Maybe Jack murdered Logan for taking the information and putting his job at risk, but by poisoning him? Doubtful.

I needed to confirm that Armon and Jack landed at Orlando Executive Airport at 2:00 a.m., which was enough past the time of the homicide to make him look good. Doc Podjaski estimated it was closer to 8:30 p.m., which, in conjunction with the time line for that night, made sense. Then there was poisoning the pizza and getting it to Logan, which moved the homicide timeframe even earlier.

If what Jack said was true, then he probably didn't murder Logan.

But if not him, then who?

52

It was 3:30 P.M. before Crevis and I stepped onto the elevator and headed up to Armon's lair. Working through the night had made my head fuzzy. But we weren't done yet.

"Just keep your mouth shut and let me do the talking," I told Crevis.

"I know the drill."

The glazed sheen in his eyes matched mine. He was young and would recover quickly. My body and psyche didn't respond well to the time warp. I wiped my face, hoping to scrape some of the haze away. My leg throbbed, and every fiber of my life essence cried out for a cup of coffee. I wanted to be at my best when dealing with Armon, but time didn't permit a stop. I'd have to do it stimulant free.

The elevator door opened, and Megan rose as we approached her desk.

"I can't believe Jack did that." She lifted her eyebrows and spoke by barely moving her lips, as if doing so would prevent her voice from penetrating the walls into Armon's den. "What did he say? Why'd he do it?"

"I'll tell you later," I said. "Let *him* know we're here."

She held her hand to her earpiece and proclaimed to His High and Mightiness that we had arrived. The door opened immediately, and Wykoff waved us into the conference room. The wear of the night had taken its toll on Wykoff as well. His disheveled suit looked more like he should be standing in line at a soup kitchen than lawyering for the rich and arrogant.

Armon hovered near the windows; he looked as if he'd been smoking his hemp jacket all night. His eyes were red and swollen, and he looked ten years older.

"You have the hard drive and all my information?" he asked.

I tossed the satchel onto the conference table with no care for the contents or the table. It slid to rest in front of Armon.

"The hard drive and data are all there," I said. "OPD is serving search warrants on both Jack's and Derek's houses for computers and storage devices, even though you're not pressing charges. I had to do some serious dancing to get that done. They weren't enthusiastic about all that work for a victim who won't see the charges through. They're going to sweep all the electronics to see if they had hidden copies. We should know by the end of the day."

"Now that Jack and Derek's activities have been discovered," Armon said, "I am not worried about copies or further problems. I know how to make this disappear from my end. Mr. Wykoff's associate will meet with them both at the jail. An agreement will be struck that is satisfactory to everyone involved. You have exceeded my expectations, Detective Quinn. You were most definitely the right man for the job. Your connections to the police department have proven invaluable. Maybe law enforcement getting involved will work out for the best, even though I was quite clear in my instructions."

"Marvelous," I said, debating if I should Cane Fu him before or after he cut my final check. "I'm having a difficult time containing my glee that things are working out so well."

Armon surveyed the city below. "Something is on your mind, Detective."

"A lot is on my mind," I said, my voice dropping to a growl. "You've been screwing me around on this case from the beginning. I delivered the guys who attempted to extort ten million dollars from you, and you're cutting a deal with them. For what?"

"I would think, with your vast experience in the law enforcement community, that the art of cutting deals would not surprise or offend you. Prosecutors and judges routinely do the same. That is how the world works. I have a business to run. Dozens of jobs and hundreds of clients rely every day on the decisions I make in this room. You have no idea the pressures of having so much responsibility for the lives around you."

"You're right. I'm just a lowly detective." I tossed in a little southern twang for effect and scratched the side of my head like an orangutan. "I wouldn't know much about those kinds of things." My angry voice took over again. "I only have one skill in life—I can spot a dirty player, a corrupt scumbag, from a mile away, no matter how good they clean up. I'm not one of your cronies." I pointed at Wykoff with my cane. "You used me and are hiding something big. I hope for your sake it isn't murder."

"I have paid for your services, Detective Quinn, so don't moralize to me. You are a hired gun, a brute who does the dirty work no one else will do—and you do it well. The world needs hired guns, but never forget that is who you are. And part of the services you provide is your discretion. Nothing that has transpired or that you have uncovered in this sordid tale can ever be revealed. Your own ethics and the contract we both signed will not allow for it. As you said, your job is to look out for your client—whether you approve of me and my business or not. Now, we need to settle accounts in this case, be done with this unseemly affair, and move on."

Armon dipped his head to Wykoff, who dutifully withdrew the checkbook from his coat pocket, dabbed the tip of his pen on his tongue, and scribbled out an obscene number. Crevis and I traded some eye work. Wykoff ripped the check from the book with more force than necessary and handed it to me, just like the first time we met.

"This should cover any additional expenses you've incurred as well as provide a bonus." Wykoff stood and straightened his coat. "Mr. Mayer feels you've earned it."

Armon placed his hands on his hips and smirked. He'd thrown enough cash on the fire to finally extinguish it, though the foul stench of corruption still lingered all around me. "That number should satisfy you."

It did. So much that I hated myself for ever becoming a private investigator. I hated myself for taking this case, and I really hated myself for not knocking Armon unconscious right then and there. A cop solved cases because it was the right thing to do, and if you did

a really good job, you got the same pay you did every other day—
nothing more, nothing less. The filthy check made my hand sweat.

"What about Logan's murder?" I said. "Don't you want me to
continue investigating that? He was your employee. Whatever else
has happened, you owe him that much. I think we're close and could
have this thing finished in a week or so."

"Our arrangement is finished," he said. "The murder of Logan
Ramsey is the police department's concern. I owe *him* nothing."

I crumpled the check in my hand, forced it into my pocket, and
let out a slow and controlled breath before I answered him. "I have
my report to finish and some DNA stuff to clear up with the lab. I
should have the final report to you next week sometime."

Crevis followed my lead as I turned to exit the palace.

"Aren't you forgetting something?" Armon said.

"Not that I can think of," I said.

He held out his hands. "You were supposed to slap my face when
you finished the case." A broad smile crossed his bearded face.

"I forgot about that." I hadn't, but telling him the truth seemed
a bit ridiculous at that point. I posted both hands on my cane. "To
answer your question, no, not now. I think this case has had a pro-
found effect on me that could reverberate deep in my innermost
parts for many years to come." I raised a finger in the air. "As a matter of fact, I think spending this time with you—being in your superior presence and absorbing your wit and acute personal insights—has
caused me to grow as a human being. I see the error of my ways and
am currently rethinking my life. I'm not sure I can slap anyone in

the face now, and I have you to thank for that. Thank you, Armon Mayer, for helping me mature as a person."

His smile retracted like a zipper, replaced with a bewildered stare.

"Good day, gentlemen," I said, taking a long step with my cane. Crevis caught the door for me.

"Let's get together later," I whispered to Megan as we passed her desk.

The elevator door opened, and Crevis and I boarded it, facing Megan. As soon as the door closed, Crevis burst into speech.

"You blew it." He pumped two jabs and a cross in the air. "You missed a good chance to pop him in the mouth, Ray. What were you thinking?"

"You're not a big Shakespeare guy, are you?"

He rolled his eyes.

"Your next lesson in police work has to do with food preparation."

"What?"

"You will learn how to serve a bitter dish, cold."

53

IN THE VAN, I opened my laptop and attempted to pick up where I'd left off on Armon's files. Wasn't going to happen. The case bounced around my mind with all the grace of a moose on a trampoline. I still had a lot to do, but I just couldn't concentrate. I closed the laptop.

Logan was still very dead, and I had no name to assign the responsibility for it. If Jack's and Derek's alibis panned out, we had no viable suspects for his murder. No scarcity of folks who wanted it to happen, but none that I could show did the foul deed. Armon was a dirtbag extraordinaire, but I couldn't see him getting his hands soiled on a murder. Actually, I couldn't see him getting anything dirty. The freak was some kind of Howard Hughes wannabe, but the fresh piece of tainted scrip in my pocket would at least keep Crevis and me in chow for a couple millennia.

The Rebel Soldiers, Jason Santos, Jack Gordon, Derek Strickland—the case ran laps in my head. Armon spent a fortune to get his hard drive back, and it still didn't seem to be enough to put this thing to rest.

A text message buzzed my phone. *Meet tonight?* Megan wrote.

Need sleep first. Call U later. I returned my phone to its pouch and rubbed my face again.

Crevis got us home, and he plopped face first on the couch without taking off his shoes. He was rumbling away in minutes.

I wasn't so lucky. For several hours I wrestled with my pillow and my soul, in and out of a delirium masquerading as sleep.

Consciousness finally won out, so I got up and showered. I traded text messages with Megan as I got ready for the night. We were meeting at the Pig & Whistle on International Drive. I'd been there once before and knew it would suit my needs.

I put on a white long-sleeved shirt with dark dress pants. At the last minute, I slipped on a coat and checked my look in the mirror. I was trying for more debonair than pathetic. Never been much for sympathy, but every time I saw Megan, she glanced first to the leg, then to my face. Most people did that. A morbid curiosity about my circumstance.

For some reason, the coat seemed to diminish the cane at my side, and it made concealing my pistol in my waistband much easier. I adjusted the coat, my Glock tucked snugly in its holster. Like a commercial used to tout many years ago: "Don't leave home without it."

I hobbled to the kitchen and stole a quick gulp of Jim. Crevis's snores were muffled by the sofa cushion he was drooling on. He was worse than a Labrador at times, though he'd at least proven to be housebroken. I didn't disturb him. He'd earned the rest.

Megan arrived early—earlier than me, anyway. She wore a short black dress that hugged the contours of her hips. She crossed her legs and smiled at my approach.

"You are one crazy man," she said. "I knew you'd get Armon's stuff back. You had that look in your eye when you first came into the office. You're a man who won't be denied."

"I still haven't found out who killed Logan." I eased into the seat next to her and propped the cane on the table. She already had a drink. I glanced around for the waitress. If I didn't have a drink soon, my lips might chap under the pressure. "Your buddy Jack Gordon is still on the list, though he might be down a few names now. I wouldn't put anything past that snake."

"He's such a jerk." Her radiant green eyes teased mine as she lifted her glass for a drink. "I can't say I'm sad that he's finally gone. Did he tell you anything?"

"Nothing I would repeat in polite company," I said. "If it makes you feel any better, Crevis knocked him silly. A sweet punch if I've ever seen one."

"Bravo." She clapped. "But maybe my company is not so polite. Did he say why he wanted to blackmail Armon? Was anyone else involved?"

I stopped our waitress as she passed and ordered a Jim and Coke. Megan doubled up on hers. The party girl was at it again and picking up steam.

"Maybe we should talk about something else," I said. "Your boss has about sucked the life out of me today. The mere mention of his name provokes very unhealthy, felonious thoughts."

"He can do that to people," she said, her happy countenance

vanishing. "But he got everything back, right? No chance Logan or Jack Gordon gave it to anyone else?"

"It's always possible, but as far as I can tell, it's all accounted for," I said. "Other than the murder, this thing is wrapped up."

"You're going to find out who killed Logan, right? I mean, just 'cause you're finished with Armon, that doesn't mean you have to stop looking for his killer."

"OPD's on it," I said. "They've got a good team. They'll figure it out."

My phone vibrated. Sleeping Not-So-Beauty was up and moving around.

Where are u?

"Sorry," I told Megan. "Crevis needs some direction."

Out with Megan. Be home later, I texted back.

Call now! Important.

It can wait.

I smiled at Megan as she emptied her second glass in my presence.

Phone records in. IMPORTANT!

I didn't answer him and tucked my phone away. The waitress returned, and we ordered dinner. Megan had the shepherd's pie, and I had a sandwich and another round of Jim.

My phone vibrated again, and I decided at that moment that I would fire Crevis only to rehire him so I could fire him again.

This time it was an e-mail with a short note. *Check number 4.*

I looked at the number. The name leaped out at me like a slap in the face. A phone number that called Logan's cell phone almost constantly had a very interesting subscriber.

Several things came clearly into focus as I slugged back the Jim. I now knew why a young, vivacious, and attractive woman like Megan was fawning over an older, broken-down ex-cop. In two swallows, I was in need of a refill.

"You never stop working, do you?" Megan flashed a spry smile that should have had me babbling like the idiot I was. But not anymore.

"Unfortunately not," I said. "Crevis just got some information that he thought was very important. After reading it, I would have to agree…Savannah."

54

SHE STOPPED THE GLASS halfway to her mouth, which froze open for the split second I needed to confirm I'd scored a bull's-eye. Her gaze shifted from predator to prey as she stole a small sip, then set the glass down. "Savannah? Who's that, an old girlfriend?"

"Nice recovery, Ms. Breeze," I said. "You played me well. Keep the crippled ex-cop drunk, flirt with him a little. Have him do your bidding. It nearly worked."

She eased back in the chair and flaunted a coy smile my way. She was working it hard. "I don't know what you're talking about, Ray."

"That might have worked five minutes ago," I said. "Before I got phone records that show you and Logan in constant contact, all the way up to the night he was murdered. You left that tidbit out of your story."

She shrugged, then crossed her arms and legs. "We worked together. He asked my advice on things."

"Here's the deal." I propped both elbows on the table and leaned forward. "We can continue to bandy one-liners for the rest of the night in this ridiculous game, and then I can call Oscar and the homicide team to come interview you as a suspect in Logan's murder. Or you can cut the crap and tell me what happened that night, and I'll see what I can do to help you through this. It's your choice."

"I...I don't know what you're talking about." She giggled and squirmed in her chair. "Kill Logan? That's ridiculous."

"Fine. I can do it that way too. You had fingerprints taken as part of your employment package at Mayer Holdings," I said. "I can compare those files to the glass and a bottle of Jack Daniel's, your drink of choice, found at the crime scene. And when they match, OPD will hammer you as a homicide suspect, with all the evidence they need—a lying statement and your fingerprints at the scene. I've made weaker cases. Either way, you're all out of charm with me."

Her eyes steamed over, moistening as she tilted her head. "I didn't kill him, I swear. I...I really cared for him."

"Then how'd he get dead?"

"I never meant for any of this to happen." She wiped tears from her cheeks and turned her head away from me as she spoke. "I just didn't know what to do. I found out some things about Armon and what he's doing. I didn't know who to turn to or what to do."

"So you went to Logan?" I said.

"Yes. We'd partied a few times. He was a lot of fun. And since he used to be a cop, I felt I could trust him. I *knew* I could trust him. I downloaded some of the files that could sink Armon and Richard. Logan said he'd get them to the right people. He was trying to do the right thing, and someone killed him for it."

"You signed him into the hotel and helped him hide?" I said.

She nodded.

"Who killed him?"

"I don't know." Her voice cracked. "I went to the room that morning sometime after 2:00 a.m. I'd had a few and thought he and I could…you know, hang out for a while. I was really drunk. The door was open, so I went in. I saw him there on the bed with that knife in his chest, and I screamed and ran out."

"And dropped your booze and glasses?"

"Yeah. I didn't know what to do then, so I—"

"Called Jack Gordon?"

"He said he would take care of it and wouldn't tell the police about me or my involvement. He said he was protecting me. I just had to keep my mouth shut and not tell anyone, especially Armon, no matter what happened. Jack said he would take care of the rest."

"Were Logan's Jeep and his satchel still there when you saw him?"

"His Jeep was definitely there," she said. "I think the satchel was on the floor when I left. I was so freaked out, I didn't even think of grabbing it. I had no idea Jack would steal it and set up."

"Were you part of the extortion?" I asked.

"No, no. I wouldn't do that," she said in a soothing voice as she rested her hand on my forearm, trying to regain a little of her spell over me. Fortunately, the truth had fully inoculated me. "I found out what Armon was doing and wanted to stop him. Why would I turn around and try to extort him? I tried to make the financials public, but I was too afraid that Armon and his people would find out it was me. Logan wasn't afraid of anything. When I told him what I'd found, he said he could get it to the right people and expose it all. He was pretty fired up about it. He said he felt like a cop again."

"Did you buy him a pizza that night?"

"No." She shook her head like she truly had no idea what I was talking about. "I just brought a bottle of Jack Daniel's and the glasses."

"What's on that hard drive that's so valuable to everyone?" I pulled my arm away from her grasp. "What's on there that would make someone kill for it?"

"I'm the only one left who knows what's going on at Mayer—the only one not involved, that is. I don't think Jack knows that I tipped off Logan and downloaded the information from his computer. I just told him that I had found Logan in the hotel room, and he was already dead. Jack knew he had me in a bad spot and that I wouldn't say anything, no matter what he pulled. So whoever killed Logan would do the same to me if they find out. I can't risk that. I tried to stop them, I really did, but I have to protect myself now. I'm going to quit this week and move on quietly."

"At some point, Armon is going to figure out that Logan didn't hack his system. He suspects as much now. That's going to narrow the suspect list for him considerably. How long before they check your computer activity and see what you've been viewing at the front desk? It's not a matter of *if*—it's *when* they figure it out. The only way to protect yourself is with the truth."

"I covered my tracks," she said. "I'm smarter than you or any of them think. They'll never know I know."

"It's your life you're betting with."

"He's got something going that he or anyone else would kill for," she said. "Tens of millions of dollars are on the line, and a lot of people are going to get burned by what he's finagling."

"If he's doing something illegal, you've got to go to the police," I said.

"I'm not going to do that. I'd be dead in a week."

I sighed and processed her story for a moment. "Okay, get me up to speed, then. I'll do what I can. I'm not a numbers guy, so I need some help. What's Armon's game?"

She paused and closed her eyes. "Okay."

For the next two hours, Megan made sense of the names and numbers I'd seen on the hard drive, and in doing that, she complicated my life in a way I hadn't anticipated.

Before she left, I got some DNA swabs from my car and took a reference sample from her. Since she had no credibility with me now, I'd verify everything she told me.

Regardless of how she'd toyed with me, I still hoped her DNA didn't come back on the pizza box.

55

AFTER DEBRIEFING MEGAN and sending her on her way, I dragged my pathetic self back into the bar, tail and pride between my legs. I lost count after five more refills but kept chugging away. The world went fuzzy, and I was sure of only one thing—I was in no condition to drive home.

I flipped open the phone and located Crevis's cell number. Just as I was about to push Send, I decided against it. I found another number and hit the speed dial.

Twenty minutes and two drinks later, Pam Winters walked through the bar—something I was sure she didn't do often—and took custody of my keys and me.

"You okay?" she asked as I squared up on my tab.

"Been better." The tangle of words that left my mouth sounded foreign to me, a sloppy slur of syllables stripping away any pretense of sobriety. But we were well past pretense. I was hammered, and we both knew it. "Thanks for the help today…couldna done it without you."

"Thanks for calling." I think she smiled but couldn't be sure.

All was quiet as we ambled out to her car. She'd kept her promise about not bombarding me with scriptures and Biblespeak. She was so silent it concerned me. I attempted to focus on the streetlights as they blurred past faster than I was comfortable with.

After fifteen minutes or so, she parked in my lot and shifted to face me with that concerned look of hers.

"Do you want me to walk you to the door?" she said.

"I think I can make it from here," I said.

"I'll come by tomorrow to check on you." She flipped open her phone and did some crazy-thumbs text messaging, then turned back to me.

"Not too early." I held a finger in the air. "I think I'm going to be indisposed in the morning. You might find me lingering around the bathroom. Just a guess."

"Ray, I'm glad you called, and you can do it anytime," she said, then broke her own commandment. "But we need to talk later. You really need to get a handle on this. The drinking is out of control, and I'm afraid of what it's doing to you. You deserve so much better."

I couldn't even face her. I'd been played like a poorly tuned instrument by one woman and had just disappointed another, one of the few people on the planet whose opinion of me I valued. All in a day's work. I was too pie-eyed to make any reasonable defense, so I didn't try.

"I'll see you tomorrow. Thanks for the ride." I opened the car door just in time to greet Crevis, who was walking toward us, probably summoned by Pam.

"What's up?" he said.

I stood quickly and wobbled. Crevis steadied me by grabbing my elbow.

"I'm good." I adjusted my coat and staggered toward the gate. Crevis escorted me to the apartment, where I lost consciousness in a way I had not in a very long time.

———

Morning never happened. It was well after lunchtime when I first suffered the effects of a foolish plunge to the depths of my own misery and crawled from the darkness of my cavelike room. I hadn't been sick like that in a couple of years. I tried every hangover remedy I knew—aspirin, coffee, more aspirin. Only the passing of hours provided relief to my racked body and spirit.

Crevis wandered in and out of the apartment, keeping a watchful eye on me from a distance. It probably had something to do with me being testy when I wasn't feeling well. He remained just out of biting range.

By late afternoon, I was capable of coherent thought and civil discourse. Pam must have instinctively known this—or she was coordinating with Crevis—because she showed up just before dinner. She feigned a smile and so did I.

"Is Crevis here?" she said, looking around the apartment.

"He was here earlier, but I have no idea where he went. Have a seat?"

I offered her a chair at the kitchen table, which held two piles of paperwork and computer printouts from Logan's case. We danced the awkward waltz of who would say something intelligent and to the point first. I moved. She deserved that.

"You were right about her. Megan. I was too caught up in everything to see it. She was neck deep in this and using me."

"I wish I hadn't been, Ray. I'm sorry about that."

"I'll survive. I always do. I'll just be a little smarter next time."

"Do you want to talk about last night?"

"Not really, but I don't think that will stop you."

"You've got a problem, Ray. A serious one. You need help. I wouldn't be your friend if I didn't tell you that."

"I have a lot of problems. Too many to count. I think I'm past any chance for help. Maybe this is just who I am and all I'll ever be."

"You have your feet in two worlds, Ray. If you don't get control of this thing, you're going to end up like Logan. I care about you too much to see that."

"It sounds easy, Pam, but life throws things at you. You can't always just pray and go Pollyanna and make everything okay. You haven't had to deal with the things I have. You just don't know."

She was quiet and stared out the window. Neither of us spoke for several minutes.

"Do you know why I want you to open your case?" she asked.

"Please, not that again." I rubbed my aching head. "I'm not up for that too."

"Hear me out." She swallowed hard and drew a cleansing breath. "I have a son, Ray." She said it as if the words had escaped her mouth without her permission. "I haven't seen him since the day he was born. I was young and thought I was in love. I was the daughter of a missionary and loved God. That wasn't supposed to happen to me, but it did. I was stupid and naive, and I messed up bad. Hurt my parents and everyone around me. I gave my son up for adoption, and there hasn't been a day that I haven't longed to meet him, to see him and know he's okay. To know I did the right thing by letting him go. I dream of the day when he's an adult and comes looking for me."

In all the years I kick-boxed, I had never once been laid out on the canvas. Now I understood what that must feel like. I didn't see that punch coming.

Pam waited for me to say something, anything, but—a rarity in my life—I didn't know what to say.

She brushed a tear away, then regained her composure. "Why do you think you're the only person who carries pain, Ray? It's not true. We all have struggles. The only question is what you're going to do with yours."

"I'm sorry, Pam. About your son. I didn't know."

"No one does. I haven't spoken about it since I gave him up. Perhaps God had me hold it until now...just for you."

I didn't answer her, but I certainly wouldn't lie. Since I'd met her and worked her brother's case, I'd felt an awareness that there might be a God in control of the affairs of men. But she was correct as well that I had been running—or hobbling—away from that possibility too.

I stared into the eyes of a woman who had shared her deepest secret with me. I'd seen her walk through the devastation of her brother's murder and now the revelation of a wounded youth and catastrophic loss, and yet she still carried herself with a strength that was foreign to me—and one I envied.

"I know it's going to be difficult," she said, "but what are your choices? You can't continue like this. The drinking is going to destroy you, and it's a symptom of a deeper problem. But first things first— you need help. I'll do what I can, but you need to take that first step."

I sighed and tapped my finger on the handle of the cane. Logan Ramsey's file was right in front of me on the table and on the forefront of my mind, gleaming like a mirror of truth held up to my soul, reflecting everything I loathed about myself. I imagined the day I found myself on Doc Podjaski's gurney, and it would all be over. I really didn't want to do life like Logan, but I had no idea how to prevent it. I didn't want to leave a legacy of pain and disappointment, even though I had no children to leave it to.

Oscar's talk about choices came to mind as well; both he and Pam were right. There was a glitch in my psyche that demanded I drink to cope with life. Since I'd never known my parents, I had no idea if I had some genetic predisposition to drink or if I was simply a weak character in need of something to blunt the pain of life. Either way, there was no denying the problem. The solution seemed a bit more elusive.

I regarded Pam, who had mustered a remarkable amount of strength to share that part of her life with me. I hesitated before I spoke, as the words were thick and hard to get out of my mouth, like spitting out mud. But they finally came.

"I know I have a problem, Pam. And even though I want to stop, I don't know if I *can*."

56

PAM AND I TALKED for another thirty minutes. She wanted to pray with me, but I wasn't ready for that. I did agree that she could pray *for* me. She hugged me and left. Her concern was real, as was mine.

Just after sunset, I drove to the office for a few hours to catch up on my report for Armon—a narrative lacking a serious suspect for Logan's murder.

I checked my e-mail. Agent Young had forwarded the lab results for the items taken from the Rebel Soldiers' clubhouse: no cyanide detected. Not what I had hoped for.

I piddled around the office with as much busywork as I could find, organizing files and typing out the grim narrative. I closed down the place and headed back to the apartment.

Crevis was still awake when I arrived, studying at the kitchen table. His OPD exam was in two days.

"You ready?" I said, not wanting to burden him with the details of my struggles and the case. He needed to focus on the test and only the test. There'd be plenty of time to bring him up to speed, and I still had many things to work through.

"I don't know." He dropped his pen on the table and rubbed his eyes. "This is all so hard. I just don't get a lot of this and am guessing on most questions. Maybe I should just forget the whole thing. I mean, we've got a good thing goin', don't we? Who's gonna look out for you if I'm working as a cop? You need good backup."

"I survived long before you got here." I released Jim from the bottom cabinet in the kitchen and retrieved a glass by force of habit. The irony of the ritual struck me, but I didn't open the bottle. "I'll be fine. Pam thinks you can do this, and she's a whole lot smarter than the both of us put together."

"Do you think I should do this, Ray?" He slid his chair around and faced me. "I really gotta know."

As sixteen sarcastic comebacks flashed through me in rapid succession, I locked eyes with Crevis, a kid who'd never caught a break his entire life, and found the herculean strength to wrestle my tongue into submission. He couldn't help the home he was born into; he couldn't help that his brain was wired different than most. So he couldn't conjugate verbs or spell *Saskatchewan*. He would swim through shark-infested waters to help a friend, and he possessed more courage than most cops I'd known. You couldn't measure heart. If he could just pass the stupid written test, I hoped OPD's review board would take that into account.

"You're gonna make a great cop," I said.

Crevis smiled, then looked back at the open textbook and shook his head.

"You should probably hit the sack," I said. "You need to get back on a decent sleep schedule so you'll be well rested for the test."

"I don't want to let you and Pam down, Ray," he said. "You guys have done so much for me."

"No chance of that." I checked my watch. "You're keeping me awake. Get to bed before I toss you outta here and make you sleep in a pool chair."

Crevis made his bed on the couch, and I limped into my room. Pain radiated up and down my leg like aftershocks of an earthquake, and I'd taken nothing but good intentions to dull it. I'd been on my feet too much.

As Crevis snored, I put on my bathing suit, grabbed a towel, and hobbled out to the pool, the tip of my cane tapping a cadence in the still, muggy night air. The traffic on John Young Parkway was barely audible. The pool light cast a faint blue hue on the water, and the horseshoe apartment complex was deadly silent. It was much too late for anyone but me to be awake.

I dipped my toe in the water. Lukewarm. Steadying myself with the metal railing, I eased down two steps and laid the cane on the cement. In a single graceless plunge, I released my weary body to the placid waters of Hacienda Del Sol. I rolled over and floated on my back. Stars peppered the night sky, and for the first time since I'd picked up Logan's case, I had a moment to fully relax. I worked my hands back and forth with just enough force to keep me afloat and my face above the waterline. My ears were below, the hollow rush of air into and out of my lungs severing any connection with the outside world.

My job was finished. My client was happy, for the most part, and he'd reimbursed me in a way that embarrassed me to consider. Logan's murder wasn't my affair anymore. Bowden and Oscar were more than capable homicide cops. I could, at this point, close the case and move on. Find some other tortured soul or aggrieved spouse—there seemed to be no lack of them—and continue to pay my bills and build my business.

But my chat with Megan didn't make that easy. I knew things, the kind of information that troubled sleep and made ex-cops crazy. I suspected other things too, which troubled my waking hours and really drove me crazy.

I knew Logan as well. We were never best friends, but he wore the badge and did it right, at least for a while. Then there was Cassy and the things she'd said about her own father. If he'd lived long enough, could they have reconciled? Was Logan just a few steps away from getting his life together?

Walking away now seemed cowardly. I owed so much more to everyone involved.

I wasn't sure how to move with Megan and her information. My stomach knotted up. I was such a moron. She drew me right into her drama like some dopey kid, and I was ripe for the picking. Since Trisha's death and dealing with my own personal issues, my confidence teetered. She read me as easily as a children's book and exploited it, attacking me where I was vulnerable to keep an eye on the investigation. That would never happen again.

I rolled over in the water and considered swimming some laps to strengthen the leg. But I didn't have the energy, so I floated around in the deep end like a broken pool toy. When I got to the verge of passing out, I paddled to the steps, got out, and toweled off on my way back to the apartment.

I desperately needed a sparring session with Jim, and I went to the bottle still sitting on the kitchen counter. My hand trembled as I reached for it. I stopped and rubbed both hands together. My body ached with no particular pain I could identify, and Jim stared at me, desiring a union. My pulse quickened, and I quivered like I was cold, but I wasn't. I was now wet with sweat, not just pool water.

I had no idea what to do. Pam's gentle voice was in my head, and I found myself saying words I thought would never breach my lips.

"God, please help me."

57

I ROLLED OUT OF BED the next morning and felt okay, yet still in some pain. My routine was the same, but different. It was my first morning in a long time without the residue of whiskey in my system.

I'd managed to sneak off to bed without any Jim. My hands vibrated well out of my control, and I felt as if I'd jump out of my skin, but I made it through breakfast and coffee without reaching underneath the sink. It was a start. If I made it to dinner, it would be a bona fide miracle.

Crevis had already left to check on his parents. I headed into the office with a mug of Joe in tow. I checked the answering machine: two messages—one from a prospective new client, the other from an old friend who worked at the Orlando Executive Airport. He'd made some contacts and confirmed Jack's story about the travel route of Armon and Jack on the night of the homicide. Lovely. I was still flying a goose egg on suspects for Logan's murder.

I fired up the computers and checked my e-mail. A message had come from my buddies in South Africa. Since I hadn't heard from them in a while I figured Mrs. Simpkins must have scared them off. They would move on to scamming someone else.

> Dearest Mrs. Simpkins,
>   I have wonderful news! One of my associates will be in the Orlando area next week. We would love to make arrangements to help you get to your bank for the transactions necessary to greatly benefit us both. Please e-mail me your address, and we'll arrange a time to meet and make the transaction.
>   Blessings,
>   Mr. Nomvete

My day was improving. I typed my response back to him and giggled as I sent it. Having never been much of a fisherman, I suddenly understood the joy of reeling in a big one.

Since my funk had lifted some, I removed my dart gun from the top drawer and decided to get in a little range time.

I took aim at Armon's profile picture on my murder mural across the office. After considering distance and elevation, I squeezed off a round that smacked Armon in the forehead, sticking to the picture. Maybe my luck would improve on the case as well.

Nothing at this point had produced a solid suspect in the case. Many had motive, but no one rose to the top as the person who committed the crime. Nikki was a nut but got there too late. Jason had an alibi, and his phone hits showed him by his house the entire night. The Rebel Soldiers were good for it, but no cyanide was found at their clubhouse, and it just didn't fit with them. Jack Gordon and Derek Strickland were alibied up. Besides, the clerk at the pizza place told Bowden a woman purchased the pizza, and the DNA on the box came back female. That put Megan at the top of the list, but I didn't feel right about her for the murder. She'd been the one to get the information to Logan in the first place, so it didn't make much sense that she would poison him. But nothing was off the table at this point. The lab would exonerate her or convict her.

I loaded another dart and smacked Armon in the head again, about an inch away from my last shot. I was on fire. Armon's picture was one of those goofy professional jobs with his hands up near his face. The jewelry on his fingers sparkled in a vain display of opulence, rubbed clean by his incessant hand wiping.

The jewelry! I dropped my head. I couldn't believe I hadn't seen it before. I logged on to the Internet and confirmed my suspicions about cyanide. I pulled out my cell phone and dialed Oscar.

"What's going on, Ray?" he said.

"I think I know who killed Logan," I said, "but I need you guys to write a search warrant, pronto."

"Why not, Ray?" he said. "We've shaken up just about everyone else in town, and it's only a Sunday."

"Yeah, but this time I have a plan," I said.

"Few things in life scare me more than hearing those words come out of your mouth."

58

OSCAR, BOWDEN, AND I approached Jason Santos's front door. The tactical team—armed with M-4s, ballistic helmets, and attitude—slipped to the side of the house to cover the backyard. Steve Stockton and Rita Jimenez backed us up with Katie ready to work the scene. We decided not to do a full-on S.W.A.T.-team warrant on the house because of the young children.

Bowden pounded on the door with the bottom of his fist and rang the bell. Less than thirty seconds later, Jason opened the door. He wore shorts and a white T-shirt with a design on it. His head cocked back as he took notice of us and the tactical officers with us.

"What's going on?" He posted his hands on his hips. "I've told you everything I know. This harassment has got to stop."

Cindy Santos appeared behind her husband, the two children with her.

"We have a search warrant for your residence." Bowden held up the paper. "We need to come in, but would like to do it quietly and with as little drama as possible because of your children."

"Show me the warrant." Cindy pushed past Jason. "I want to see it now."

Bowden handed her a copy. "Ma'am, we need to come in now, and we don't want to frighten the kids. So please step aside, and let us do what we need to do. I'll explain everything inside."

Cindy scooped up their older daughter with one hand while reading the warrant with the other. Jason grabbed their younger and pulled her close to his chest. The six-man entry team filed in and scurried through the house, securing each room. We could do no searching until we knew the house was under our full control.

We led the Santos family into the living room. An officer searched the couch, lifting the cushions, before we sat them on it. Katie Pham started videotaping the house.

"This is harassment." Cindy crossed her arms and seethed, her face turning crimson. "When I get through with you and your entire department, all of you will be fired. We will own this—"

"Please just let them speak." Jason rested a hand on her knee.

His felonious education had served him well. He seemed to know that the homicide unit didn't show up at your house for no reason. He swallowed hard as he searched the faces of everyone in the room.

"What are you looking for?" Cindy said.

"Cyanide," I said.

Both stayed quiet.

"And I want your DNA," I said.

"You already have mine," Jason said. "You took it when you were here before."

"I'm not talking about you." I pointed to Cindy with my chin. "I need hers. And I have a warrant to obtain it in any way necessary."

Cindy squared on me and silently assaulted me with her glare. Then she sat back against the couch, her head hanging. Reality crushed down on her.

"This is out of control, Detective Quinn," Jason said. "You've got to tell me *something*. I don't understand what's going on. I've cooperated. I've done everything you've asked. This doesn't make sense."

"We don't want to tear apart the house," I said. "We just want to know where the cyanide is."

"I work with metals," Jason said. "I have cyanide in my shop to polish some of the bronze sculptures and clean jewelry. What does that have to do with anything? Logan was stabbed to death. That's what the news said. Why are you looking for cyanide?"

"Mrs. Santos," I said, "would you like to tell him or should I?"

"I can show you what you're looking for," Cindy said as she handed her child to Jason.

"I assume we'll find your DNA or prints on the bottle?" I said.

"She doesn't use that. I do," Jason said.

"My fingerprints will probably be on it and my DNA," she said, almost monotone, tamed by the reality of our presence. She had no reason to lash out anymore, to be the mother lioness protecting the pride. It was over.

"I know they will," I said. "I think we need to have a talk in private."

"We do." She leaned down and kissed Jason on the forehead.

"Take the children in the other room. I need to talk with Detective Quinn."

"You can't be serious," he said. "What are you talking about? You can't—"

"Not in front of the girls." She touched his lips with the tip of her finger. "I love you, Jason Santos. I always will."

Jason carried one child in his arms and led the other by the hand into the kitchen with Rita Jiminez.

"Your DNA is gonna be on that pizza box," I said. "You know it, and I know it. I only want to know if this was Jason's idea or yours."

"He doesn't know about it at all," she said. "He didn't do anything."

"How can I be sure? It's his cyanide. How do I know you weren't both in on it?"

"I'll tell you everything. Just leave Jason out of it. He knows nothing."

"Prove it to me. Because right now you both look pretty guilty."

She sat on the sofa in the living room with her hands on her knees, staring at a family photo on the wall. It was several moments before she spoke.

"He was going to destroy us, everything we worked for. Jason's on life probation. One slip, one allegation, and he's back in prison for the rest of his life. Then our girls have no father. I have no husband. He's a good man, a good father and husband. I couldn't raise my girls knowing their father was in prison, especially because of *him*. That man had no right to come to our home and threaten us.

He would have destroyed our family. Him, you, anyone who had the chance—I couldn't allow it."

"So you sought him out and killed him?"

"No." She shook her head. "I wasn't looking for him at all. I was driving to my class at UCF the Monday before, and I saw him walking along Colonial Drive like he didn't have a care in the world. I couldn't believe it was him. I followed him to that hotel. I never planned to do this. I never dreamed I could. But when I saw him, the rage, the fear… I knew it would only be a matter of time before he came back. I wouldn't let him destroy us."

"How did you do it?" I asked.

"I had class on Wednesday, so on the way there I ordered the pizza." She motioned with her hand like she was shaking a salt container. "I sprinkled the cyanide on it. It's in liquid form, so I carefully dripped it over the pizza."

"How much?"

"More than enough to do the job. Then I went to his room and knocked. I told him the management had sent him a free dinner. He didn't recognize me. He didn't care. He just grabbed the pizza and shut the door. It was easier than I thought."

"I guess so."

"What do we do now?" she asked.

"Well, you're going to go with these men," I said. "And if you want to keep Jason out of prison, I would suggest that you tell them the same story."

She nodded, her hands clasped in front of her. "Can I have five minutes with my husband before I go?"

I regarded Bowden. Since it was his case, it was his call.

"Yeah, that's fine." Bowden escorted her into the other room to see Jason. Rita brought the children out so their parents could have the most important conversation of their lives.

"What tipped you off that it was her?" Oscar asked.

"Cyanide can be a byproduct of crystal meth, but it's also used to clean precious metals and bronze. Doc Podjaski told me that, but I got tunnel vision with the Rebel Soldiers and their operation. I should have taken a step back and looked at the case differently from the beginning. Anyway, when I saw a picture of Armon's shiny jewelry, it hit me what I had been missing. It all made sense then."

"You did all right, Ray," Oscar said. "For a PI."

A few minutes later, Jason's sobs carried into our room. Cindy emerged from the kitchen, brushed her hair back, and composed herself.

She directed us to Jason's workshop. As we entered, Jason's latest masterpiece stood in the middle of the room: a life-sized bronze statue of a man grabbing both sides of his head and ripping it in two. His work was stellar.

Cindy pointed to a cabinet and told us which shelf the cyanide was on. Katie Pham photographed the bottle and took it into evidence. Cindy accompanied Bowden and Oscar to the homicide unit's interview room, where she laid out in great detail the murder of Logan Ramsey.

59

I PARKED A FEW HOUSES away and collected my thoughts before I got out of the truck. The adrenaline of the case had faded, and I didn't have much energy left. I kept my usual snail's pace up Cassy's driveway to her front door.

After a short knock, Cassy opened the door, and I saw her for the first time in casual attire—shorts, no shoes, and a gray T-shirt.

"Detective Quinn?" She smiled. "I'm surprised to see you here on a weekend."

"Can I come in? I have some news that's kind of important."

"Of course." She opened the door, and I followed her through the hallway to her kitchen. A golf game was on television. "You look sad."

"I'm not. I have news to tell you, and I know there's no good way to talk about this."

She folded her arms and continued listening to me.

"Orlando PD arrested a woman for your father's murder," I said.

"Again?" She raised an eyebrow. "Not the same woman, I hope."

"No. A different one this time."

"Another woman he hurt, I take it. Another life my father wrecked?"

"Not exactly that either." I explained about Jason and Cindy Santos, about a woman driven to extremes to protect her family, or so she believed.

"Don't get me wrong, I am relieved," Cassy said. "I wanted the person caught, but I didn't know what to expect. But I'm okay with this."

"There's one more thing." I pulled the picture out of my file folder, the one of her sitting on her father's lap, smiling and hugging her dad like he was the only thing that mattered in the world. The one he'd kept with him while on the run. "He had this picture with him on the day he died. He had it in his coat pocket. It must have really meant something to him."

I handed it to her. She smiled and chuckled. "I remember when we took that. It was in the living room of our old house." She ran her fingers across it.

"I found out a lot about your dad while I was investigating this. He didn't steal what his employer said he stole. It's a little complicated, but I think he was trying to help people. And, if everything goes well, his work there will help protect a lot of people from ruin. He was trying to do one good thing, and then this happened. I don't know if that means anything to you, but it's true. He was sober and trying to make things right. You should know that."

———

The lobby of the Autumn House Retirement Home was decorated with a couch and two sofa chairs. A serene painting of a couple rowing a boat across a lake covered one wall. A long reception desk faced the glass double doors that opened to the lobby. A tune from the big band era echoed softly through the room.

A young woman who introduced herself as Ashley waited behind the counter. An octogenarian couple holding hands shuffled past the desk, through the lobby, and to the elevator. They smiled at Agent Tom Sloan and me as we stood off to the side, waiting patiently for our guest. The staff at Autumn House were more than happy to assist us, once they heard the nature of our visit.

I checked my watch. He was ten minutes late.

I spent a couple of free minutes texting Crevis to see how his test went. He didn't sound confident, although he wouldn't get the results for a day or two. He was going to be tough to live with until then.

As I put my phone away, a black man in his thirties hurried down the sidewalk toward the double doors. He wore long khaki pants with tan boots and a gray shirt. He broached the doors with purpose and hurried straight to the counter without even glancing our way.

"I have an appointment to see one of your residents," he said with a thick African accent and a very large grin.

"Who are you here to see?" Ashley said on cue.

"Mrs. Marion Simpkins," he said. "She should be expecting me."

Tom Sloan and I shuffled in behind him, placing ourselves between him and the door.

"Mr. Nomvete?" I said.

He turned and cocked his head. "Yes, who are you?"

"I'm Marion Simpkins," I said. "Pleased to make your acquaintance. I'd like you to meet a very good friend of mine, FBI Agent Tom Sloan. He investigates fraud and white-collar crimes here in the Orlando area. I'm sure you two have a lot to talk about."

Mr. Nomvete's grin disappeared.

60

"THEY WERE SUPPOSED to call by now." Crevis paced through the office and checked his watch at least three times a minute. I reached carefully into my top drawer and removed my dart gun. I figured I could take some potshots at him, like a duck at a shooting gallery. As I raised the gun, Pam's scowl forced me to tuck it back into the drawer.

I noticed the time on my computer screen. "We need to turn on the TV. The five o'clock news is on." I picked up the remote to the flat-screen television on the wall.

"Why waste your time watching that stuff?" Pam said. "Nothing good ever comes on. It's depressing."

"Sometimes," I said. "But I'm much more civic-minded now and like to keep up with the goings-on in the city. You never know, I just might pick up another case this way."

Pam chuckled as Crevis passed by us for the umpteenth time, wearing a path between our desks.

I clicked on the television to a male newscaster chattering away. Then a long shot of the Mayer Holdings logo on the front of

Armon's building appeared on the screen. I turned up the volume and snickered.

"Just after noon today, the FBI raided the offices of Armon Mayer and Mayer Holdings. Early indications are that Mayer Holdings was involved in a large pyramid scheme that was ready to implode, potentially bilking investors out of tens of millions of dollars. The FBI made their bust just in time to seize all the assets of the company, possibly rescuing much of the duped investors' assets.

"FBI Agent Tom Sloan was quoted as saying that Mayer Holdings has been under investigation for some time, and they expect federal indictments for Richard Wykoff and CEO Armon Mayer, as well as several others."

Armon was led out of his building in handcuffs, Tom Sloan's imposing frame behind him, guiding him through the knot of reporters. Armon seemed smaller in the light of day, standing next to Sloan. Tom glanced toward the cameras, covered his mouth and coughed, then grabbed Armon with the same hand. He winked at the camera. Armon Mayer looked as if he would faint.

"Boy, that Tom Sloan seems to be everywhere," I said. "I'm really beginning to like that guy."

Pam pointed to the screen and scrunched her face. "Did you have anything to do with that? This whole thing smacks of Ray Quinn."

"Pam, Pam, Pam." I steepled my hands and rocked back and forth. "It would be highly improper for me to take copied, privileged information from my client and deliver it to an FBI agent in an untraceable fashion so he could then thwart a large, ongoing criminal enterprise. That would be a gross violation of the Private Investigator's Code of Ethics and a disservice to my client, not to mention a breach of my contract, which could place me and my business in serious legal jeopardy. I'm offended that you even brought it up."

"That wasn't a *no*," she said.

Crevis's phone rang, and it was out of his pouch in a flash. "Crevis Creighton. Yeah…okay. I understand…okay…thanks."

Crevis sighed and eased his phone back into the pouch. He staggered over to his chair and plopped down, dropping his face into his hands.

"Was it the testing board?" I said.

"Yeah," he said, offering nothing else.

"I'm sorry, Crevis. You can take the test again in six months. We'll make sure you're ready by then." I nodded to Pam. She would be on board with that.

He let out another exaggerated sigh. "It's not that."

"What is it, then?"

"I passed."

"You what?"

"I passed the test," he said, his head still down. "I'm supposed to take my physical next week."

"You'd think you'd be a little more excited." I sat up in my chair. "That's great news. You did it."

Pam leaped from her seat and nearly tackled Crevis, latching herself to him with a monster hug.

"I knew you could do it, I just knew it! I'm so proud of you," she said, her voice muffled by her face pressed into his chest.

"I guess I should go tell my folks," he said, Pam still latched on to him like a tick.

"Try to do it with a little more enthusiasm," I said. "You've worked hard for this for a long time. Enjoy the moment."

He feigned a smile as Pam released him. He thanked her and turned toward the door to leave.

"Crevis," I said.

He stopped but didn't face me.

"You're gonna make a great cop. Don't lose sight of that."

He pushed the door open and headed to the parking lot.

"You did good with him," I said. "You brought him a long way in a short time."

"I've prayed every day for this. He should be proud of himself. He worked really hard to make it happen." She exhaled and dropped into the chair in front of my desk. After a few silent moments, she turned to me. "I'm really sorry about what happened with Megan and everything."

I shrugged. "Not like I wasn't warned. You've been very good about not telling me, 'I told you so.'"

She didn't respond. She wouldn't. She had more class than that.

"It's been four days," I said. "I haven't had anything to drink since Friday."

She smiled. "How are you holding up?"

I held out my hand and tipped it back and forth. "So-so. A little shaky, but I'm managing. I'm not sure how this is going to go, but it's been four days. I'm trying not to look ahead too far. Just taking it day by day."

Tremors racked my body now and again, and I filled the void of Jim in my life with more coffee and copious amounts of aspirin. I had no idea how far this would go, if it was permanent or just another hiccup in my life. But the last hangover hurt me like no other. I'd had worse physical ones, but this cut me deep. For the first time, I had to admit Jim had more control over me than I had over him. I hated that and wanted it to change. *I* wanted to change, not just the drinking but many other aspects of my life.

"It's a start," Pam said. "I know of some ministries that can—"

I held up my hand. "I'm taking this slow. It's been four days. I'll let you know if I'm ready for anything else."

She backed off yet continued to give me that silly grin. I didn't share that I had mumbled a prayer and not dropped dead on the spot. It wasn't as hard as I had anticipated. And it got easier the next couple of times I tried it. Pam didn't need to know that, though.

"Since you're here, I've got something to discuss with you. I have a case I'm going to need your help with."

I rolled my chair over to the filing cabinet and worked the combination. I opened the drawer and lifted the brown envelope from the file—the same file Pam gave me months before, from the Department of Children and Families.

The manila envelope contained the earliest records of my abandonment and trek through the foster care system. The folder was unopened. Delving into this truth could sting a bit, but it was time.

I slipped the letter opener into the top of the envelope and sliced across it. I spilled the mystery of my beginnings onto my desk top.

There could be no backing down now.

ACKNOWLEDGMENTS

Once again I am so very grateful to the many people who helped nurture this story from seedling idea, through the developmental process, and ultimately into the production of this novel. It truly is a team effort, and the wonderful staff at WaterBrook Multnomah Publishing Group has made this project a work of joy. There's a fear in naming people in that I might overlook someone. If I do please forgive me, but I would like to give special thanks to Cindy Brovsky, Pam Shoup, Melissa Sturgis, Renee Nyen, Jessica Barnes, Joel Ruse, Carie Freimuth, Stuart McGuiggan, Lori Sturgeon Addicott, Amy Haddock, and Ken Petersen. I am also indebted to my superb editor, Shannon Marchese, whose skilled eye and vast knowledge have been a huge blessing.

I would also like to thank my wife and children, who bless and support me and make my life richer than I could have ever imagined.

Many thanks also to the men and women in law enforcement whom I've had the privilege of serving with these last twenty-three years. I only hope the stories I write accurately represent the honor and sacrifice you give every single day.

When everything is taken away...

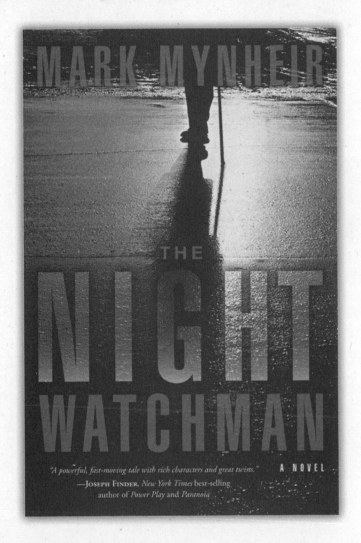

MARK MYNHEIR

THE
NIGHT
WATCHMAN

A NOVEL

"*A powerful, fast-moving tale with rich characters and great twists.*"
—JOSEPH FINDER, *New York Times* best-selling
author of *Power Play* and *Paranoia*

A barrage of bullets leaves detective Ray Quinn
crippled and the love of his life dead. Ray gives
up on life—until a murder-suicide emerges that
may be linked to his own ambush.

Read a chapter excerpt at www.waterbrookmultnomah.com